MAZE

A. H. GARNET

MAZE

TICKNOR & FIELDS

NEW HAVEN AND NEW YORK

1982

Library of Congress Cataloging in Publication Data

Garnet, A. H.
Maze.

"A Joan Kahn book."
I. Title.
PS3557.A7167M3   1982   813'.54   82-5878
ISBN 0-89919-091-X   AACR2

Printed in the United States of America

S   10   9   8   7   6   5   4   3   2   1

For Pat and Al
For John and Deborah
For Elizabeth, for Ben

MAZE

1

The showpiece of Mid-East University was the law quad-
rangle. Sometimes called Michigan Gothic, it had been
donated in the 1930s by a wealthy Chicago corporation
lawyer.

The law quad consisted of residence halls on one side,
the law library and faculty offices on another, a classroom
building, and finally the impressive Lawyers Club, consist-
ing of lounge, dining room, and the food-preparation
areas.

It was the food-preparation areas that interested Arthur
Browne that fall afternoon. He had entered the Lawyers
Club through the main entrance, as he usually did, where
everything was ornate and resplendent: luxurious leather
couches, stately mahogany cabinets, tables, and chairs,
massive gilt-framed portraits of old law professors and
distinguished jurists.

Arthur Browne walked proprietarily through the sump-
tuous dining hall with its high, ornate ceilings, stained-
glass windows, long teakwood tables and dining chairs,
and the intricate Belgian chandeliers brought over from
Europe by a former state supreme court justice and graduate of the school.

The dining hall, the lounge breathed tradition, power, and privilege. (Mid-East was ranked in the top five of the nation's law schools.)

The law club kitchen breathed life.

And life was what Arthur Browne was interested in that day, as he was every day.

He pushed open the swinging doors and knew immediately he had come to the right place for his model of hell.

The kitchen and baking area — a huge T-shaped room . . . In front of Browne were large, steaming cauldrons. There were lights glowing on huge broilers and fryers. To Browne's right a conveyor belt carried dirty dishes to an immense dish-washing machine. There were people everywhere in white uniforms. The attendants in the hell he'd create on stage should dress in white. He made a note on his pad to always have at least three or four white-clad figures moving around in the steam (dry ice? a motor to drive its vapor around the stage?) in the back — scurrying back and forth, gesturing to each other, workers in hell . . .

He looked up at the kitchen. Beyond, in the back, in the baking area he saw an immense oven spewing out heat with a deadly electronic hum.

"I love it, I love it," Arthur Browne murmured, and he began to draw a quick sketch of the kitchen. Something that would entice Connie. Words didn't move Constantine Poulos.

The stout, phlegmatic supervisor of the food preparation was a woman named Lydia Nolan. She knew who Arthur Browne was, of course. And she was worried about his visit. Yesterday he had called asking for a tour of their kitchen and bakery. At first she'd thought it was an inspection. But they'd just had and passed with flying colors a health department inspection two months ago.

2

And why would someone of Arthur Browne's stature want to inspect our kitchen, she had wondered. Arthur Browne was on the Board of Governors of the Lawyers Club. He was also an adjunct professor in the law school, heading up the school's clinical law program. In addition, he had his own private practice and directed, at a dollar a year, the city's legal aid program. Finally, if all that weren't enough, he was one of the founders and directors of the City Players — the city's well-known civic theater.

He directed two plays a year that were always well received.

The Arthur Browne who now stood in her kitchen taking notes was one of Harbour Woods's most prominent citizens. Just last year the mayor had officially honored him with the city's Citizen-of-the-Year Award.

When Lydia Nolan had told her husband the night before that Arthur Browne had asked her for a tour of her facility, Tom replied dourly: "Keep the girls under cover. From what I hear, he's a big girl-chaser."

So far Arthur Browne wasn't interested in the girls. Just the machinery.

"Let me explain, Mrs. Nolan. You've been exceedingly patient . . . " His eyes were alive, his manner almost charming, she thought.

"This spring I'm directing Marlowe's *Faustus* for the City Players. It's a play set in Hades. And always in my head I keep coming back to Orson Welles's production of *Macbeth* — the witches' hell, the witches' cauldrons. Where can I find cauldrons on campus? Where can I find hell? A kitchen. A marvellous, marvellous kitchen. And that's why I'm here now. Looking for a model for my set designer. Tell me now about that oven back there. Why is it so large?"

His quick sketch of the room was done.

"It's large," she replied, "because we bake for all the dorms on central campus."

"I love it. I love it. You're marvellous people here. And those pots?"

"Stockpots for soups and gravies."

"We'll need those. I'll bring Connie Poulos here tonight. I'll need a key, of course. I'll get one from you before I leave . . . "

His arrogance matched his charm, she thought. Was it really all right to let him have a key? Probably. *Her* supervisor reported to the Board of Governors.

"Connie's my scene designer. He'll want to do his own sketches in addition to these. Now . . . what is that delightful machine over there?"

"A deep-fryer."

"Of course. What else would it be?" He laughed, and she had to laugh with him, despite her misgivings.

There was a hiss from the fryer. Steam rose from the stockpots. All the instruments spoke as though on cue. A girl darted over to adjust a control. Arthur Browne watched her. His eyes gleamed.

"Marvellous, marvellous," he murmured.

He says everything twice, Mrs. Nolan thought.

"I'll also have to come back in the daytime to make a tape recording of these sounds. Just how many people do you feed each day, Mrs. Nolan?"

He wasn't really interested, she knew. He was just being polite about her job. His pencil flew over his pad. The stockpots, steamers, broilers took quixotic shapes.

"Three hundred and forty law students three meals a day," she said grimly, determined to give him the information anyway. "I have a staff of twelve, including three bakers . . . "

All of whom, she might have added, need supervision. Especially at this time of day.

4

"And now the *pièce de résistance,*" Arthur Browne said, not listening to her as he advanced on the huge oven, "tell me about this marvellous thing."

The oven was the single biggest piece of machinery in the kitchen. Fifteen feet high, ten feet wide, and twenty feet deep, it dwarfed everything: the dishwashing machines, the conveyor belts, the broilers, pots, sinks, counters. It was big and substantial. Like the law buildings themselves.

Tending it right now was one of the bakers — Edna Poole.

Mrs. Nolan began to tell Arthur Browne about the oven — why it was a reel-type — when she suddenly realized he was no longer at her side. The tall, stout lawyer was standing next to Edna Poole.

The young black woman wore a tight-fitting white jump suit. She had a long paddle in her hands. *Keep the girls under cover,* Tom had said. Edna might have to defend herself with that paddle, Mrs. Nolan thought.

"Arthur Browne, my dear," the lawyer introduced himself, smiling, "I just adore your baker's uniform."

Edna smiled. "You do?"

She looked at him boldly. Breasts quivering, inviting, challenging: touch me, steal me . . .

Perhaps I'm getting old, Mrs. Nolan thought, joining them.

"How deep is your oven, my dear?" Arthur Browne touched Edna's shoulder lightly. He was one of those men who could not keep his hands off women, Mrs. Nolan thought.

"Deep enough," Edna said, with a throaty laugh. "Ain't it, Mrs. Nolan?"

"We have here," Mrs. Nolan said stiffly, "a reel-type oven. So called because the trays cycle within it slowly.

5

The trays can cycle some five hundred loaves of bread at one time."

"Open it, my dear," Arthur Browne said to Edna. Edna glanced at Mrs. Nolan who, reluctantly, nodded.

Edna pulled up on the control bar. The oven door swung upwards, counter-balanced like a garage door. The heat came blasting out. Arthur Browne's eyes lit up. A child at a carnival, Mrs. Nolan thought.

Not a bad image, because inside the trays were circling like ferris-wheel gondolas . . . swinging toward the front of the oven, rising, and then moving slowly back to the rear, where they lowered and made another trip forward.

There was something distinctly odd, Mrs. Nolan thought, about the way this Harbour Woods Citizen-of-the-Year was staring at it.

"From here," she said loudly, "the breads are taken to be cooled, fed into slicing machines, then bagging machines, then racked for deliveries for the freezer. Would you like to see these other machines, Mr. Browne?"

"No, Mrs. Nolan. I think this machine will do. It is a thing of beauty. We'll build an abstract model of it and the damned will tend it and it will represent life in hell with its endless circles. I love it. I love it."

He put his arm casually around Edna's waist. "Do you like this job, my dear?"

"Sure," Edna said, not moving. She glanced questioningly at Mrs. Nolan.

"We'll need someone on stage to tend our abstract oven . . ."

Edna didn't know what the man was talking about with his mouth but she sure was getting the message from his hand.

What a figure, Arthur Browne thought. A bit old for me, but a superb creature.

"I want you to act, my dear. Perform. You won't have

6

any lines. All you'll have to do is walk about magnificently, tending your machinery, a goddess of hell."

Edna Poole laughed nervously as his hand caressed her hip. "Mister, I don't know what you're talking about. This ain't hell. This is a good place to work."

Arthur Browne laughed heartily. "Wonderful, wonderful, wonderful," he said.

Threes, Mrs. Nolan thought, and stepped between the two of them.

2

They worked as a team. They arrived as a team. Each morning at 6 A.M. The chief baker, Steve Gruzinski. Anthony, older than anyone in the kitchen, had been working there since World War II, when he had been an Italian POW brought to Harbour Woods with fifty other POWs to cook and clean for the Army's Judge Advocate School. And there was the youngest of the bakers — Edna Poole.

Their routine was a set one. Before they left each afternoon at 3:30, they mixed their vats of flour and salt, yeast and water. The mixture was dumped, filtered, and put into a big hopper. Then in the morning it would be mixed, divided, molded, rounded, and put on conveyor belts to the proof boxes where the dough would rise.

They made five different kinds of breads: rye, pumpernickel, whole-wheat, raisin-white, and white.

From the proof boxes the breads would be put into the big reel oven.

The big reel oven would be turned on around noon.

Turned off around two o'clock.

As the three of them entered the kitchen from the rear

loading dock entrance that morning, they each heard the steady low hum of the oven.

"Who the hell left that on?" Gruzinski wanted to know.

"I turn it off before I go home, Steve," said Anthony.

"Hey, I know," Edna said. "Mrs. Nolan was giving a tour to this man. Some smooth-talking big-shot lawyer ... " She grinned, remembering how his hand had moved from her waist to her hip and how she could sense its itching to move elsewhere. "He was talking about coming back here last night."

"Jesus, what a waste of energy," Gruzinski said. "And you know who's gonna catch hell for it? Us peons."

He sniffed. He smelled something. They all smelled it now.

"Was the asshole going to bake something in there?"

Edna shook her head. "I don't think so. He wanted to know how it worked and all but it wasn't to use it really. But you know what those guys are like. You can't figure them out."

"Well, let's take a look." Steve lifted the oven door up. It swung up smoothly on its ball bearings.

The trays were cycling normally, swaying without the weight of breads on them, coming toward them, rising, and the heat came pouring out, reaching them, as the cycle completed.

They missed it the first time.

They almost missed it the second time.

It was so obvious, so large, so gross.

The one tray that wasn't swaying. That was absolutely rigid.

"Jesus Christ," Gruzinski said.

They stared at a sight their minds refused to acknowledge. The horror was cycling again for the third time. They stood there frozen in shock.

Anthony crossed himself.

Edna bit her lip. She swayed suddenly as a wave of nausea swept through her.

The blood had drained from Gruzinski's face.

The body rose majestically in front of them.

"Turn it off!" Gruzinski yelled. "Close the door and turn the goddam thing off!"

Anthony moved quickly. Hadn't he seen men die in the war? But not like this. Never like this. Nothing like this.

He pulled the door down and turned the oven off, pushing the switch on the control bar. The light went out.

"My God," Gruzinski said, wiping his face. He was wet. The heat . . .

Edna leaned against the wall. "Steve," she mumbled. She was starting to gag. "Steve — "

"Don't get sick here. For Christ's sake, don't get sick in here."

"It was him, Steve."

"Who?"

"The big shot. The horny big shot."

She turned her face away from them.

"Get her to the toilet," Steve snarled at Anthony.

"You be OK, Edna," Anthony said softly. She was taller than he. She leaned down on his shoulder, gasping, crying.

Gruzinski stood there. His heart was pounding. It's not true, he thought. If I go outside to the loading dock and come in again, everything will be all right.

But then he heard Edna throwing up and Anthony talking softly to her.

And he could smell death.

Call the cops. You got to call the cops.

But he couldn't move. Cops would be all over. Work would stop. Questions would start. They had to make three hundred loaves of white and pumpernickel today. They couldn't stop.

He went into Mrs. Nolan's office. He dialed 8 to get an outside line. His fingers were calm. You're all right. They'll use the oven on West Campus. After you call the police, you call West Campus food preparation.

"Police Department. Officer Johnson speaking," a voice said.

Gruzinski cleared his throat. He told Officer Johnson there was a dead body in the big oven at the Lawyers Club kitchen.

Silence.

The police officer said, "Say that again."

Gruzinski said it again.

The cop said, "We'll be right over. But if this is a gag . . ."

After that he called West Campus. No one was there yet. He'd call them later. Then he went to see how Edna was. She looked awful. So did Anthony. So did he, for that matter. But none of them as bad as the guy in the oven.

3

It was neither the ringing of the phone nor the pounding on the wall that woke up Cyrus Wilson that morning. It was the voice of the pounder.

"Cyrus, for God's sake, will you wake up and answer your phone!"

"Yes, my love," Cyrus murmured into his pillow. He had been having a delightful dream. Indeed, he'd been nursing it along. In the dream one member after another of his Ph.D. committee was congratulating him on a tremendously lucid and spirited defense of his doctoral dissertation.

"Cy, you're the first one to make sense of Whitman's catalogues," Geoff Goldstein, his chairman, was saying.

"I have a whole new view of Walt Whitman," Roger Englander was saying.

"Cyrus!" Eileen shouted through the wall.

"Quite right. I'm awake now," Cyrus said, and opened his eyes. He put on his glasses and reached for the phone. For some reason he always heard better with his glasses on.

"Wilson here," he said.

"Cyrus," came the deep voice of his uncle, "I'm sorry to have wakened you."

Although barely awake, Cyrus detected the sarcasm in his uncle's voice. Cyrus looked at the expensive little Seth Thomas alarm Eileen had given him for his birthday. A little after nine o'clock.

"I worked late last night, Uncle Harold."

"You weren't the only one. Cyrus, I want you to wash your face with cold water immediately and get dressed. I'm sending Detective Guiterrez over to pick you up and take you to the morgue."

A bit of cold water already, Cyrus thought. He examined the ceiling of his bedroom. It was a once elegant room in a once elegant Greek revival mansion. Now the paint was peeling and you couldn't revive a Greek in it if you had to.

"Did you hear me, Cyrus?" his uncle asked.

"Yes, Uncle Harold, but I'm not going to get involved. I haven't the time."

And that, God knows, was the truth. Besides the continuing effort on his dissertation (this was his eighth year with it now), he was teaching a full load: his Whitman-Dickinson class, a beginning English lit survey course, and an English composition class.

The very last thing Cyrus needed was the kind of problem his uncle usually presented to him. All in all, he thought, it had been a mistake solving the Lawrence Bandemer murder on campus last year. Afterwards he had been quietly told by the dean that he was to make himself available to campus security and the Harbour Woods Police Department should a need for his "unique talents occur again."

Unique talents indeed! Cyrus had come to Mid-East University from a stint in military intelligence, but that would not have been held against him were he also not known as the author of the John Agate, Boy Detective, books. Four juvenile mysteries that had brought him little money and a lot of raised eyebrows from his colleagues. "Juvenile mysteries don't quite count as publications, Cy," Geoff Goldstein once murmured to him at a party.

Even the above items might not have propelled Cyrus from his accustomed grooves had not his Uncle Harold been chief of the Harbour Woods Police Department. The Wilsons were an old Harbour Woods family with almost everyone in it connected with the university except Uncle Harold, a black sheep, who had become a policeman.

"Cyrus," said Uncle Harold, "I am not asking you for your help as a detective. I'm asking for the kind of aid any responsible citizen should be glad to give."

When his uncle got this devious there was hardly any point in further resistance.

"What's up, Uncle Harold?"

"Someone who lives in your house has been murdered."

Cyrus quickly reminded himself that the only person who lived in this house who meant anything to him had just awakened him. She was very much alive.

"Who is it, Uncle Harold?"

"Arthur Browne."

"The lawyer?"

"Yes."

I don't believe it, Cyrus thought. Browne was one of Harbour Woods's well-known inhabitants. An aging, swinging bachelor, a man of intelligence, erudition, and wide-ranging interests. It was a little like living above a historical landmark. All kinds of people came to visit him; Eileen thought he was charming, a kind of Renaissance man. He was what Cyrus's mother used to call a "toney fella." He had loud tones too, Cyrus thought. Whenever he talked in the downstairs hall, you could hear his voice all over the house.

14

Well, Cyrus thought, I won't have to hear that anymore.

"Cyrus, are you there?"

"Yes. Why do *I* have to see his body, Uncle Harold?"

"We need an identification. He has no living relatives as far as we can determine. He happens to have lived in your house. I assume you knew him."

"Knew him and didn't like him. I'm sure there are several thousands of other people in town who knew him and didn't like him."

"I haven't the time to call all those other people," his uncle said severely. "Detective Guiterrez will be at your place in fifteen minutes. He'll run you over to the morgue."

John Guiterrez, with whom Cyrus had worked on the Bandemer murder, was the grouchiest of Harbour Woods's senior detectives.

"Uncle Harold," Cyrus said softly, "you're as opaque as a sheet of clear glass. I'm not going to let you do it to me, though. I don't want to get involved. I don't want to identify a body you could identify yourself. I don't want to find out who made Arthur Browne dead either. I'm not paid to do that; I don't have the time. I'm paid to teach classes and sit on committees. Read papers and, hopefully, squeeze out enough time to write my dissertation too. I'm up for tenure and the way I've been — "

"Thirteen minutes now," his uncle said, and hung up.

"How was he killed?" Cyrus asked into the dead phone.

And then swore quietly. When he stopped he heard the sounds of typing on the other side of the wall. It was damned unfair, Cyrus thought. She went on with her work after having propelled him into a mess.

He balled his hand into a fist and hit the wall with a short, powerful hook.

The typing next door stopped.

"And what's the matter with you?" Eileen yelled through the wall.

"You've just got me into a mess," he said, unreasonably. "Make me some coffee."

"Make your own. I'm writing."

In response he thumped the Greek revival wall three more times. Stick beat dog, dog bite cat. The problem was: the cat had a good bite herself.

"Stop that," Eileen said ominously.

"Black, no sugar," he replied.

He was shaving when she appeared in the bathroom with his coffee.

"You have a lot of nerve," she said.

She set the cup down on the edge of the sink, turned down the toilet seat and sat on it.

"What mess have I got you into?"

"Forget it."

"Don't tell me to forget it. You interrupt my writing and make me make coffee and then tell me to forget it. Who called?"

He hesitated. She didn't care for his Uncle Harold. She neither cared for nor understood the instinct for detective work that seemed to run in the Wilson family. She thought it was child's play. Much like writing juvenile fiction.

"Who called, Cyrus?"

"Uncle Harold."

She made a face. "What did he want this time?"

"You put chicory in the coffee," he said accusingly.

"It stretches it, and since you contribute nothing to our coffee bill . . . "

"I will be contributing. I'm expecting a royalty check from New York this month."

She smiled gently. "Cyrus, haven't you heard about birth control? Nobody is buying kids' books these days."

"Kids are being born every day," he said, glad to have the subject of his uncle changed. "I expect to be revived around 1990."

16

"I hope to God I'm published by then."

"What were you working on?"

"My third story for the Hillman competition. The judging committee in the department wants everything in by Friday at five o'clock. Hillman herself is in town already. She's starting her seminar today."

It was Hillman week at Mid-East University. The Hillman Foundation in Connecticut had announced a week ago that it was giving Mid-East University a gift of three million dollars to build a poetry manuscript addition to the general library. The announcement had received national publicity. The gift was to be formally presented during the two weeks that the poet Mary Louise Hillman, after whose father the foundation was named, would be on campus to read from her poems, conduct writing workshops, and award prizes in the Hillman creative writing contest. Her visit would culminate in her address to the annual fall honors convocation at Stockton Auditorium. It would be a gala period on campus for poets, writers, and librarians who rarely shone in a sky dominated by engineers and scientists. Hillman, whose title would be Poet in Residence, would also receive an honorary degree.

Eileen badly wanted to win a Hillman award. It wasn't the prize money she said she wanted as much as the recognition from Hillman, whose poetry Eileen had long admired.

At a time like this, thought Cyrus, I shouldn't be distracting her. But obviously he had.

"Cyrus," she persisted, "what did your uncle want?"

He nicked himself with the razor. "Damn. Get me a piece of toilet paper, will you?"

"Here. What did he want?"

"He's got a problem."

"What sort of problem?"

The toilet paper wasn't staunching the cut. He found a

Band-Aid and applied it. He could remove it in five minutes. He was a good healer.

"What sort of problem?" she repeated.

She was like a squirrel nibbling away on something that was not good for her.

"He wants me to go down to the morgue and identify a body."

"Whose body?"

"Somebody's body."

"Why you?"

"He thinks I know him."

"Do you?"

"Yes."

"Who is it?"

"For pete's sake, Eileen, must you know everything? Stop being a writer for a while."

"Is it someone I know?"

"Yes."

"Who?"

He sighed. It had been a mistake to bang on the wall for coffee. The price was going to be high. Still, she'd have to know sooner or later.

"Our neighbor downstairs."

She stared at him. "You mean . . . Paul? Marie?"

Paul and Marie Genthon were a French couple who lived below her apartment.

There were five apartments in the Greek revival house known in architectural texts as the Watson house. There were Eileen's small flat next to his, his own, and Ernst Mayer's — Mayer was a retired chemistry professor who had the apartment facing the backyard. Below Eileen lived Paul and Marie Genthon. They had come from France about five years ago. Paul was a graduate student in electrical engineering, Marie an administrative assistant at City Hall. Marie and Eileen had become good friends.

Marie had recommended Eileen for a lucrative free-lance writing assignment. Eileen was helping prepare a color brochure for the Chamber of Commerce that touted Harbour Woods as a new center for high technology.

The Genthons were also caretakers for the house, receiving a rent reduction for shovelling snow, cutting grass, raking leaves, that sort of thing.

By far the most luxurious apartment in the house belonged to the well-known Arthur Browne. The vultures would be after his apartment in droves. Or was it flocks?

"No, I don't mean Paul and Marie."

She studied his face. "Arthur?"

He nodded.

"That's not funny."

"I'm not being funny."

Her face froze. He should have anticipated this. Eileen was fond of the creep downstairs. She often had coffee with him in the late mornings. They talked about the theater: O'Neill, Camus, Sartre, Ionesco. The theater, Cyrus firmly believed, was Arthur Browne's ploy for getting women.

"Look, I don't know for sure it's Arthur Browne. That's what my uncle wants me to find out."

"Oh, Cyrus . . ."

Her eyes filled with tears.

"Eileen, for God's sake." A nasty thought flashed through his consciousness. Was it just talk between them in the mornings?

"Cyrus," she said, trying to stop her tears, "does this mean Arthur was killed?"

"Apparently."

She winced. She shivered. And then with the tears still warm on her lovely cheeks, she started to freeze on him. Damn writers for being sensitive souls and wanting to know everything.

"Eileen, the day my uncle became chief of police in this burg was the day I should have shed its dust forever."

A car horn sounded outside.

"Eileen . . . "

But she was somewhere else already.

"Eileen, that's Detective John Guiterrez out there. Would you like to come along?"

Madness. Perhaps he could reach her by appealing to the writer in her.

But she was mute.

Then feed her terror! Kill dandelions by growing them to death! He'd once seen an ad to that effect on the garden page of the Sunday *Times.*

"You might need a description of a morgue for one of your stories some day."

It worked. She blinked. And then looked at him. "Cyrus, you're unfeeling and you're gross. You go to hell!" She ran out of the apartment.

He was relieved.

Outside the car horn sounded again.

"You go to hell too," Cyrus yelled down at the detective.

And got dressed.

20

4

The morgue for the city of Harbour Woods was the morgue of Mid-East University Hospital. Located in the subbasement of that large complex, it consisted of three battleship-gray-painted rooms. The outer room was an office with a table and registration book. The middle room was the morgue proper, a series of drawers in white-painted metal cabinets, each drawer wide and long enough to contain a body. The third and final room, behind a pair of swinging doors, was an autopsy room.

The main door could only be opened from the inside or with a key from the ambulance office.

Detective First Grade John Guiterrez rapped on the frosted glass. "Guiterrez, Police Department," he called out.

A moment later the door opened and a tall, thin black man in green hospital pants and a green jacket stood there.

Guiterrez showed him his badge and the attendant stepped aside. There was no way of knowing from this brief ritual, Cyrus thought, that these two actually were well acquainted.

"Sign in, gentlemen," the attendant said.

Guiterrez checked his watch and then signed in, writing in the time. Cyrus scrawled his name under the detective's.

They went through the inner doors into the morgue proper. On one wall was a row of lockers where personal belongings were kept until claimed by relatives. On the other wall, the filing cabinets for bodies. Plus a chain and hoist for larger bodies going to higher trays.

"Who you be wanting to see today, gentlemen?" the attendant asked.

"Come on, Judkins, I'm tired. I been up all night," Guiterrez said sourly. "The one that come in this morning."

"Two come in this morning, John," the morgue attendant said cheerfully. "Which one you be interested in?"

"Quit farting around, Judkins."

"I guess you be interested in the brown bread." Judkins chuckled.

His laughter echoed insanely in the clean and polished empty room.

Judkins opened a drawer and pulled out a tray that moved easily on ball bearings. The body was covered with a clear plastic.

"Done to a turn, ain't he?" Judkins asked.

Cyrus peered at the body. It looked like Arthur Browne all right. Wrinkled and brown like a dried peach.

"Know him?"

"His name is Arthur Browne," Cyrus said formally. "He lived at 310 Division Street, Harbour Woods, Michigan. Zip: 48104."

"Man, you even know his zip," Judkins said, impressed.

"It's the same as mine," Cyrus said.

"All right," Guiterrez said, "let's get the fuck out of here."

"Tch, tch," said Judkins.

Cyrus wondered whether morgue attendants developed their humor before or after taking the job.

"Some shit," Guiterrez said as they walked into the bright sunlight and toward his car. He yawned.

"Did the medical examiner say he was dead when he got shoved in the oven?"

"No. Doc Hollins says he was alive when he got shoved in."

Cyrus winced. "Horrible."

Guiterrez grinned wolfishly. "A long way from the classroom, eh, Prof?"

"Thank God, yes."

"We found a lump on the back of his head. Not enough of a blow to kill him. He was hit with something hard. Stone, or metal. There was leaf stuff on his clothes. We figure he was hit in or near some bushes and dragged inside."

"Any shoe prints in the dirt?"

"No. There were too many leaves on the ground. The lab boys are still going over the area but I'm not hopeful."

"Does anyone know what Browne was doing in the area last night?"

"He was meeting someone in the kitchen."

Cyrus looked startled. "Are you saying he was in the kitchen, left, got conked, and dragged back?"

"No, Prof. I'm just saying he was supposed to give someone a tour of the kitchen. We got that from the head lady, who said he'd been in earlier that day and got a key from her."

"Did the key turn up?"

"In his pocket. The lab boys have got that too but first report says it was wiped clean."

"Who was Browne meeting?"

"One of his theater people. Someone named Connie Poulos. We're going to check him out."

"We?"

"Yeah — we. Your uncle wants you in on this."

"No way," said Cyrus. "I identified his body. Now you just drop me off at my place."

"Sorry, pal. My orders are to drop you off at headquarters."

"I haven't had breakfast yet."

"Tough. I haven't been to bed yet. I came on duty at midnight. Listen, Prof, if you think I want you in on this case you're cockeyed. You had a piece of luck last spring on that rape-murder and now your uncle thinks you can do anything. Boy detective grows up. Well, I don't like it. I didn't like it last spring and I don't like it now. I can run this one down without you."

"I couldn't agree with you more, John," Cyrus said cheerfully. "So drop me off at home."

"Aw shut up," Guiterrez snarled and drove them to the police station.

5

Guiterrez left his white Buick in the basement garage of the police station. He unlocked an unmarked door.

"I always wondered where the back door was," Cyrus said.

Guiterrez grunted no response. He had stopped talking to Cyrus. Cyrus was a necessary evil.

They walked up three steps and down a long corridor with offices on both sides. The detectives and squad chiefs got the window offices. The other rooms were secretaries' offices, file rooms, interrogation and detention rooms, a communications center. That was the long part of the L. The short part was the city jail.

The chief's office was large and on the window side, facing the *Harbour Woods News* building across the street. The blinds were drawn. No matter, the media would be here soon enough.

Three people were waiting for Cyrus and Guiterrez in Chief Wilson's office. There was the chief — Cyrus's uncle — big, sly-eyed, easygoing. Cyrus resembled his mother's side of the family, slightly better looking but infinitely more eccentric.

Seated next to Uncle Harold was Rollie Mazur, former head of the Michigan State Police and now in charge of campus security for Mid-East University. Mazur was a short, barrel-chested man with a boxer's battered face.

His own days as an on-line cop were over. Campus security was a retirement job for him. Except for the unusual homicide, all that concerned campus security were occasional thefts, vandalism, and keeping the drug dealers off campus and out of the dormitories.

In addition Mazur was coming off a cancer operation on his throat, in the course of which his vocal chords had had to be removed. He was still learning to use a mechanical voice box, and it was very difficult to understand him when he talked.

Thus it was out of the question for him not only to handle a homicide on campus but to talk to the media about it.

This time the suggestion to employ Cyrus for both tasks came not as Guiterrez thought it would, from the chief, but from the third person in the room — Tom Whelan, Vice President for University Relations.

Whelan and Cyrus were the same age — thirty-three — but whereas Cyrus was an untenured assistant professor making $19,500 a year, Whelan, who had shot up through the ranks of academe, was making $55,000 a year as a university administrator.

Curiously, Whelan with his pipe, tweeds, and leather elbow-patches looked like a professor. It was, Cyrus decided, a case of protective coloration. It's very hard for faculty to shoot down a university administrator who wears elbow-patches.

"Nice to see you again, Cy," Whelan said, taking the pipe out of his mouth to convey sincerity better. "Kind of you to be willing to help us out again."

"I'm not willing to help out at all, Tom. I was dragged

out of bed by a certain relative of mine who'll go unnamed and strong-armed into going down to the morgue. I'm now about to go back to bed."

"Not a chance, my boy," Uncle Harold said cheerfully. "You've had your beauty sleep. I'm surprised the university allows you to get away with it at all."

"They won't," Whelan said, smiling. "Cy, I'm just coming from an emergency meeting of the executive officers. Everyone concurs with my recommendation that you once again represent the university in the investigation of this tragic incident."

He talks like one of his press releases, Cyrus thought.

"Good," said Uncle Harold briskly, "we've got that settled. John" — he turned to the detective whose chair was tilted against a wall, whose eyes were closed, whose chest was rising and falling with slow regularity — "you'd better take a coffee break and then locate this Constantine Poulos. You can nap while Cyrus is talking to the media and then I want you two to check out this Poulos."

Uncle Harold was pulling the strings . . .

Guiterrez answered with his eyes closed. "Who's in charge of the investigation, Chief?"

"You two made a great team on the Bandemer case. I see no reason why you can't do it again. Get yourself some coffee, John."

He hadn't answered the question, which, Cyrus thought, was how he'd made chief.

Guiterrez looked at Cyrus, shook his head, and left the room.

Rollie Mazur began to talk. Everyone sat up, concentrating, straining to understand. It would make a good classroom gimmick, Cyrus thought.

"Cyrus will get all the cooperation of campus security," was what Rollie Mazur brought forth.

Signed, sealed, and almost delivered, Cyrus thought.

Tom Whelan tapped his pipe in an ashtray. "Cy, I've spoken to Geoff Goldstein, your chairman. He's happy to get you all the help you need, including teaching assistants to grade papers in your comp and survey courses. The important thing now is to manage the media. They're over at the Lawyers Club. I've got some people with them and Rollie has staff there too. But they'll be humping over here any second. Given Rollie's physical problems, Cy, it's out of the question for him to represent the university on TV. I don't have the time. You're the logical one. And, as we both know, there's more than one path to tenure . . ."

Thus the carrot. Whence the stick? What its shape?

"So I'm asking you to tell them you'll be representing the university in getting to the bottom of this tragic incident, which has occurred at an especially difficult time for us. We've got financial problems right now with the state legislature, with our alumni, and with the foundations in Washington. Cy, I know you'll do the job for us. My oldest boy is beginning to read your juvenile mysteries. (With what condescension they pronounced the word "juvenile", Cyrus thought.) And I must say he's very admiring of John Agate, boy detective, and your literary style. I believe his real life progenitor will be every bit as effective as John Agate. Incidentally, the fact that your contract is up for renewal this spring should be of absolutely no concern to you."

The stick at last.

Mazur's rasping voice erupted. "A TV truck just pulled up, Harold."

"Good," the chief said, "let's get the bastards in and out of here with a minimum of fuss."

"Thank you, Cy," said Tom Whelan, rising.

"I'm coming with you," Rollie said.

And that left uncle and nephew alone.

"Well, my boy."

"Don't say a word, Uncle," Cyrus warned.

"Shan't then," Uncle Harold said. "Never was much of a talker. Unlike you. But I will say this, Cyrus. You may look and talk like a professor, but deep down, you know what you are?"

"What?"

"A cop."

The chief's secretary buzzed that TV people were invading her office.

"Tell them to come right in," the chief said. He smiled at his nephew. "We're all set."

6

"Wake up, John," Cyrus said, "we're here."

He turned Guiterrez's Buick into the drive leading to Mid-East University's botanical gardens.

Guiterrez woke up with a start and blinked. He cleared his throat. "What time've you got, Prof?"

"Eleven o'clock."

"Secret of success in the cop business, Prof. You got to be able to sleep in spurts."

"I'd never make it on the force," Cyrus said blandly. "I like to read before I go to sleep."

"I bet you do at that."

They drove by a small orchard. Ahead of them loomed a series of low-slung modern brick buildings with a series of large greenhouses in the middle. The university's botanical gardens covered some fifty acres just north of the city. There were brooks, bridges, wild areas, a pond, a swamp, English and French gardens. The exhibit greenhouses were visited by school children and garden clubs from all over the state.

There were four exhibit greenhouses, each designed to imitate a specific environment and climate: the American desert, with several hundred varieties of cactuses; next to it a tropical rain forest, with lush vegetation and birds; a greenhouse designed to contain and maintain plants, flowers, trees, and shrubs of the North American temperate zone; and finally a greenhouse given over to the pebbly gardens and flora of Japan.

There was also a research greenhouse for use by university students and faculty: a world of exotic hybrids, strange grafts, seedlings . . .

Guiterrez was familiar with the gardens because once he had arrested a dope peddler there.

"The guy was making his connection under a banana tree."

"What's Poulos using it for?"

"Background. It's too expensive to fly down to Arizona for picture taking. You know him?"

"No."

"Art director at Chapman-Adams. Ad agency downtown. He's a character. We got a complaint on him a couple of years ago. A dumb flake called in to say he'd stolen her husband."

"Kidnapped?"

Guiterrez leered. "Poulos couldn't kidnap a flea. I told her to put some lipstick on and buy a sexy nightgown and get her man back. She got abusive with me. No wonder the husband became a pederast."

Cyrus parked near the front entrance. "You go to college, John?"

"No. I just picked up those big words from hanging around smart guys like you. Look, Prof, before we jump all over the little Greek, let's get one thing straight. This is *my* investigation. You represent the fucking university; I represent the fucking law."

Here we go again, Cyrus thought. They'd been through this on the Bandemer case.

"I'll give you this much, Prof," Guiterrez went on. "I don't have the words you got. I heard the tail end of that press conference. You were smoother'n shit. You told them nothing and they were taking notes on it."

"I get paid to do that every day by the university."

"Yeah, well you can play professor and John Agate, boy detective, with the newspapers and TV all you want. But when we're on the job, I'm taking charge. You're welcome to trail along so long as you stay the fuck out of my way."

The four-letter word was as much to emphasize class distinctions as anything else.

"Fair enough, John," Cyrus said amiably. Investigations had a way of running their own course, Cyrus knew. What would happen would happen. He knew that Guiterrez was aware of this too, but self-esteem demanded a speech, and so Cyrus had received one.

They entered a large lobby filled with plants. On the walls were paintings of plants and trees.

An assistant curator named Jonathan Feld was waiting for them.

They followed Feld through various greenhouses — the North American temperate zone, into Japan, across a South American jungle (the centerpiece of which was a banana tree — Guiterrez looked at it fondly) — and finally into the arid world of the American Southwest.

At the far end of the desert, they saw stands of lights and a tall, skinny model posing in a sunsuit. Off to one side was a group of onlookers: gardeners, tourists, students.

"You do this kind of thing often?" Cyrus asked the assistant curator.

"*We* are not doing this, Mr. Wilson," said Feld carefully. "The university is happy to cooperate with private industry. These are times of severe budget constraints, as you may know."

"What do they pay you?"

"One hundred dollars an hour."

"Cheaper than flying to Arizona."

"Considerably."

As they came up to the picture-taking group, they heard a high voice giving orders.

"No, no, darling. You are to fondle the needle. You are one who loves the sensation of pain. Tempting pain. Smile at it. Now, George, now!"

A large camera clicked away.

They saw him then: a small, dark-haired man bounding this way and that as he directed, cajoled, threatened both model and photographer. Large expressive hands made virtuoso movements in the air. Done as much for the spectators as for the performers.

"Better, darling, much better. You *love* summer. You adore the *chaleur* because you are wearing this perfectly *marvellous* piece of fluff. Don't laugh with your mouth. Only your eyes are amused, haughty, indifferent. Imperious! Neither sun nor cactus nor hail nor wind can — "

The model burst into laughter. As did the photographer. And the spectators broke into spontaneous applause.

Constantine Poulos acknowledged the applause with a small, precise bow.

"I say, Mr. Poulos," Feld said, taking advantage of the interruption, "you have two visitors here."

"Not now."

"Now," Guiterrez said.

The flat tone of the single word turned Constantine Poulos around. Alert, sensitive eyes took them in.

"Yes?"

"Talk to you in private," said Guiterrez.

"Young man, I am working."

"So are we. Harbour Woods Police."

"Ah, my car is not parked in the correct space. All these university rules. Who can keep up with them?"

"Someplace private," Guiterrez said.

Poulos gazed into Guiterrez's face and did not like what he saw. "All right," he said, "costume change. The swimsuit, Lise. The orange one. George, you can set up by that big cactus there. I want her kneeling, looking up at it. Paying homage. Where can we go, Feld?"

"The rain forest is empty, sir."

The assistant curator began to follow them into the adjoining greenhouse. Guiterrez blocked his path.

Feld blushed. "Of course. I'll close off this area for you."

"Hmmm . . . " Poulos said, looking wary. "Gentlemen, you have exactly ten minutes. What can I do for you?"

"You can stop allotting time for starters," Cyrus said mildly.

Poulos looked at Cyrus for the first time. And then looked back questioningly at Guiterrez.

"This is Professor Wilson from the university. He's working with the Harbour Woods P.D. right now."

Cyrus's face was expressionless. "Mr. Poulos, we understand you were a good friend of Arthur Browne."

"And I still am. There is no past tense about it."

"When did you see him last?"

"Excuse me," the little man said nervously, "but what is this all about? Has something happened to Arthur?"

"Yes, something has happened to Mr. Browne. When did you see him last?"

"I insist on knowing what happened. I saw Arthur only last night. He has talked me into designing scenery for his new play. I insist on —"

"Where did you see him last night?"

" —knowing exactly what is going on."

34

"We'll tell you," Cyrus said quietly, "as soon as you tell us where you were with Browne last night."

Poulos's dark eyes darted from Cyrus to Guiterrez, who was sitting on a brick ledge, his eyes closed.

"We visited the Lawyers Club kitchen . . . " As he said it, it sounded silly to his ears. "I was to use it as a model for a set for Marlowe's *Faustus.* Please, you must tell me what — "

"What time was that?" Cyrus asked.

"Perhaps ten. I had to meet my photographer at eleven o'clock. So I must have left Arthur before then."

"Where did you meet your photographer?"

"At my house. Now I will answer no more questions. I have a right to know what is behind all this. Something has happened to Arthur, hasn't it? Something terrible . . . "

Alarm showed in his dark eyes.

"Two more questions, Mr. Poulos. When you left the Lawyers Club kitchen, did you leave with Browne?"

"Yes. He walked me to my car, which I had parked . . . illegally . . . " He glanced at the immobile Guiterrez, "in the service drive. I will not say another word. I have a lawyer. A good one. I wish to call him immediately if — "

"Did you at any time see anyone else either inside or outside the Lawyers Club kitchen?"

Poulos looked as though he wanted to cry.

"Did you?" Cyrus asked.

"No! Now tell me. I've told you what you've asked. Now you tell me!"

Guiterrez opened his eyes. "Your friend Browne was murdered last night. We found his body this morning in an oven in the Lawyers Club kitchen. He'd been baked to death."

"Connie," came a shout from the desert. "We're all set here."

35

Cyrus moved quickly. He caught the little Greek before his head could strike against a retaining wall.

"You've got a tactful way of breaking news, John," Cyrus said.

Together they dragged Poulos over to the artificial waterfall.

"Connie! We're ready!" came the impatient call.

"Connie's going for a swim," Guiterrez yelled as he and Cyrus took turns throwing water onto the face of the unconscious Constantine Poulos.

7

Sounds of typing from Cyrus's apartment. He understood immediately. Eileen had moved her typewriter into his place. She didn't want to miss him. She wanted to *know.*

She would have to know and she would also have to tell him all she knew about Arthur Browne. And he'd be caught between wanting to know a lot and hoping, as her lover, that she didn't know much.

Cyrus didn't go immediately upstairs to his apartment. He walked through the front hall to Browne's apartment and tried the door. It was locked.

The police hadn't sealed it yet. And it wasn't much of a lock. A credit card slipped against the latch and a quick hard shove would force it. But undoubtedly one of the Genthons would hear him. And that could make for complications.

Cyrus stepped across the hall and knocked on the Genthon door. Paul opened it immediately. Which meant he'd been listening. Well, that was why he received a rent reduction. They had a genuine French concierge.

"Hello, Cyrus. What can I do for you?"

Paul was a pointy-nosed Frenchman with a pencil mustache and slightly soiled superior airs. Eileen suspected he cheated on Marie with a variety of Harbour Woods women who might think Frenchmen were great lovers. Eileen's suspicions were reinforced one day when she'd seen Paul driving a Lincoln Continental accompanied by an older woman. Arthur Browne, Cyrus thought, went for younger women; Paul Genthon went for older ones. If Marie suspected anything she gave no public sign of it. But then she was a Frenchwoman and very proud.

"Paul," Cyrus said, guessing that Genthon hadn't heard yet about Browne, "I left one of my books in Arthur's apartment. He's not in, and I need the damned thing. I wonder if you could let me in."

"Of course, Cyrus," Paul said. And added with that superior air of his, "I did not know that you and Arthur were pals."

"We're not," Cyrus said, irritated. He was a bad liar. "Eileen had my book and . . . " He started to let the sentence trail off, wondering if he looked embarrassed because Paul had begun to smirk knowingly, "she seems to have left it down here."

It turned out to be the right thing to have said to Paul Genthon.

"What kind of book, Cyrus?" Paul smiled sympathetically.

Damn you, Cyrus thought. "A C. P. Snow novel," he replied, grabbing an author out of thin air.

He was hoping Paul would let him wander through the apartment alone.

"It could be in any room, really." Cyrus stepped past Paul into Browne's apartment.

"But, hopefully, not in the bedroom. Hein?"

Go to hell, you goddam frog, Cyrus thought.

Chuckling, Paul followed him through the apartment.

At first there was nothing extraordinary about Arthur

Browne's pad. Typical for an older, educated single man. Books, records, some nice paintings — originals apparently. Wood sculpture. African stuff. Modern lamps: thin, gleaming, tubular. Modern furniture. Danish blonde wood. Then, oddly, on a wall was a poster made up from a still frame from a movie, a nude, the pose: sensual innocence. A pin-up nymphet.

Paul lingered appreciatively in front of it. His lips pursed in silent admiration.

On Browne's bureau a silver-framed photograph of a woman and a girl about fifteen. It caught Cyrus's eye. The girl especially. She was smiling boldly at the person holding the camera. The woman looked faintly unhappy.

"Arthur was married once, you know," Paul offered.

"Is that so?"

"Why don't you try looking for your book in a bookcase, Cyrus?" Paul asked in an amused tone.

He thinks I'm looking for traces of Eileen here, Cyrus thought.

"Right you are," Cyrus said. He made a show of looking in a nearby bookcase. No law books but a lot of stuff on theater. Bentley, Brecht, Ibsen, Stanislavski, Pirandello, Shaw, Pinter, Wesker, James Barrie, and on a lower shelf a group of past and present best-sellers.

"See it?"

"No. I — yes, it's right here."

There, unbelievably, in front of him was a copy of C. P. Snow's novel *The Affair.*

"This is it. Thanks much, Paul."

The Frenchman was astonished. But not as much as Cyrus.

*

Eileen met Cyrus at his door. She looked into his eyes. Trying to read the news there.

"Was it?"

"Yes."

"Oh God, Cyrus. That's awful. That's just awful."

She sank into his old green morris chair and buried her face in her hands.

"Eileen," he said gently.

"I'm all right. I was prepared for it. It's just so hard to believe. We live such insulated lives here in Harbour Woods. In a lovely old house, surrounded by books . . . Who would want to kill someone like Arthur?"

"Somebody would and did. Detective Guiterrez and I are working on some leads."

She gave him a look. "Detective Guiterrez and you?"

"Yes. I'm helping on the case."

"Oh, my God, no. More madness."

"I didn't want to, Eileen. I didn't ask for it. The university has bludgeoned me into it."

"Cyrus, don't get mixed up in it. Let *them* find out who killed him. You're a teacher. You've got to finish your dissertation."

"I know. But . . . "

She stared at him. "You mean," she said slowly, "you *want* to."

He was silent.

"Cyrus, are you crazy? Who are you? Cyrus Wilson, English professor? Or are you going to remain John Agate, boy detective, all your life?"

He took her hands in his. "I'll be Cyrus Wilson," he said gently. "This case won't last forever, Eileen. The town is too small for someone as prominent as Arthur Browne to get bumped off in and the killer get away — "

"Bumped off," she repeated. "Already you're making it casual. Cold. Professional."

"Eileen, does the name Constantine Poulos mean anything to you?"

40

"And now you're interrogating me. Am I a suspect?"

"For pete's sake, just answer me."

"He's Arthur's scene designer. If you'd gone to any of the plays Arthur directed you'd know that. Just yesterday I was having coffee with Marie at the city hall coffee shop and Arthur was telling everyone how his friend Connie Poulos was going to design a magnificent set of hell for him."

"Poulos is a homosexual. He seems to think Arthur was a suppressed homosexual. What's your reaction to this?"

"It can't be."

He looked at her uncomfortably, and then looked away.

"Eileen, do you know someone named Karen Bjorkland?"

"No."

"She's a freshman at the university. After we woke up Poulos from the shock of the news, he told us Bjorkland had tried out for a part in the new play. She was terrible but Arthur made her his assistant."

"So?"

"To Poulos that meant Arthur was sleeping with her."

"He probably was. What's wrong with that?"

Cyrus frowned. "A man in his fifties? She's barely eighteen."

"Arthur liked his women young."

Cyrus hesitated. He was trying very hard not to think of Eileen and Arthur as a couple.

"According to Poulos, the Bjorkland girl had a boyfriend, a football player who used to come to auditions with her. But he hasn't been seen recently."

"Arthur never mentioned him either. As far as I knew, Arthur had no enemies."

"Middle-aged lechers always have enemies."

"He wasn't a lecher."

"That's not what we've heard."

"You've been talking to the wrong people."

Cyrus looked at her, walked away, and then turned and said with a cold tone: "Well, I'm glad I've come to the right person at last. I guess maybe I *ought* to know about you and Arthur Browne."

"Who's asking? Cyrus Wilson or John Agate?"

He didn't have the answer to that.

She looked away from him. "Cyrus," she said quietly but with firmness, "I don't want to fight with you. Not about Arthur Browne. I liked him. I found him charming, widely read, interested in many different sorts of things. And I admired him. He was a lawyer who defended the underdog, the unpopular . . . "

Cyrus, gratefully, seized upon her lead.

"Did Browne ever talk to you about his legal aid work?"

"At times."

"Poulos seemed to think he had problems with his clients."

Eileen thought about it. Outside the traffic roared by, going toward the depot and beyond it the river bridge and the expressways north and west.

"I remember now he once told me about a drug pusher he'd got off with a light sentence. The man seemed to think he shouldn't have been sentenced at all. He was very upset, ranting and raving."

"Did he mention his name?"

"No. I wasn't interested in his name. I wanted to find out about the world of drug pushers."

"Why?"

"One of my stories for the Hillman competition is about the drug culture. I didn't know anything about pushers."

"And he did?"

"Yes. Arthur Browne moved in many different worlds. That's what I'm trying to tell you, Cyrus. He wasn't an ivory-tower intellectual."

"Thanks."

42

"I didn't mean it that way."

"I'm taking it that way."

"Cyrus, are you done playing John Agate with me?"

"Not quite. Did your pal Browne ever talk with you about his marriage?"

Eileen was silent a moment. Then she shrugged. "Yes." Her voice took on a matter-of-fact tone, as though she wanted to undermine her intimate knowledge.

"The marriage didn't last long. Arthur said it was a mistake. He used to quote a line from a Graham Greene novel. Something about pity masking as love. I think he felt sorry for one of the many women who fell in love with him. And he married her."

"Did he also tell you about their sex life?"

"Come on, Cyrus. You asked me a question and I answered it."

"Christ, Eileen, you and he seem to have had close talks on just about everything."

"Well, we were close."

He looked at her and suddenly he was scared and now it didn't matter who was asking, him or John Agate. I should stop right now, he thought. I should get over to the search committee luncheon.

"How close?" he asked.

"Are you asking me if I ever slept with him?"

"That's exactly what I'm asking you."

"You've got no right to ask that, Cyrus. You don't own me. And you don't own my past."

"Cut the women's lib shit, Eileen." His fingers dug into her thin shoulders. "I'm Cyrus Wilson. I love you. And I want to know!"

"Cyrus, you're hurting me. Let go . . . please. Oh, Cyrus —" She burst into tears.

"Eileen," he whispered. "I'm sorry." He held her. He kissed her hair.

She sobbed. "He wanted to. I never let him. I liked him,

43

Cyrus. I admired him. But I didn't understand that part of him . . . and now he's dead."

She went on weeping. For Arthur. For intelligence and philandering, and for the mortality that surrounds us all the time, even in a wonderful world characterized by books and culture.

Cyrus picked her up and carried her into his bedroom. There they made love violently and passionately. And, together, they made death disappear.

For a little while.

8

The administrative wing of Mid-East University Law School is a warren of oak-panelled rooms emitting a powerful feeling of money and tradition.

The dean's secretary had an office twice as big as the one Cyrus shared with two other English instructors.

"I'm Cyrus Wilson from the English department. I don't have an appointment with Dean Russell, but I'm hoping he can find time for me now."

"Dean Russell does have a meeting in a few minutes."

"I've got a class to teach at two so I won't be long."

The secretary disappeared into another office. Cyrus examined the pictures on the oak walls. Eighteenth-century color etchings of barristers. The Law School ranked in the top five of the country and existed in lofty isolation from the rest of the university.

The door opened. "Dean Russell can see you now." She held the door open for him, looking at him curiously, so that Cyrus guessed Russell knew why he was here and had told her.

Tall, craggy, wearing a herringbone-tweed jacket, Frank Russell came around a huge desk, his hand extended.

"I was half expecting you, Mr. Wilson. The fact is: I've had little else on my mind other than the dreadful Arthur Browne news."

The handshake was firm; the expression on the dean's face, worried. The law school was involved in a fund-raising campaign of its own. Cyrus could only conjecture as to the damage the news of a murder in the law quad would have on that campaign.

Russell did not go back to his seat behind the desk, but sat down in an elegant yew parsonage chair. The sun came in through leaded windows and shone on volume after volume of law tomes.

"May I ask when you learned about it, Mr. Russell?

The dean reached for his pipe on the desk. "My secretary heard about it on her coffee break. Art Browne was a part-time member of our faculty. It's been a terrible shock for everyone here. I don't think much work has been getting done in the administrative offices."

He lit his pipe.

"Was Browne well liked by the staff?"

"Oh, yes. Art was one of our more lively adjuncts. You're going to want an answer to the usual question: did he have any enemies on the staff? No, not so far as I knew. We're all quite specialized in the law school; we don't really compete with each other for students the way you people do in the literary college. Art was respected as a go-getter, a live wire. He ran the legal aid clinic and that, as you know, was what he taught: clinical law."

"Any problems with students?"

"We all have problems with students. Law students *are* problems. If I were investigating this dreadful business I'd look at his clinic. They get some pretty unsavory types down there."

46

"We'll be looking there, too. As far as you know then, Arthur Browne had no special problems with faculty, staff, or students?"

Russell examined his pipe. He smiled mournfully. "No special or unique problems," he said, "that we all haven't had from time to time."

"For example?"

Russell hesitated. "You understand that what I'm about to tell you must be held in strictest confidence."

Cyrus nodded. Nothing was confidential in a murder case. The dean knew that as well as he did, but the nod was salve enough for his conscience.

"This semester a second-year student, female, came to me and complained, reluctantly, about Art." Russell looked pained. Motes danced in the golden shaft of light between them. "It wasn't anything I took very seriously, you understand. Until . . . Earl Freeman also talked to me about it. Do you know Earl?"

"No."

"He's our development officer. In charge of our alumni fund-raising programs. The gist of the young lady's complaint was that Browne, she alleged, offered to give her an A in the clinical law course if she would . . . " Russell looked *very* unhappy now, "would uh . . . sleep with him." He pronounced the word "sleep" with distaste.

"What was the student's name?" Cyrus asked, wondering why Russell was shocked. Was the law school *this* farther removed from the facts of life than the rest of the university?

"Her name is Sylvia Minkus. And two things are disturbing about her allegation. One is that she seemed to me to be a fairly level-headed girl. She was reluctant to confront me with this. And only did so on the urging of her father. Our second disturbing item. The father is a graduate of our school and a prominent Philadelphia attorney. Which was how Earl Freeman came into the picture. Minkus senior called Earl about this and wanted to know what kind of faculty his money was supporting."

A damn good question, Cyrus thought.

"Did you talk with Browne about this?"

Russell nodded. He looked at his pipe. No refuge there. And then at Cyrus. "Rather off-handedly, of course. But I knew he'd get the point. 'Young women imagine a good many things these days,' I said."

"And his response?"

"He laughed and denied it. As any sensible person would."

"What did you think?"

"I accepted his denial. Though, frankly, between the two of us, I didn't quite accept it in my heart. Art has always been an oddball on our faculty. We're all, for the most part, teachers rather than lawyers. Art was probably our one true lawyer teaching. As such he came with quirks. He said what he thought, which is always a dangerous thing to do on a college campus. And there were the rumors — a swinging bachelor, and his civic activities, not quite what you'd expect a law professor to be engaged in. Theater . . . "

Russell pronounced the word with scorn.

"Did you get back to the girl?"

"Of course. I called her back here and told her that Professor Browne denied it and that, indeed, it was a very serious charge to bring against a faculty member. I told her she could make a complaint, which would then institute a regular procedure. There would be an investigation, a hearing . . . By that time she wanted out, of course. Which is practically the point of the procedure. I suspect she was more afraid of her father than anyone else in the first place."

48

"Why?"

"I didn't go into it. But fathers being fathers and daughters being daughters, you can draw your own conclusions." Suddenly Russell looked startled. "Surely you're not thinking that Minkus senior came out here — "

"I'm not thinking anything, Mr. Russell. Not yet. What was your gut impression? Did you find her allegation credible?"

Russell was silent. "I don't know . . . Excuse me, I didn't know Art Browne very well. There were the rumors. The theater business I never found attractive, but certainly understandable. Our profession is filled with frustrated actors. From a dean's point of view, he was a conscientious teacher, unlike some adjuncts we've had in the past. He met his classes regularly. He was also a model board member of the Lawyers Club." Russell looked at Cyrus for a moment. "Was his body really found there in . . . an oven?"

"That's right."

Russell shivered. "How gruesome. It's clear we're dealing with a maniac."

"Do you happen to know the name of Sylvia Minkus's father?"

Russell sighed. "Lawrence. Lawrence Minkus, Class of '51, law. With the very prestigious firm of Hopkins, Pennypacker, and Waltrous. Really, Mr. Wilson, Minkus is hardly the type to bake a fellow advocate no matter what lewd propositions were made to his daughter." He eyed Cyrus dolorously. "I take it that Minkus will now become part of your investigation?"

"I'm afraid so."

"Could you bear in mind, Mr. Wilson, that Larry Minkus has through the years been a most generous giver to our alumni fund?"

"I will bear that in mind, sir." Cyrus rose. "But look at

49

it this way, Dean Russell. If innocent, Mr. Minkus may be delighted with the news and double his donation."

Russell's face brightened. "I hadn't thought of that. Well," he smiled, "let's just hope you're right."

They shook hands.

9

Guiterrez was waiting for Cyrus after his two o'clock class. He looked more tired than he was before. A short nap will do that to an exhausted man.

"I been listening in the hall to you, Prof. You didn't tell them a damn thing."

"Secret of good teaching. It keeps them coming back."

"And my taxes go for that? Jesus, let's get out of here."

"John, I want to go down to the legal aid clinic."

"What for?"

"A friend of mine told me one of Browne's clients threatened him. I want to find out which one."

"What friend told you that?"

"A girl who lives in our house."

"Your girl, Prof?"

"Yes."

"She knew Browne?"

"Yes." Cyrus gritted his teeth. After all, he thought, it had only been a matter of time.

Guiterrez yawned. "Let's go."

"I also want a check run on a Philadelphia lawyer named Lawrence Minkus. Browne apparently propositioned his daughter, who was a student of his. Minkus was furious when he found out. We might as well find out where Minkus was last night. And we've got to check out Karen Bjorkland's boyfriend."

"You got his name?"

"Not yet. I thought we'd talk to Bjorkland first. She lives in Blackwell Hall."

Guiterrez looked at Cyrus thoughtfully. "You been busy for a guy teaching classes, Prof."

"That's why I don't tell them anything. I don't have the time."

Guiterrez smiled. "Let's go."

*

The city's legal aid clinic was lodged in a small office on the second floor of the city hall, adjacent to a nest of larger offices that were all part of the city manager's domain.

They found the door of the legal aid office closed and locked.

"It's a part-time operation," said Guiterrez. "We can get a key next door."

"I know someone who works there," Cyrus said.

They passed a counter covered with brochures and notices about city licensing practices, minutes of the last council meeting, Harbour Woods bicycle regulations, parking structure fee schedules . . .

From the counter Cyrus could see a row of cubicles. Marie Genthon's cubicle was off to the right. Cyrus had dropped in here once before to pick up Eileen after a meeting on her free-lance writing assignment for the Harbour Woods brochure.

He saw Marie alone in her cubicle, sitting there staring at the wall in front of her.

Cyrus beckoned to Guiterrez, who followed him around the counter and back to the cubicles.

"Marie," Cyrus said softly.

And still she almost jumped. "Cyrus," she said, and tears appeared in her eyes. "Isn't it awful? I can't get over it. Paul called me with the news. It's so terrible. What is this world we live in, Cyrus?"

She was a slim, attractive woman and sorrow made her even sexier, Cyrus thought. Behind him he sensed Guiterrez looking at Marie with interest.

"Arthur was so nonviolent, so charmant. Why, Cyrus, why?"

"That's what we want to find out, Marie. I'd like you to meet Detective Guiterrez from the police department."

Marie looked at Guiterrez. She dabbed at her eyes with a handkerchief that was already pretty wet. "Yes, I've seen you in the building."

"Same here." Guiterrez smiled crookedly.

"Marie," Cyrus interposed, "we're looking for the name of one of Browne's legal aid clients. The clinic's locked."

"They went home when they heard the news."

"You have a key, Miss?" Guiterrez asked.

"*Mrs.* Genthon," Cyrus said.

Guiterrez laughed. "Prof looks out for young women," he said. "Married or not, you got a key?"

Marie blushed. "No. But there is a spare one around here somewhere. I will go find it."

She brushed by them both.

"Cute," Guiterrez said. "Where's she from?"

"France."

"Funny how she found her way to your house, Prof. And Browne too."

"Those things happen."

"How well did *you* know Browne?"

"Not too well," Cyrus said, resenting feeling uncomfortable with the question. He shrugged. "My girl liked him. So I didn't."

"Maybe I ought to check your alibi for last night."

"I don't have one."

"Could be a twist, no?" Guiterrez said. "Investigating detective is the killer."

"Twist maybe, first no," Cyrus replied. "Back in 1887, Roul Fouchon, a Sûreté inspector investigated a case in which he was the killer."

"Did he know it?"

"No. He was a schizoid personality."

"Then it doesn't really count. What happened anyway?"

"He was guillotined."

Guiterrez shook his head. "How the hell do you know things like that, Prof?"

"Research. Once I was going to write a John Agate mystery in which Agate was the killer."

"What stopped you?"

"It would have ended the John Agate series."

"Mercy killing, huh?"

Marie came back with a key in her hand.

"Do you know what you're looking for?" she pointedly asked Cyrus.

"Not exactly."

They stepped into an office with stacks of papers all over the floor and filing cabinets tilted in all directions. Legal aid for the oppressed and the poor, Cyrus thought with dismay.

"Perhaps you ought to call Shirley Martin," Marie said. "She's Arthur's secretary and knows where everything is. She's home now. I'll get her on the phone for you, Cyrus."

A moment later he was talking to Shirley Martin, who was, by the sound of her voice, black.

Cyrus apologized for disturbing her and described to her the man Poulos had described to them.

After a silence, Shirley Martin said: "That would be

Ricky Andrews. He's a hot-tempered young punk. If there's anything dirty or illegal going on in Harbour Woods, he's likely to be involved in it, Mr. Wilson. He manages the adult bookstore on Warren Street when he's not in jail."

"What happened between Mr. Browne and Ricky Andrews?"

"Ricky ran a drug operation in the county and he got caught selling cocaine to two undercover deputies. That's how smart he was. Not one. Two. Arthur got him off with only a six-month sentence. Andrews blew up in court." She was silent. "Do you think he killed Arthur?"

"I don't know, Ms. Martin."

He heard her breathing on the phone. "Arthur Browne was a wonderful boss, Mr. Wilson. And a wonderful man . . . " She broke down and started to cry.

"Ms. Martin," Cyrus said, "where does Ricky Andrews live?"

"Out toward Ypsi," she sobbed. "In the Village Apartments off the expressway." She fought for and got control of herself. "I'm sorry, but it's such a shock. You're in our office right now, aren't you? Well, you face the front door and on your left you'll see a green file cabinet. Right? OK, bottom of that file there's a drawer. In it, Arthur kept a folder of what he called his problem children. Ricky Andrews should be in that folder. But if he killed Arthur, he wouldn't be staying in his apartment, would he?"

"We'll find out. Thanks."

"I hope you catch him, Mr. Wilson. The legal aid program never had a more dedicated person trying to help the poor people of this town than Arthur Browne. I hope you catch his killer. I only wish we had the death penalty in Michigan. I'd like to see him burn."

*

His uncle gave Cyrus a temporary office next to his. In it, they had the first meeting of the new investigative team: Cyrus, Guiterrez, the chief, and two detectives assigned to them — Tom Tinker, a solid, careful black man who had been on the force for over twenty years, and Hal Layne, slim and good-humored and perhaps the best dresser on the force.

"What do you have so far, Cyrus?" the chief asked.

"Someone's got to go out and check this Ricky Andrews, the Village Apartments out by the expressway."

"I'll take it," Tinker said. "I know the manager out there."

"Tink and I get a lot of trouble from that place, don't we?" Layne said. "They got amateurs and pros living out there. John, you remember we had a fatal OD out there New Year's Day?"

"Yeah."

"I've got a lawyer in Philadelphia who needs checking out," Cyrus went on. "He's got a daughter who was a student of Browne's. Apparently Browne propositioned her and Papa was supposed to have been pretty sore. Name of Minkus, Lawrence."

"Me," Layne said. "I did a favor last year for a guy on Center City homicide there."

"Then there's Karen Bjorkland, eighteen years old, freshman at the university. According to Poulos, Browne's latest mistress. She has a boyfriend who's a football player — "

"We're getting a profile here, aren't we?" the chief said.

"Of a candidate for an oven," Guiterrez said.

"John, you want to check out Bjorkland and the boyfriend?"

"Why don't we take it together, Prof?" Guiterrez asked casually. He wasn't going to let Cyrus out of his sight. Not to foul up things or to solve things by himself.

56

"Suits me," Cyrus said. "Let's get going."

"Gentlemen," the chief said, picking up some telephone messages left for him, "may I remind you of the not inconsiderable pressure we're under from the media, the university, and — "

But he was talking to an empty office. They were gone.

10

The housemother at Blackwell Hall was an elderly, southern lady named Madelon Cross. She greeted them in her apartment-office on the first floor.

"When I heard the news, gentlemen," she said softly, "I knew it was only a matter of time before you were here."

"Why, ma'am?" Cyrus asked.

"Because we were all upset about Karen. You know, gentlemen, there are dorms and there are dorms on this campus. Blackwell is an honor students' dorm. We seek and accept a certain type of girl here. We still call them 'girls' and not women. There are coed dorms on campus, there are apartments, co-ops, single rooms where rules are bent because of the times in which we live. This is not true at Blackwell Hall and there is no pressure on us to make it that way. When a girl applies to Blackwell Hall she is almost always a serious, high-minded girl of good morality. Karen Bjorkland came here that way six weeks ago."

"And what happened?"

"She got involved with a detestable man. Through a theater course. And she only a freshman. I spoke to her about it several times. Her boyfriend was terribly angry. If her father knew, he would be terribly angry too. She comes from a small town upstate — Gladwin. I told her that she was behaving in a fashion that didn't suit either Gladwin *or* Blackwell Hall."

"What did she say?" Guiterrez asked.

Mrs. Cross's handsome face looked severe. "She moved out of Blackwell Hall last week."

"Where to?"

"To an apartment in town. I don't have the address. But I believe it's on Hill Street. She shares it with some other girls from the theater department. Perhaps that detestable man was paying for the apartment. I don't know. I don't want to know. All I can say is that while I don't approve of anyone being murdered, I can't think of anyone who deserved it more than Mr. Arthur Browne."

There was still a lot of venom left in the old South, Cyrus thought.

"Karen's boyfriend," he said mildly, "what's his name?"

"Gary Dunning."

"Could you tell us about him?"

Mrs. Cross hesitated.

"In a case of murder, ma'am, we must consider everyone and everything. Could you tell us a little more about him? For instance, how did you know he was 'terribly angry'?"

The housemother was silent. "All right. I don't like to eavesdrop on people, but one night I was making myself a cup of tea in the kitchen and I heard some raised voices in the lounge. I went out to tell whoever it was to hush. It was Gary and Karen, arguing. He was yelling at her. Before I could make my presence known, he . . . slapped her. And then he ran out of the house. I was absolutely shocked. It's not the kind of thing one sees in Blackwell

59

Hall. It wasn't the kind of behavior I would have expected from a boy like Gary Dunning. I didn't think he had that kind of temper. To me he was a nice farm boy, gentle, thank God, for someone of his size. And always, always polite."

"What did Karen do after he slapped her?" Cyrus asked.

"She just stood there. I tried to talk to her. To tell her that one thing always leads to another. That the kind of life she was leading was bound to bring on incidents like that. That was when she told me she was moving out."

"Do you know if she saw Gary again?"

"I don't know. The fact is, I haven't seen her since."

"Do you have Gary's address?"

"He lives at North Quad. That's the freshman football dorm. I'm sure he's at football practice right now."

Cyrus looked at Guiterrez, who shook his head. He had no questions.

"We'll be getting in touch with Karen, Mrs. Cross. If she should call here, would you please tell her that we have to talk with her. She can call either Detective Guiterrez at the Harbour Woods Police Department or me. Here's my card."

The housemother read his name and then the blue eyes fixed on him. "Why are you, a professor, investigating a murder?"

Cyrus sensed Guiterrez's silent amusement.

"The Harbour Woods Police Department needs assistance, ma'am," Cyrus said.

Guiterrez rose. "Let's move it, Prof."

"Many thanks for all your help, Mrs. Cross," Cyrus said.

"I hope you're successful, Professor Wilson, but Arthur Browne will not be missed. Not around here anyway."

*

"Do we look up the boy or the girl first?" Guiterrez asked.

"The boy," Cyrus said. "Poulos told us he threatened to punch Browne at the theater rehearsal. He's already slapped his girlfriend. With a temper like that and the kind of strength he's got, we'd better check on him right away."

They headed south down State Street to the university's football practice fields.

"By the way, what was that crack for about the police department?" Guiterrez asked.

"I was looking for a quick exit," Cyrus said. "I knew that you'd get us out of there fast."

Guiterrez yawned. "You're funny, Prof."

*

The head football coach glowered at them. He wore a baseball cap and a sweat shirt that said MID-EAST FOOT-BALL, and carried a whistle on a black ribbon around his neck. His face was an ancient road map of wrinkles, grooves, roadbeds in the flesh worn by a hundred thousand practices in sun, wind, rain, and snow.

"Dunning's a kid," Wally Lassiter growled, "a freshman. Eighteen years old. What the hell do cops want with him?"

They stood on the edge of Mid-East's practice fields —a huge complex of artificial turf fields adjoining the university's stadium.

As always when watching a Mid-East football practice, Cyrus was both awed and resentful. More than one hundred and fifty players, almost all huge, in a variety of uniforms, were scrimmaging or running through plays. A dozen assistant coaches, some paid, some volunteers, were working with their special units: offensive line, defensive line, receivers, centers, defensive backfield, offensive backfield, punters, kickers, punt return men, special teams . . .

61

There were punting machines for those who ran back punts; at the far end of the field, kickers were practicing field goals, holders practicing receiving center snaps.

It was an industrial complex worthy of General Motors and had, Cyrus always felt, no place in an educational institution. But it brought in money and the man who ran it — Wally Lassiter — was a virtual dictator, reporting only to a businessman athletic director who left him alone as long as every seat in the stadium was filled.

Lassiter, National Coach-of-the-Year ten years ago, looked with narrow, mean eyes at Guiterrez's silver-plated badge.

"What is it? A pot charge?" he asked with contempt.

Guiterrez stiffened. "Not quite," he said. "We want to ask Gary Dunning some questions."

"What about?"

"About a murder that took place last night," Cyrus interjected. Guiterrez and Lassiter were like two big dogs sizing each other up before battling.

Lassiter looked at him. His stare was penetrating. "You're the professor, aren't you?"

"That's right."

"The kid wouldn't kill anyone."

"That's your opinion," Guiterrez snapped.

Lassiter's eyes narrowed. For a crazy moment Cyrus thought the old coach might just throw a punch at Guiterrez.

"We think," Cyrus said quietly, "that Gary might be able to help us with some information."

Lassiter didn't take his gaze from Guiterrez. "You got a court order to talk to him?"

"Not yet," Guiterrez said.

"Gentlemen, we're holding up practice," Cyrus said.

Lassiter looked away first. Cyrus's words seemed to have given him an approach to the situation. "Look, boys," he said, his voice softening, "I got a tough schedule this year. We haven't had an easy time in or out of the conference the past two years. My job might be up for grabs. I'm not ready to retire and I'm too old to look for another line of work. You get what I'm saying? Like the prof here says, I got a practice to run."

"Five minutes," Cyrus pressed. "Just give us five minutes with this student."

The word "student" was intentional. Lassiter looked at Cyrus for a moment and then at his clipboard. He shouted at an assistant coach.

"Where's offensive line 2A?"

"South end, working on . . . " — the coach consulted *his* clipboard, looked at his watch — "pass blocking."

"Get Dunning over here. Don't tell him why. Just get him here."

"You bet."

The assistant coach summoned one of many student managers who also wore uniforms and cleats. The boy dashed across the field with the élan of a player entering the game.

"You got five minutes with the kid. That's all," Lassiter said. "A kid loses more than five minutes he moves to a different subgrouping." He shouted at a group of players. "All right, white shirts, let's get going. You looked like my Aunt Mary's church team on that last series. Get your ass in gear, Willie. Last year's press clippings ain't gonna help you out none this year. Those guys from Ohio State can't read anyway."

A laugh went up. Cyrus understood then that while talking to them the coach had been carefully observing a series of plays. Despite his misgivings about the football program, Cyrus found the coach impressive. His changes of language. Educated talk, black English, blue-collar white English — the coach could probably lecture in the linguistics department.

What was truly impressive was that, despite going from

a top-ten national ranking year after year to several mediocre seasons and, last year, a losing season, Lassiter's teams continued to fill the 98,000-seat stadium for every home game.

Shrewd, hard-driving, Lassiter was America's last old-fashioned football coach. The players, apparently, adored him.

*

"You're Gary?" Cyrus asked a big, perspiring kid wearing a purple pullover jersey. He looked as though he'd just stepped off the farm. And weighed about two hundred and sixty pounds.

"Yes, sir. I'm Gary," the boy said, glancing at Lassiter for instructions.

"They got five minutes with you, Dunning. After that, back to your unit."

"Sure, Coach. How can I help you fellas?"

He thought they were reporters. And yet, he wasn't sure. No pencils. No cassette recorders. Gary Dunning's youthful eyes contained a wariness beyond their years. Maybe these kids experience more than we know, Cyrus thought. These prize recruits who come to manhood dealing with avaricious alumni, fast-talking recruiters, reporters, promises of pie in the sky. Maybe you grow old very fast at eighteen when you're six foot five and weigh two hundred and sixty pounds. You develop a sense of your own dollar-worth. Right on the hoof.

Cyrus waited till Lassiter drifted off with his clipboard. Beads of sweat stood out on Gary Dunning's broad brow.

"We'd like to know where you were last night, Gary."

It seemed like a question he almost had expected.

His face grew more guarded. "What for?"

"A man you didn't like got hurt last night," Guiterrez

said. "We want to make sure you didn't have anything to do with it."

There was a subtle shift in the boy's face but Cyrus couldn't tell what it meant exactly. A new set of gears began operating in the kid's head.

"Who got hurt?" Gary asked.

"A man named Arthur Browne."

Gary Dunning's face was blank. And then an expression of distaste — pure, ethereal, unadulterated distaste — passed over his otherwise stolid features.

"Him. What happened to him?"

"He was murdered," Cyrus said.

"Jesus." There was no feigning here, Cyrus thought. But fear. For whom? Himself? Karen Bjorkland?

"We heard you once put on quite a show at the City Players threatening to beat him up," Guiterrez said.

The boy didn't hesitate. "That's right. I did that," he said. "He took my girl from me. I was pretty sore. But I'm not sore no more." He hesitated. "Does Karen know about this?"

"We haven't seen her yet. We're going to. Where does she live now, Gary?"

"Twelve-hundred Hill Street." Gary looked away from them. His eyes were thoughtful. Players yelled and whistles blew. But he wasn't watching the practice. "You know, this could be the best break she ever got. I hope she sees it like that."

"That sounds like you're not seeing her anymore," Cyrus said.

"I ain't. I got another girl now. Karen and I were high school sweethearts." He blushed. It was touching, Cyrus thought. Standing there as big as he was, blushing. "We come down here together. But it's no big deal for a jock to get a girl on this campus."

He managed to look even a little pleased with himself.

Guiterrez's lips curled with contempt. "What's the name of your new girl, kid?"

"Mary Lee Johnson," Gary said, looking at Guiterrez, surprised at his tone. "She's from Battle Creek."

"Where were you last night?"

And there it was again. A subtle shift of expression. A thin curtain coming down over his eyes.

"Back at the dorm."

Guiterrez caught it too.

"Got any witnesses to that?"

The boy's eyes locked stubbornly with Guiterrez's. "Sure. The whole dorm. The whole floor. My roomie."

"Who's your roomie?"

"Alex Franke. He's a defensive lineman."

"You're an offensive lineman," Guiterrez snapped. "Since when does he room offense with defense?"

Gary shrugged. "We're roomies."

"What's your phone number?"

"Seven-six-something."

"Don't you know your own number?"

"I never call myself."

"Where were you till midnight?"

"I was around."

"Around where?"

"Like I said: the dorm. With a lot of guys maybe."

"Doing what?"

"Studying. Maybe horsing around."

"Was Alex Franke with you?"

"He could've been. You know how it is in the dorm. Guys come. Guys go."

"Is Alex Franke on the field right now?"

The boy's eyes were mockingly blank.

"No. He's got a bad knee. He's been off practice for a couple of weeks now."

"Where can we find him?"

66

"I dunno. Sometimes he's in the tub over at the field house. But I don't know where he is right now."

"We'll check with him. And the others, too," Guiterrez said.

For a moment again the veil lifted and a slight expression of concern appeared in the boy's eyes.

"Hey," he said, "you don't think I'd do anything to an old guy like that?"

"You threatened him in public," Guiterrez said.

"And someone pretty strong knocked him out and dragged him into an oven," Cyrus added quietly.

"And baked him to death," Guiterrez wrapped it up.

The boy looked sick.

"All right," Wally Lassiter growled, closing faster than any of his defensive backs, and Cyrus knew he'd had an eye on them all the time. "You had your five minutes and more. Now you got my boy here disturbed. Get back to your unit, Gary. I'll take care of the rest of this."

"Yes, sir." Gary wheeled and ran off.

"All right," Lassiter said softly, "what the fuck is this about?"

"A man Gary once threatened bodily harm to got killed last night, Mr. Lassiter. And someone big enough to do it hauled his body into a bake oven."

Lassiter's pale blue eyes went from Cyrus to Guiterrez and back to Cyrus again. "Am I supposed to believe that?"

"It'll be in tonight's papers."

Lassiter turned to watch a play being run off. They were hitting hard in practice. You could hear the pads a long way off. And then the shouts and the hand-slapping.

"Listen, both of you," Lassiter said softly. "Listen to me carefully. My kids only kill people on the gridiron. You got that?"

He stuck a forefinger into Guiterrez's chest. "I recruit kids who like to hit people. I recruit kids who like to hurt people. But they don't go around killing people off the field." He jabbed rhythmically with his finger.

"Coach," Guiterrez said softly, "you get your finger off my chest or I'll break it off."

Lassiter looked at him. "Where'd you play ball, son?"

"Ypsi," Guiterrez said.

Lassiter nodded. "You looked familiar." The finger came away. Lassiter smiled bleakly. "A little small for a big man," he said. "Just a little small." The smile vanished. The blue eyes bore into Guiterrez's dark eyes. "Get off my field, son," he said icily. "If you want to come back, get a court order."

Guiterrez's face was a mask but Cyrus knew how close to the surface lay the detective's violence.

"Let's move along, John," Cyrus said. And to Lassiter: "We *will* have that court order next time, Mr. Lassiter."

"Fuck off," Wally Lassiter said. "You too." He spat on the ground between them and then walked away from them.

Only when they had left the artificial turf and were on natural grass again did Guiterrez produce a string of oaths that would have done honor to even a major college football coach.

When he was done, Cyrus asked, "Feel better?"

"No."

"I didn't know you played football."

"I didn't. They took away my scholarship after my freshman year. I hurt my knee. I had to quit school. That's when I became a cop."

"How'd he know you played ball?"

"Bastards like him know everything. I hate them."

They got into Guiterrez's car and drove over the grass toward the gate.

"I get like this when I'm around guys like him. It brings back memories of what I could've been."

"You know," Cyrus said as they left the athletic complex and turned up State Street toward campus, "I went through school and I'd still like to be a cop."

"You are a cop, Prof," Guiterrez snapped, and then he breathed out. He tried to put a grin on his face. "A cop's a way of looking at life, Prof. Guys lose jobs because they're cops in jobs they're not supposed to be cops in."

He was beginning to come unwound. The adrenalin that Lassiter had pumped up inside him was going now, leaving the old fatigue just a bit deeper.

"What did you think of Dunning?" he asked Cyrus.

"He's got the size, the strength, and the desire."

Guiterrez laughed.

"But he's also got a new girl and half the dorm alibiing for him. Maybe," Cyrus added.

Guiterrez yawned. "I hate seeing cases widen."

"In the end they narrow."

"Only in your books, Prof."

"You read any, John?"

"Both of them."

"There are four."

"Two was enough."

They went through the amber light at State and Packard and headed up toward Hill Street. Guiterrez's eyes were closing as he drove.

"I was thinking," Guiterrez said slowly, "about this Arthur Browne guy. He was really a piece of shit. Any way you looked at him. The guy spent his days getting dope pushers and murderers free on technicalities and back onto the streets where they can fuck up and kill young people. Nights he fucks young people personally. Girls young enough to be his daughter. I think maybe it's good riddance to bad rubbish, Prof."

Cyrus studied Guiterrez's profile. Was he being told something?

"Maybe," Cyrus said, "but in this town you've got to have a license to collect rubbish."

Guiterrez yawned. "That's what the law says."

They stopped at 1200 Hill. Karen Bjorkland's roommates reported that she had left town. She'd gone home to Gladwin.

Cyrus got behind the wheel of the car. "I'll drive, John. You sack out. Tomorrow I'll go up north and check out the girl. You can check out Gary's new girl, the roomie, and all the dormitory alibis."

Guiterrez had no objection. He was asleep already.

11

"Who are you and what do you want?"

The words were flat and unfriendly. The speaker was a tall, thin, grizzled farmer in his late fifties. He wore a checkered mackinaw jacket, coveralls, an orange cap with the letters CAT on it. Behind him, in crisp November sunlight, a row of maples led down a dirt driveway to a large farmhouse with peeling paint everywhere you looked. Beyond the house was a weathered barn, and alongside and beyond the barn a pasture and cornfields.

All of it, Cyrus thought, was in stark contrast to Karen Bjorkland's life in Harbour Woods: the world of the theater, Arthur Browne, Constantine Poulos, make-up, scene design, rehearsals, *Faustus*.

"I'm Cyrus Wilson, Mr. Bjorkland. And this is my associate Eileen O'Hanrahan. We've come up from Harbour Woods —"

He got no further.

"If you're from Harbour Woods you can git right back there," Farmer Bjorkland said, and spat onto the grass. "Karen's not going back there."

Eileen nudged Cyrus, but he had already glimpsed a

girl's face in the second floor window. The curtains closed again.

"We haven't come up here to bring your daughter back to the university, Mr. Bjorkland. It's something more serious. There was a murder in Harbour Woods Monday night. I've been asked by the university to work with the police in investigating it. We feel Karen may be able to shed some light on it for us."

He offered Farmer Bjorkland the police identification card his uncle had made up for him yesterday. Bjorkland ignored it. He spat again. His stubbly jaw worked some kind of chew.

"I would like to talk to Karen, if I can," Cyrus said.

"You can't," Farmer Bjorkland said.

"Why not?"

"She ain't here. No one's here but me."

"I believe she's in there, sir, and I'm asking again to see her."

"And I'm telling you, son, get the hell off my property."

Cyrus sighed. "All that means, sir, is that I will have to return with a court order permitting me to talk with Karen as a material witness in a homicide investigation. Or, what's more likely, have the state police bring her down to Harbour Woods for the prosecuting attorneys to question her."

Cyrus paused. The old farmer looked at him with hate. And then with equal dislike at Eileen. She looked grimly back at him. She didn't like him either, Cyrus thought. Eileen was quick and accurate in her likes and dislikes.

He hadn't brought Eileen with him to rural Roscommon County to confront a balky old farmer. He'd brought her because he thought she might be of help with Karen. Especially if the young girl was, as he suspected, frightened. And had left Harbour Woods in fear.

In addition, Cyrus had thought Eileen could use a break

from her work. She had finished the revisions of her stories for the Hillman competition. They were being photocopied right now in Harbour Woods. Eileen had no classes on Wednesdays. It was only a two-hour ride up here; she could fix a picnic lunch for them and they could also make a fall color outing of it, since the leaves were just turning.

"All right," Eileen had agreed, "I'll go with you, Cyrus. But I have to get back in time for dinner. Marie, Bob, and I are meeting the new assistant director of the Chamber of Commerce at the Swingletree Restaurant. The brochure was his idea. Something that worked for him back east and that he believes will help Harbour Woods."

"I'll get you to your free-lance job in time," Cyrus had promised.

"What'd you say your name was, son?" Bjorkland asked. The prosecuting attorney threat had done its job. His tone was different.

"Cyrus Wilson," Cyrus said politely.

The old farmer nodded as though the name had an intrinsic meaning.

"Mr. Wilson, let me ask you something. That man down there that was killed. You know about him?"

"Yes, sir."

"He wasn't a very good man. She told me all about him. She didn't want to. But I made her. What he did with her wasn't nice. A man his age. A girl her age. How I see it, Mr. Wilson, someone did the world a favor getting rid of a man like that. You follow me?"

The old man looked away from them. At his barns, at the fields beyond bathed in sunlight.

His voice was low. "A varmint gets into your fields you shoot it before it destroys your whole crop. And you done the right thing." He looked at the two of them. "You look like nice folks. Why don't you leave and go back home? My Karen's been through enough."

"You didn't happen to kill Mr. Arthur Browne, did you, sir?" Cyrus asked, almost cordially, suggesting by his tone that he wouldn't be entirely without sympathy or understanding for Farmer Bjorkland if he had done it.

"No, sir," the jaw wagged, "I didn't. But I would of if I had the chance." And then the anger thrust itself unformed into his voice. His Adam's apple bobbled. The words came exploding out.

"I sent that girl down there to get an education. You know the kind of education she got? In sin. That's what she got. She got an education in sin. Karen was a good Christian girl what went to Sunday school all her life. She taught Sunday school till this year. What happened to her down there, Mr. Wilson? That's what I want to know. What did you people with your fancy ways and your fancy books and your fancy clothes do to her down there? And you want me to help you find the one who destroyed the varmint? No, no, NO!"

He coughed and spat violently. A tractor had appeared in one of the fields and moved peacefully over the rows of corn stubble.

The old man watched it. Its movements seemed to relax him. His lips moved, his jaw waggled, his Adam's apple bobbled, but no words came out. His engine was running down.

Eileen looked uneasily at Cyrus.

"Mr. Bjorkland," Cyrus said gently, "either we talk with Karen now or the state police will take her back to Harbour Woods."

The threat, for the old man, was not the cops; it was Harbour Woods.

He breathed out. "All right, but you upset her, Mr. Wilson, and I'll make you sorrier than you ever been."

74

He headed toward the house, not waiting for them to follow.

"Let's go," Cyrus said.

"You were very good, Cyrus," Eileen murmured.

They followed the old farmer toward the decaying farmhouse.

"I hope you don't mind being my 'associate,' " Cyrus said. "I was going to say 'friend' but it might have sounded to him as though we were living together."

"I can see that," she said.

They went up four wide and sagging porch steps that hadn't been painted in many years into a glass enclosed front room with wicker chairs in it that looked like they hadn't been sat on in many years.

And finally into the house proper: cold, empty, the touch of a woman's hand long absent. In checking on Karen Bjorkland's history at the dean of students' office that morning, Cyrus had learned that her mother had died when she was twelve. That she had two older sisters who did not live at home. That she was the first one in her family ever to attend college.

Bjorkland stood in the hall, one hand on the newel post of a stairway.

"Karen!" he shouted up the steps. "Git down here."

Eileen shuddered.

Moments later Karen Bjorkland came down the stairs. And neither Cyrus nor Eileen were prepared for her beauty. Her eyes were large and luminous, her skin fair and clear. Blonde hair tumbled down her shoulders. She had a slight but lovely figure. She looked of the theater. It was difficult to perceive how she was related to the tall, grizzled farmer who was her father.

Her voice was quiet, deep, self-assured.

"I'm Karen Bjorkland," she said. And held out her hand. First to Eileen. Then to Cyrus.

75

"I'm Cyrus Wilson, Karen. This is Eileen O'Hanrahan. We teach at the university."

She frowned, puzzled. "You're not from the dean of students' office then?"

"No. A lot of students leave school suddenly," Cyrus said. "The dean's office will undoubtedly be in touch with you. But that's not why we're here."

She hesitated, glancing at her father, and made up her mind about something. She was obviously concerned to know why they were here. "Won't you sit down, please? Would you like something to drink? Some tea or coffee?"

"They won't be here that long," the old man said gruffly. "They're wanting to ask you about that boyfriend of yours."

Karen winced. "Dad, please — "

"Just answer their questions and I'll send them on their way."

Karen turned to them helplessly. "It's terrible . . . I'm so sorry. How can I help you?"

What was "terrible," Cyrus wondered? Browne's death or her being stuck here with her father?

"When did you learn of Arthur Browne's death, Karen?"

Her face composed itself, as only an actress can make it do. "I heard it on the radio Tuesday morning."

"Why did you leave town?"

She hesitated. "I was going to quit school anyway. I . . . " she glanced at her father, "I was getting pretty mixed up."

Farmer Bjorkland opened his mouth to say something, thought the better of it, and clamped his jaws shut tight.

"Do you know of anyone who might have wanted to kill Arthur Browne?" Cyrus asked gently.

She shook her head, and then after another glance at her father, replied, "No. He had no enemies. He was a very kind man. I can't think of anyone who hated him."

"Kind," Bjorkland said. "You call a man who'd take advantage of an eighteen-year-old girl kind?"

She faced her father bravely. "He was kind, Father. And he was nice. And he was intelligent and — "

A hard, callous hand came through the air and made contact with her face. Karen staggered back with the force of the slap. Tears sprang into her eyes. She held a hand to her cheek. It was red.

"You didn't have to do that," Eileen said angrily.

"You stay out of it, Miss. I don't know what your father thinks you do down there in Harbour Woods, but I know what she was doing. And I blame her mother for it. Always putting fancy ideas in the girl's head. Act in plays, read books, go to college. I know why she really went to college. That damn Dunning boy was going down there. I never liked the two of them being together. I never liked him. He was always getting in trouble with that temper of his. But that's why she really went down there. To be near her stud. But she found another one down there. An old bastard devil she found down there. And that old bastard devil turned her into a whore. A scarlet woman!"

Karen's composure finally broke. She burst into tears.

"Do you really have to go on like this?" Eileen said to the old farmer. She put her arm around the girl. "Sit down, Karen. You *can* give us something to drink. I'd like tea. Cyrus?"

"The same," Cyrus said, falling in love with Eileen again and again for those marvellous instincts of hers.

Karen shot a fearful look at her father. The old man's jaw worked in suppressed rage but no words followed. Angrily he stomped out of the room. They heard an inside door slam and then the outside door.

"He didn't really mean to hit me." Karen started weeping again.

Eileen soothed her. Cyrus made the tea. He wondered if the girl was a masochist of sorts who invited slapping around. There was a softness about her that could bring out violence in men.

He brought the tea to the two women. Eileen told him to get the picnic lunch out of the car. It would be getting warm in there and it looked as though they'd be in the Bjorkland house some time. Eileen had taken over the investigation without quite knowing it. But she was doing admirably.

They ended up sharing the lunch with Karen. There wasn't a lot of food in the Bjorkland kitchen. Karen talked to Eileen. She talked about Arthur Browne and all that he meant to her. She wept afresh every few minutes and to Cyrus's disapproval Eileen got tears in her eyes also.

Karen talked about how kind Arthur had been to her when she had been rejected for a part in the play.

"I felt like I'd been waiting to meet him all my life, Eileen. He had books, records, paintings. Things I'd only heard about growing up around here. He'd gone to the theater in New York and London. He let me in on his world. Maybe what we did was wrong, but it didn't seem wrong. It seemed clean and wonderful . . . "

Cyrus drank the tea and ate the cheese and sausage sandwiches.

Eileen asked Karen about the university. Would she ever go back? Not now. Perhaps later. She still wanted a career in the theater. Her mother had almost gone to college when she was Karen's age, but a lack of money had forced her to stay on the farm. And after that she'd married.

"My older sisters never wanted to go beyond high school. They're married now and live over near Gaylord. But I wanted to go. Mother would have wanted me to go. She used to take me to school plays and as a treat to the

78

summer playhouse in Traverse City. She loved books too, though he didn't like them around. But he's not as bad as you saw just now . . . " She touched her cheek. "He didn't really mean that. He's so upset. He just never wanted me to go to Harbour Woods; we had terrible fights about it."

"Were you going because Gary got a football scholarship there?" Cyrus asked.

"No. I was going because my mother would have wanted me to go there."

"When did you and Gary first start going together?"

"Our freshman year in high school."

"What's Gary like?"

"Have you met him?"

"No," Cyrus lied.

She was silent a moment. "He's nice. Or he was nice. I don't know what's going to happen to him with all this football business. Up here if anyone is as big as Gary he's expected to play football and when high school is over go to work on a farm. But I think Gary's going to go on playing football."

"He's got a pretty bad temper, hasn't he?"

"How did — oh, my father said so. Yes, he has a temper."

"Gary hit you in your dorm, didn't he?"

She looked at Cyrus. Eileen flashed Cyrus a warning look. Cyrus ignored her.

"Who told you that?"

"Mrs. Cross."

"She shouldn't have. But, yes, it's true." She smiled wanly. "I seem to be the type men hit."

"No, you're not," Eileen said.

"Thanks. But he did hit me. He was frustrated. Just the way my father is. Gary wanted our relationship in Harbour Woods to be the same as it was in Gladwin High School.

And it couldn't have been. I was growing, changing, and he wasn't. He was in a jock world, full of macho boys, but deep down he was still the same person he was in high school."

Karen looked up at Cyrus. "You won't believe it but Gary's a very shy and timid person. People think that because he's big he isn't afraid of things. But he's afraid of a lot of things."

"Like what?"

"Like sex. Gary and I never did anything. We never made love. I'm sure he's still a virgin."

A tiny element of disdain showed in her face for a second. And Cyrus wondered why.

"Gary was in love with you though, wasn't he?" he asked.

"Not really. He thought he was. I was the first girl he ever went out with."

"He threatened Arthur Browne, didn't he?"

"Yes. But he only did that because of his new macho image. He didn't really mean it. Someone on the team must have been teasing him about losing his girl to an older man. And he couldn't take it."

She blinked. She was suddenly aware of what Cyrus was getting at. "You surely don't think that Gary —"

"He's a suspect."

"But Gary wouldn't."

"He has a temper."

"But not for killing anyone. Gary wouldn't. He's a farm boy. He just wouldn't ever do a thing like that."

She turned pale. The farm-boy line rang false. Farm boys learn to kill long before city boys do.

"Gary's whereabouts Monday night are being checked out right now in Harbour Woods," Cyrus said. "Can I ask you, Karen, where *you* were Monday night?"

But the girl was still shaken with the thought of Gary Dunning a suspect.

80

"Karen," Cyrus repeated.

"I . . . had a film class in the foreign language building. I was watching a movie." She spoke woodenly.

She thinks Gary did it, Cyrus thought.

"What movie?"

"I don't remember. *The Grapes of Wrath*. It's an old movie."

"Did anyone take attendance?"

"I don't know. The T.A. did." She looked at him in anguish. "You don't believe he would hurt Arthur."

"I don't know, Karen."

"Cyrus," Eileen broke in, "don't you think it's been enough by now?"

"Just one more question, Karen. Do you know where your father was Monday night?"

"I kin tell you that myself," said Farmer Bjorkland from the doorway of the kitchen, where he stood holding a shotgun in his hand. The barrel was pointed to the floor. But its presence was palpable.

"I was at a grange meeting in Gladwin, Mister. Now I want you and your woman to clear out. You been here long enough."

"Dad, please — "

Eileen ignored the farmer and his shotgun. She walked over and kneeled by Karen. "Karen, listen to me. If you do come back to Harbour Woods, I want you to call me. Here's my address and my phone number."

Eileen wrote down her name, address, and phone number on a piece of paper she took from her purse. When Karen made no attempt to take it from her, Eileen put it in her lap.

"Now," said Farmer Bjorkland, waving the shotgun triumphantly, "get the hell out of here."

Cyrus and Eileen left.

*

They drove silently down one dirt road after another until they reached a stop sign and a paved road running east and west. A sign told them Gladwin was eight miles to their left; the I-75 expressway leading to Harbour Woods was fifteen miles to their right.

"Turn right, Cyrus. I've got that dinner meeting to go to, and I have to get ready for it. I have to get my copy for the pictures. And afterward I've got reading to do for my Hillman seminar tomorrow. Please turn right."

The motor ran. Cyrus stalled. "How did your meeting with Hillman go yesterday?"

"Good. She's nice. But she won't be nice if I'm not prepared for tomorrow. Turn right, Cyrus. Let's go home."

"I thought you were wonderful back there, Eileen. The girl wouldn't have opened up to me alone."

"Cyrus, turn right!"

"She's scared right now. She thinks he may have killed Arthur."

"No. I believed her when she said he wouldn't."

"I'm not talking about Gary. I'm talking about her father."

"Cyrus, for God's sake, I've had enough for one day. As it is I'll have nightmares for a long time about that poor kid trapped in that house with her monster of a father. Now please turn *right!*"

Cyrus turned the car left.

"Look," he said quietly, "I've got a lot of work to do too. I've got my Whitman-Dickinson class to prepare for tomorrow. I've got papers to read, a report from the presidential search committee to go over. I won't be getting a lot done over the weekend. We're going to the football game Saturday. Remember, it's band day."

Band day was the only football game Eileen wanted to attend.

82

"Cyrus, don't lay this on me. You want to go on playing John Agate."

"I'm not playing, Eileen," he said, and stepped on the gas.

She was silent. "Suppose we don't find anyone at the grange in Gladwin."

"We will. By the way, I love you."

"I don't love you."

"Yes, you do. You love me and I love you. And as soon as I get tenure I'm going to propose marriage to you."

Despite her vexation, she had to laugh.

Cyrus was hurt. "What's funny about that?"

"To think I'll be an old maid all my life."

"That's not funny and you won't be," Cyrus snapped.

He was in an ill humor when they reached Gladwin. An ill humor that grew when the grange master, the owner of a farm implement store, told them yes, John Bjorkland had been at the grange meeting Monday night.

"We couldn't have a meeting without John," said the grange master. "He's our secretary. Only one of us can read and write decent enough."

They drove home without speaking.

12

"Yes, madame," the maître d' said, "they are waiting for you. But they said only one more was expected."

"I'm just staying for a drink," Cyrus said.

"You really don't even have to do that," said Eileen as they followed the maître d' through the labyrinth of rooms that made up the sprawling Swingletree Restaurant.

"Come on," Cyrus said, "I got you back in time. I've left word with Guiterrez where I am. I'd *like* a drink."

Eileen made an exasperated noise. She knew she was being unreasonable. It wasn't Cyrus's fault the trip to Gladwin hadn't produced results, nor was it his fault that she'd have nightmares for weeks about Karen Bjorkland and her father.

"I think this is your party, no?" the maitre d' asked.

Marie Genthon and a stranger were seated at a table set for three. The man, short, middle-aged, with alert eyes, rose with a smile.

"Cyrus," Marie said, "what a nice surprise."

"I'm only staying for a drink, Marie."

"Cyrus, this is Mr. Evans from the Chamber of Commerce," Marie said.

84

"Wilbur Evans," said the man, pumping Cyrus's hand energetically. He had a friendly, puppylike air about him. "I'm sure glad you made it, Miss O'Hanrahan. I was getting a little worried about you." He winked at Cyrus. "Miss O'Hanrahan is a hell of a writer, you know."

"I do know it," Cyrus said, as an extra chair was brought to the table. "I'd like to treat everyone to a drink."

"Did you strike oil up north, Cyrus?" Marie asked, eyes twinkling.

"No," Eileen said, "he just has a guilty conscience for what happened in Gladwin today."

Wilbur Evans flashed a smile. "I'm very new in these parts. Where is Gladwin and what happened there?"

"Gladwin is a two-hour drive to a terrible experience," Eileen told him. "We saw a girl there living alone with a monster of a father."

Wilbur Evans's eyes looked merry. "And what does a monster of a father look like, Eileen?"

"Just like a Mr. Bjorkland." Eileen paused while drink orders were taken and then she described, with accuracy, Cyrus thought, the scene in which Farmer Bjorkland slapped his daughter.

"How horrible." Marie shuddered.

Wilbur Evans frowned. "I find it hard to believe a father would strike a grown-up daughter like that."

"This one did," Eileen said flatly.

"Well," said Evans, "you never know what lies behind a scene like that, Eileen. Hell, you could be seeing the tip of the iceberg. For all you know, the girl could have driven him to it."

"We were there and she didn't," Eileen said firmly.

"She didn't while you were there," Evans corrected her gently. "You kids are all young," he said, including Cyrus and Marie. "Let me tell you something. Until you've had children you never really know what's going on. You can take my word for that."

"I can't accept that," Eileen said. "I saw what I saw, I felt what I felt. Anyway, enough of that."

The drinks came and the talk shifted to the brochure Eileen was writing for the Chamber of Commerce. And the need for pictures for it. Picture sources were the Chamber of Commerce, which had a slide collection Eileen could exploit, the *Harbour Woods News*'s picture file, Mid-East's university relations picture and slide files, athletic department, and band department.

"I take pictures myself," Evans said modestly. "I hope to be taking some in the stadium this Saturday."

"That's band day," Eileen said. "It would be nice to get some new pictures. We'll need slides rather than stills."

"I'll get you some slides," Evans said. He laughed. "The truth is, when I was a kid I wanted to be a photographer, and now in middle age I'd give my right arm to become a professional photographer. I'm sure I have a case of midlife crisis."

"You're not alone," Eileen said, her face bland. "Cyrus has the most advanced case of midlife crisis I know. He's been working on his Ph.D. dissertation for ten years now —"

"Eight," Cyrus said.

Everyone laughed except Cyrus.

" — and now it turns out he really wants to be a detective."

"And he'll never make that either," a new voice said.

They looked up. Guiterrez was standing there. Cat's feet, Cyrus thought. Guiterrez had a silent way about him.

"I've come to collect your pal, Miss."

"Eileen, this is John Guiterrez, about whom you've heard. John, Eileen O'Hanrahan, Marie Genthon, whom you know, of course, and Wilbur Evans from the Chamber of Commerce."

"Nice to see you again," Guiterrez said to Marie. His

grin was mirthless and hard. "Mr. Evans." And finally he turned to Cyrus. "C'mon, Prof, we've got work to do."

"So do we," Eileen snapped. He was the enemy all right. She turned her back on both Guiterrez and Cyrus. "We'll have to talk about the *kind* of band day pictures we'll need. Verticals, horizontals, close-ups and —"

"No, you don't, young man," Evans said. He had caught Cyrus putting money on the table.

"I insist," Cyrus said.

"No," Evans said, quietly but firmly, "the Chamber is taking care of this."

"You sure?"

"Positive."

Cyrus retrieved his money. "Will I see you later?" he asked Eileen.

"Only if I'm at the scene of some crime."

Outside the restaurant Guiterrez slapped him on the shoulder. "You got yourself a looker there, Prof, but you'll have to tame it."

"I know.

"She's competing with you. And that won't buy you nothing but trouble. I *know.* "

"Are you married, John?"

"I was. I've been there."

"What happened?"

"She found it too tough being a cop's wife. She's married to an accountant now. She can bookkeep the book-keeper and all the columns tally. Get in."

"What's up?"

"We're taking the Dunning kid in. His alibi didn't stand up. He wasn't in the dorm Monday night. And the roomie finally broke down and confessed that Gary came in after 1 A.M. that night. We're gonna take him down to the station and sweat him a bit. I think we got our man, Prof. Yes, sir, I think we got ourselves a crazy baker."

"Where is he now?"

"At the student union. The team is eating there. Steaks probably. I had a hot dog but those kids get steak. Where the kid is going he won't be getting steak. No, sir. They got big ovens in Southern Michigan Prison at Jackson. Maybe they'll let that baby tend the ovens since he likes 'em so much."

Guiterrez was in a good humor as they drove to the Mid-East student union.

*

Although on the practice fields the players separated into their specialty units — offense with offense, defense with defense, receivers with receivers — at dinner they grouped along racial lines. Blacks with blacks at small, round tables, whites with whites.

In the jumble of oversized boys, their muscles bulging from T-shirts with MID-EAST FOOTBALL stencilled on them, Gary Dunning was hard to isolate. Cyrus was aware that, standing there in the alcove of the union cafteria, he and Guiterrez were conspicuous.

"Can I help you?" a kid wearing a manager's T-shirt asked them.

"We're looking for Gary Dunning," Guiterrez said.

"Over there," the boy said, pointing to a far corner.

They moved toward the corner, past big bodies getting bigger, past massive hands holding tiny knives and forks, past plates with mounds of mashed potatoes, vegetables and, not steaks, but prime ribs. There were small hills of butter and rolls and pitchers of milk on each table.

The boys worked hard; the boys ate hard.

Gary Dunning had two huge portions of prime ribs on his plate.

Guiterrez beckoned him with his finger. Gary didn't move. He looked up blankly. The other kids at the table

88

looked curiously at the two strangers. And, Cyrus thought, divested of their bulky pads and helmets, that is exactly what they looked like: kids. Oversized to be sure, but still kids.

"Wally says no reporters at the training table, Mister," a boy said.

"They ain't reporters," Gary mumbled.

"Who are they?"

"What gives, Dunning?"

"C'mon, Gary," Guiterrez said in a cold tone, "let's go."

Gary rose reluctantly. He picked his football jacket off the back of his chair.

"Hey, Dunning, where're you going?"

Gary didn't answer. He followed Cyrus and Guiterrez away from the tables. The noise level in the cafeteria dropped as all eyes followed them.

"Excuse me," Gary said, quietly, when they'd gone past the tables and were moving near the exit door, "but where're we going?"

"Police station," Guiterrez said.

"What for?"

"You'll find out there."

"Do I have to go there?"

"Yeah, Gary," Guiterrez said contemptuously, "you got to go."

Gary looked at Cyrus.

"You can call a lawyer from there," Cyrus said.

The boy's face turned pale, but he fell in behind Guiterrez. Cyrus brought up the rear, thinking how quickly and naturally they all fell into a guards-and-their-prisoner pantomime.

They didn't quite make it to the exit door.

Wally Lassiter, coat over one arm, squired by two assistant coaches, cut them off.

89

"I thought I told you to keep away from my kids," he snarled at Guiterrez.

Somehow, though, Cyrus thought, the hard leathery look didn't contain the same strength and malevolence it had outdoors. Or maybe it was the absence of the baseball cap, the whistle. The outdoor turf was his domain. Indoors, Wally Lassiter looked a little insecure, despite the snarl in his voice.

"Well, coach," Guiterrez said amiably, "we're taking your boy down to the police station."

The assistant coaches gaped at them. Wally waved them away impatiently. They moved reluctantly out of earshot.

"Horseshit," Wally said. "You better have a hell of a reason for taking him in."

"We got one," Guiterrez said, enjoying the upper hand. "His alibi for Monday night didn't hold up. I checked every one of his friends out. A man Gary Dunning threatened was killed Monday night. Gary's lied about where he was Monday night. That's enough for me right there."

Gary Dunning was sweating now. Everyone in the dining room was looking at them.

"Coach," Gary said hoarsely, "I can explain everything." He turned to Guiterrez. "I wasn't where you think I was. I was . . . " His face turned red. "I was somewhere else."

"We know where you were, kid. You were stuffing Arthur Browne in an oven."

"No, sir. I didn't do that. I wasn't there."

"Tell them where you were, son," Lassiter said.

Gary shook his head. "Could we . . . talk somewhere else?"

There was genuine agony in the boy's features. He didn't want to talk in front of his coach, Cyrus thought.

"We'll find a room upstairs," Cyrus said. "Coach, you stay here. If we take him to the police station, we'll let you know."

90

"You're goddam right you'll let me know," Wally Lassiter snapped.

"We're taking him in, coach," Guitterez said softly, "whether you like it or not."

"Let's talk first," Cyrus said. He took Gary's arm. They left the cafeteria. Guiterrez followed slowly, reluctantly. Resenting Cyrus's taking over. He wanted to sweat the kid downtown.

*

The Briggs Room was a small, elegant private dining room named for the first president of Mid-East University, Nathaniel Briggs, whose stern portrait in oil hung on a brown panelled wall.

The room was lined with hand-carved oak chairs with orange cushions. In the middle there was a long table covered with a yellow linen cloth. The table was flanked by a dozen or so oak dining-room chairs.

Guiterrez pointed at one of the chairs along the wall.

"Sit down," he said to Gary.

For himself Guiterrez pulled a chair away from the table, reversed it, and sat down straddling it.

Gary remained standing.

"I said: 'Sit down.' "

Gary shook his head. He stood there very large and inert in front of them. And then slowly his right hand moved into his jacket pocket. For a mad second Cyrus thought the kid had a gun in there. Guiterrez froze.

But from the jacket pocket Gary took out, incredibly, a pair of white jockey shorts. He held them toward Cyrus and Guiterrez, holding them at each end with his fingers, pulling them apart. The crotch of the shorts faced them. On the crotch flap was a bright red lipstick imprint of a mouth.

"What the fuck is this?" Guiterrez snarled.

91

Cyrus was just grateful the door was closed.

"It's where I was Monday night, sir," Gary said calmly. He seemed in control of himself at last.

"Where were you?" Cyrus said.

Gary tossed the jockey shorts onto one of the orange leather seats just below the oil portrait. The lipstick mouth fell rightside up, facing them.

"It wasn't my idea, sir. I didn't want to do it. It was a mistake. All of it."

With a rush of words the boy's story came out. It would end with Gary Dunning calm, relieved, purged of all emotion.

Gary Dunning, self-confessed virgin, it turned out, had pledged the most popular macho jock fraternity on campus.

The shorts in his pocket tonight were there because tonight was pledge night. Each candidate was to produce a pair of jockey shorts that had been kissed on the crotch by a college co-ed while being worn by the pledge.

But the farm boy from Gladwin had been too shy to ask a girl to perform this task.

"I just couldn't ask a nice girl to do a thing like that," he told them. "I didn't know what to do. Then I saw in the *Free Press* those ads for stripper clubs on Woodward. I knew prostitutes hung out around them. The guys on the team from Detroit talked about that a lot. So I drove to Detroit Monday night. I . . . picked up a prostitute on Woodward Avenue near one of those clubs."

He's lying, Cyrus thought.

"I guess," Gary amended, "she picked me up. She took me to a motel."

Guiterrez was silent. He glanced at Cyrus and then, reluctantly, took out a pencil and pad.

"What motel?"

"The Begley."

"There's no such motel. You're lying again."

"No, sir. That was its name. I remember because I know a family in Gladwin named Begley. That's why I remember it."

"What name did you use when you registered?"

Gary looked surprised. "Dunning," he said.

That took some of the wind out of Guiterrez's sails.

"You used your own name?" he asked incredulously.

"Yes, sir."

Guiterrez shook his head. "What was the hooker's name?"

Gary hesitated just a second. "I didn't ask."

"You're lying."

"Yes, sir. Her name was JoAnne."

"Why'd you lie?"

"I didn't want to get her in trouble."

"Jesus," Guiterrez said. "Was she white or black?"

"She was white." The boy seemed shocked at the question.

"Okay, a hooker named JoAnne picked you up on Woodward Monday night and took you to a motel you're calling the Begley. What time?"

"About eleven."

"How convenient for your alibi. How long were you in the motel?"

"Not too long."

"How long?"

"About an hour. Maybe longer. But I didn't do anything."

"What the hell do you mean, you didn't do anything? Do you mean you didn't kill her the way you killed Browne?"

"I didn't kill anyone, sir. I mean . . . " Gary looked away from them. He wanted to use the right words, but what were they? And as the boy searched in his head, Cyrus suddenly knew what had happened to him in Detroit. He recalled Karen's description of Gary Dunning as a lover.

"You mean," Cyrus said gently, "nothing happened between you and her?"

The boy looked at him with gratitude. "Yes, sir. That's what I mean. Thank you."

"Bullshit," Guiterrez snapped. "You picked up a hooker and you didn't screw her. Are you trying to tell me that?"

Gary's face reddened. "Yes, sir," he said.

"I don't believe a goddam thing you tell me, Dunning. I think you're a professional liar. You killed Arthur Browne and your first alibi didn't hold up and now you're looking for another one."

"No, sir," the boy said calmly, "I'm telling the truth this time."

"Keep talking, Gary," Cyrus suggested.

The point was that Gary Dunning wanted to talk and Guiterrez's pressure was making him shut up.

Gary looked at Cyrus. "When I . . . couldn't do it, she said maybe whiskey would help me. She told me the clerk at the desk sold whiskey. I got dressed and went to the office and bought a pint of whiskey."

"What kind?" Guiterrez snapped.

"Wild Turkey."

"What'd you pay for it?"

"Ten dollars."

"For a pint?"

"Yes, sir. I thought it was steep, but . . . "

As a cure for impotence, Cyrus thought, it would be damn cheap.

"How much money did you have?"

"A hundred bucks."

"How much did the hooker want?"

"Fifty."

94

"What did the clerk look like?"

"He was an older man."

"White or black?"

"Black."

Interesting, thought Cyrus, that a farm boy from Gladwin would mention age before race. It might have something to do with playing football with black students from Detroit.

"What did you do with the whiskey?"

"I drank it."

"Did it help?"

"No, sir. I got sick. She was real nice to me. She held my head."

"Then what happened?"

"I paid her."

"How much?"

"Fifty dollars."

"For what?"

"Well, it wasn't her fault I couldn't do it."

"How'd you get the lipstick on the shorts?" Cyrus broke in.

Gary looked relieved. "She asked me why I'd come into Detroit. I told her about pledge night. She thought it was funny. She told me to put my shorts on. Then she put on a lot of lipstick and kissed me."

There was a silence. The fifty-dollar crotch kiss, Cyrus thought.

"Didn't that get it up for you?" Guiterrez's voice was harsh.

He wanted Gary for Browne's murder, Cyrus thought. He wanted Gary badly.

Gary's face turned red again.

"No, sir," he said.

"What are you — a fag?"

The boy looked at Guiterrez. Guiterrez was a big man

but not in the boy's size and weight class. On the other hand, with a pro like Guiterrez the big farm boy wouldn't stand a chance.

Don't lose your temper, son, Cyrus prayed.

Gary breathed out. "No, sir," he said calmly.

Guiterrez put the pad away. "You stay here, Dunning. I'm going to check out this new story of yours. I'm going to see if there's a Begley motel, a hooker named JoAnne, a clerk who sells whiskey to minors. If there isn't, you're dead. You've run out of all alibis."

Guiterrez nodded to Cyrus and left the room. Cyrus sat with the boy while Guiterrez went to a phone at the front desk. Gary sat looking straight ahead of him. His face held no expression at all.

The two of them sat silently for a few moments and finally Cyrus broke the silence.

"Gary, were you going through with the initiation tonight?"

"No, sir."

"Why not?"

"I decided I didn't want to join after all. I got a lot to learn in college but I don't think I'm gonna learn it there."

Either the farm boy was coming of age or he was lying again.

"Why did you have the shorts with you then?"

Gary nodded. "I didn't want anyone riding me about not being able to find a girl to do it."

The kid had covered all bases. Cyrus decided to give him another one to worry about.

"I was up in Gladwin yesterday, Gary."

Gary looked at him. "Yes, sir."

"I visited the Bjorklands. Karen's back home."

The boy said nothing.

"She's probably not coming back to school for a while."

"Is she upset about . . . *him?*"

"Yes."

Gary looked upset. And then the expression passed. "Did she talk about me?"

"Just to say you wouldn't kill anyone."

"I didn't, sir." And then came the line Cyrus would always remember. "I came to Harbour Woods to play football."

The door opened. Guiterrez, looking irritated, entered.

"His story checks out," he said curtly. "Dunning, you were either dumb enough or smart enough to register in your real name. The clerk gave me a good description of you. I called the Highland Park cops. That end of Woodward is in Highland Park. They'll pick up your JoAnne. The clerk knows her real name. You can go back to your goddam prime ribs. But don't leave town. You're still involved in this."

"Yes, sir." Gary rose.

"And take your goddam jockey shorts with you," Guiterrez said.

Gary's face was one of unchanging calm. He picked up the shorts and walked to the door. There he dropped the shorts in a wastepaper basket. He closed the door behind him. He hadn't looked back once. He could not have managed it better, Cyrus thought. A boy had just grown up.

"What do you think, Prof?"

"He never was a good suspect, John."

"Nuts! He was a beauty. He had the motive, the size, and the temper."

"It wasn't temper that made a man drag Browne out of the bushes and stuff him into a bake oven."

"What was it?"

"Hate."

Guiterrez was silent. He looked at his pad. "Maybe.

Anyway, back to square one." He pocketed his pad. "At least I won't have to deal with that bastard Lassiter anymore."

They left the room. Cyrus wondered what the person who dumped the trash would make of the item in the Nathaniel Briggs wastepaper basket.

13

They were waiting for the chief to get off the phone before starting the Friday morning meeting.

Detective Layne looked at Guiterrez. "You know, John, I'm glad the kid's off the hook."

"Why?" Guiterrez asked.

"Because Mid-East's got a tough game against Duke Saturday. They might need the kid. I hear Lassiter's pretty uptight about the game."

"You go to football games, Prof?" Detective Tinker asked.

"Just the one tomorrow," Cyrus said. "It's band day. My girl adores band day."

"You couldn't get me to watch a thousand kids blow on their bugles, but I'd go to watch Wally swallow pills." Layne grinned. "You don't see that on TV. Or his players popping them either."

"Drop it," Guiterrez ordered.

A year ago Detective Layne had worked with a federal narcotics team investigating drugs in college athletics. Mid-East had received a clean bill of health. No one at the Harbour Woods P.D. knew why.

Chief Wilson hung up the phone. He looked worried. "That was someone named Arnie Newman at Channel 3. He wants to know what's new on the Browne case. I've also had calls from Channel 8, the all-news radio, and the cable news people. It's been four days now and they want to know what we have."

"Not too much that's solid," Cyrus admitted. "Poulos has no alibi but he doesn't have the muscle. Dunning's new alibi, as you know, checked out. Karen Bjorkland's father has an alibi. I haven't had a chance to tell you about my trip up there."

Cyrus then filled them in on his trip to Roscommon County, Karen Bjorkland, her father, and the father's presence at the Gladwin grange that Monday night.

Detective Hal Layne spoke next. The Philadelphia lawyer had been in court all day Monday and at a dinner party that night. Layne had decided student complaints might be a good angle to pursue and had gone over to the law school. He'd talked his way into a confidential file in the dean of students' office.

"Browne wasn't in it," Layne grinned, "but some other profs were."

Guiterrez had spent yesterday checking with the juvenile squad and the vice squad. "Browne liked his meat tender so I checked with Mary Phelps. She opened her Complaints and Offenders book to me. He didn't make it."

"Pity," the chief said.

"I popped up to Legal Aid. I figured Browne probably defended some teenage hookers along the way and maybe took it out in trade. They were very offended at the notion up there."

"They didn't know their boss very well," the chief said. "You should have tried some of the girls on Warren Street."

Warren Street was Harbour Woods's attempt at a red-light district. The adult bookstore, a few bars, a cheap motel, and the omnipresent hookers.

"I did," Guiterrez said. "They knew all about Browne. He was a big hero to them. They were pretty upset about his being offed. I talked with Sully in Vice. He didn't have anything on Browne except he was glad the S.O.B. was dead. Browne was too damn clever at getting pimps and hookers back on the street. He got a court order last year keeping the bookstore open on a freedom-of-the-press defense."

"Which," Cyrus said softly, "leads us to one Ricky Andrews."

"All roads lead to Ricky Andrews," Guiterrez said.

"Gentlemen," Tom Tinker said in his deep, amused voice, "I am on the Ricky Andrews road."

The best for the last, they thought, as Tink flipped through pages in his note pad. The ex-con, pimp, drug dealer, the one suspect who could be associated with violence.

"Ricky is a good-looking suspect," Tink pronounced. "For one thing, he's disappeared."

"Do we have enough to put out an all points on him?" the chief asked.

"Yes, sir."

"Then get it out as soon as we're done here."

"What'd you find at his apartment complex, Tink?" Guiterrez asked.

"I talked to the manager and just about every neighbor of Andrews I could wake up. Ricky, it seems, wasn't a popular citizen out there. Even in a swinging joint like that he swung too much. Wild hours, wild parties, he brought in low-lifes from Detroit. And," said Tinker with a sigh, "he's got a new Alfa-Romeo that excites envy."

"Pimps and white Alfas go together," Guiterrez grunted.

"He must be getting a whopping salary from that bookstore," Layne said, grinning.

"Indeed," Tink said, "but he hasn't been putting his time in there of late. The clerks there got no idea where Ricky is. I asked Sully over in Vice to tell his undercovers we're looking for Ricky Andrews. I think we might want to stake out the apartment and the bookstore, Chief."

"I'll get people there," Guiterrez said.

"Sully busted Andrews on drugs in January, if I remember," Layne said.

Guiterrez nodded. "That's the one Ricky got six months on, thanks to Browne."

"And threatened to get him for it," Layne said.

"And maybe did," Guiterrez said.

"He's got a record longer than that," Tinker said. "The first pinch on Andrews was made last fall but it didn't hold up."

"I remember that too," Guiterrez said. "One of his girls was going to testify he was arranging johns for her through the bookstore. She was sore at him about something."

"Why didn't it hold up?" Cyrus asked.

"She O.D.'d in the Village Apartments New Year's Day," Guiterrez said.

"Maybe someone shot stuff into her," Layne said. They were all thinking the same thing. The M.O. on Ricky had not been that he was a killer. Now the Browne murder might change the M.O.

"Doc Hollins's report said the hooker did it on her own. But maybe we ought to look into it again."

"You say she O.D.'d out at the Village Apartments. Was she living with Andrews out there?" Cyrus asked.

Tinker answered for Guiterrez. "No. Just working for him out there. In a different unit than the one he lived in. Andrews might have had three or four girls working for him out there in different units. Prof, there might be as much as twenty pros operating in that complex. It's a regular sandbox. The manager ain't too happy about it but he says what can he do so long as the girls pay the rent. Besides," Tinker couldn't resist adding with a grin, "he says you can't always tell the pros from the amateurs."

"Ricky's record says he's a petty criminal. But maybe," Cyrus said, "he's got a different record and a different M.O. in a different place."

"I thought of that, Prof," Tinker said, beaming. "I ran a check on our boy. He's petty criminal all the way. Andrews is from New York City. Queens. I called Homicide down at Center Street in the Big Apple. It took me some more calls before I got the records people. They got Ricky Andrews for car theft when he was fourteen, drugs when he was fifteen, burglary when he was sixteen. All suspended sentences because he was a juvenile. I got his home address in Queens. I called the family making out like I was an old friend. I don't think it fooled them very much. But I think they were telling the truth when they said they hadn't seen him in years, didn't know where he was, and didn't want to know where he was."

"We'll get that all points out on him," the chief said, "and ask New York to keep an eye on his house. John, who was Andrews's lawyer in that pimping charge? Was that Browne?"

"No. Ricky drew a third-year law student out of Legal Aid. Student name of Harvey Burke. I haven't been able to get hold of Burke yet. Anyway, they didn't get very far with each other because of the girl O.D.'ing."

There was a silence.

"Cyrus," the chief said, "where do we stand now?"

Cyrus looked down at his notes. "I agree, M.O. or no M.O., Ricky Andrews has got to be our number-one suspect. Constantine Poulos has got to be number two. He lacks fifty pounds maybe; on the other hand, he could have been freaky jealous."

"That's right," Layne cut in. "Give someone enough motive and you get enough muscle. You remember that little grandmother down in Tampa that lifted a Buick off her three-year-old grandson?"

"Yeah, but it was a downsized Buick," Tinker said.

Everyone laughed except Guiterrez.

"Christ," Guiterrez said, "we got the media on our necks and you guys are making jokes. We got a dead lawyer who was a part-time professor, part-time theater freak, part-time legal aid — "

"The dude's got too many parts to him, that's for sure," Tinker said.

"And we know he liked his women young," Cyrus said, "and he was probably last seen with a known homosexual — "

"Another part," said Tinker.

" — before the murderer got to him, if the killer wasn't Mr. Poulos himself." Cyrus looked again at his notes.

"I got some stuff yesterday from friends and neighbors and his colleagues at the university. Browne had a wife who died about four years ago. His stepdaughter name of Cindy left him after that. No one I've talked to, and that includes Poulos, the legal aid people, Karen Bjorkland, his colleagues at the law school, my own girl Eileen — he lived in our house" — discreet winks and grins from the policemen to each other, which Cyrus ignored — "the Genthons, people who lived next door to him downstairs, no one knew anything about his wife and daughter except that he mentioned having them. They're whole areas of mystery in Browne's life. I'm going to keep digging at them. But first, we've got to find Andrews."

The phone rang. The chief answered, said, "Okay," and hung up.

"Channel 3 wants an update on the Arthur Browne investigation for the noon news. That's you, Cyrus."

Cyrus rose.

"One second, Prof," Guiterrez said. His face was bland. "Chief, what about us checking out Cyrus?"

"For what?"

"The Browne killing. His girl was nuts about Browne."

Uncle looked at nephew. "Is that right, Cyrus?"

"Yes," Cyrus said mildly. "The only problem was that he wasn't interested in her. Not that way. She was too old for him."

Tinker and Layne laughed. The chief just shook his head. "To think that man headed this city's legal aid services. What is this world coming to? Cyrus, you better get on that statement. I'd like to look it over before I read it to a camera. Tink, get the all points out for Ricky Andrews immediately. Incidentally, Cyrus, we're not telling the media about that yet."

"Yes, sir," Cyrus said.

He left. Wondering why Guiterrez made the kind of jokes he did.

14

With thirty seconds left to play in the first half, the score was Mid-East, o – Duke University, o. In the end-zone seats over ten thousand high school bandsmen were on their feet, poised to march down aisles, through narrow entrances in the brick wall, and onto the playing field.

The rain was letting up a bit, though every once in a while it blew like an angry curtain around the stadium. But you forgot about rain at an interesting football game. Especially when you were jam-packed. Gary Dunning had played about five minutes in the first half. He was slow, Cyrus thought, but strong as an ox. Better on pass blocking than on blocking for the runner.

Eileen was bored with the game, but her eyes glistened as she watched the colorful bandsmen in the end-zone aisles.

"Cyrus, it's like a huge, undulating animal . . . "

She was always writing, he thought. Always seeing life as material, in metaphor. This particular metaphor was apt. The bandsmen made a gigantic rippling movement in the aisles as they crowded down on each other and then rippled back up again, restrained from marching onto the field by security people.

The crowd roared. On the field the incredible had just happened. Seeking to run out the clock with the ball deep in its own territory, the Duke quarterback had just fumbled. Mid-East recovered with less than six seconds to play.

The Mid-East offense raced back on the field.

And then ten thousand high school bandsmen who had just rippled forward were forced backwards against each other. The anticipatory drumming that had started now ceased. One sensed an anger on their part at being deprived of their field.

It was mad, utterly mad, Cyrus thought.

"The poor kids," Eileen murmured.

There was time for only one play. It began now to rain harder, as though the gods had lined up for Duke. Cyrus peered through the rain at the coaches on the Duke side shaking their fists at their players, screaming at them.

Now the Mid-East quarterback was fading backwards with the ball. It was to be an all-or-nothing pass.

Everyone in the stands rose to their feet.

The ball was lofted into the rain. A clap of thunder rent the air. A Mid-East player caught the ball at the ten-yard line and, to the accompaniment of 98,000 screaming people, carried it across the goal line.

Now did the drums go bang and the people yell and pound each other. Now were the bands coming on the field. Nothing could stop them. They broke through the ranks of the security guards.

Quickly the ball was set down for the point after touchdown. The kick was up. It was good. The first half was over.

And not a moment too soon, as an inexorable flood tide of ten thousand youngsters were on the march.

Into the gap between the two armies of bandsmen quick-stepping toward each other to a rapid and loud drum cadence, ran the Mid-East players, heading for the tunnel across the field. They were followed by a host of assistant coaches, trainers, assistant trainers, equipment managers, assistant equipment managers, team doctors, cheerleaders — and the last man to leave, making sure no one was left behind, the head coach, he who was responsible for this tremendous spectacle — Wally Lassiter — running easily, his hands balled into fists chest high.

The band professor from the university had climbed to the top of his conducting scaffold from where he could see and direct the ten thousand musicians. A battery of cameras was aimed at the field.

The conductor raised his baton.

A gasp went up in the stadium.

Lassiter stumbled. And then fell forward. The leading edges of the bandsmen, the drummers, tried to halt. But they were pushed forward by those behind them until, unwilling, panicking, flailing at their drums with tasselled sticks, they marched over Wally Lassiter's body.

The assistant coaches had heard the stadium gasp. They were returning now, fighting their way through the bandsmen.

Security men were also battling the tide from both end zones.

Meanwhile, oblivious, beaming, standing at the top of his scaffolding, if not at the pinnacle of his career, the professor brought his baton down. One hundred high school bands struck up "The Stars and Stripes Forever."

"What's happening, Cyrus?"

"Lassiter fell down."

Cyrus saw Guiterrez running into the bandsmen from the sidelines, clubbing his way through them to the knot of people now bent over Lassiter.

"My God," said Eileen, "what a time to fall down."

15

Cyrus worked his way around the stadium, dodging security people. There had been a flurry of announcements calling for doctors. The sounds of sirens, police and ambulance.

The teams had come back on the field and were doing warm-ups on the sidelines. Lassiter hadn't returned with them. He had been carried off on a stretcher.

On the west side of the stadium, in the general area where Cyrus and Eileen had their seats, he had noticed a growing number of policemen appearing at the exits. The Mid-East bench was on the west side of the field.

Cyrus worked his way down the steps and into the tunnel. There he found chaos. Police everywhere with walky-talkies. He saw Guiterrez talking with Doc Hollins, the medical examiner. They both looked worried.

Cyrus started toward them when a uniformed arm barred his progress.

"Where do you think you're going, bud?"

"I'm working with Detective Guiterrez." Cyrus took out his police identification card.

The arm dropped.

"John, what's going on?"

Guiterrez looked at him as though he were a painful reminder of the past.

"Lassiter's dead," Guiterrez said. "Shot in the back. Doc, you remember the chief's nephew, Cyrus Wilson."

Doc Hollins nodded at Cyrus. "Someone killed a football coach," the little pathologist said. He shook his head. "What the hell is this country coming to?"

A paramedic carrying a folded up stretcher walked by them.

"You got my bag, Sam?" Doc Hollins asked, and walked after him.

"I saw him fall," Cyrus said.

"Where were you sitting?"

"The west side."

"Did you see someone stand up and point a gun at him?"

"A lot of people were standing, moving. It was halftime."

"Well, we're going to have to screen everyone who sat on the west side of the stadium. Jesus, that's got to be a shitload."

"You're talking thirty thousand people, John," an older uniformed policeman with a worried face said.

"Cyrus. Cy Wilson," a voice called out. It was Tom Whelan, looking shaken as only a vice-president for university relations can look when disaster strikes his school.

"A lunatic is on the loose," Whelan said, fingering his tie nervously. "Cy, I can't believe this is happening to us."

"Another lunatic you mean," Guiterrez said. "Don't forget Browne."

A roar erupted from the field. The game was going on. Cyrus had left Eileen in the stands, promising to return as soon as he found out what was going on. He wouldn't get back to her now. He could imagine the John Agate diatribes that would issue now.

"Has anyone told the team?" he asked Guiterrez.

"We had an assistant coach tell them Lassiter had a heart attack and was going to be okay in the hospital." Guiterrez's grin was deathly. "He told them they had to win it for Wally."

"What about the press?"

Whelan shook his head. "They'll find out. They're already following the ambulance to the hospital. It will only be minutes before the word murder is out . . . across the nation. My God, our capital campaign, our development work, it's all going to go up in smoke."

"I want to talk to the coaches and players after the game," Cyrus said.

Guiterrez looked at him. "You weren't asked to get involved in this one, Prof."

"Of course he's asked," Whelan said. "He represents the university in these kinds of things. Cy, this has priority over everything. Browne. Anything. This is a horrible thing to have happened. This too is an assassination — the first on any university's campus."

Whelan was becoming a victim of his own rhetoric.

Cyrus turned to Guiterrez. "What about the TV, John? They must have videotapes of what happened. They're always shooting halftime."

"I've got people in the TV truck right now," Guiterrez said. He turned to Whelan. "You really want the prof involved in this one too?"

"Absolutely."

"All right." Guiterrez looked irritatedly at Cyrus. "You can start screening people, Prof. There's only thirty or forty thousand people that could have done it."

Guiterrez was upset, but his description of what now had to be done was not inaccurate, Cyrus thought. This murder could be solved through massive and detailed policework. Someone had stood up in the Mid-East stadium with a gun in his hand and shot a football coach. Someone else must have seen him.

Unless everyone was looking at the bands, the conductor, or at Lassiter as he made his last trip across the field to the locker room.

Who watches the watchers?

The president of Mid-East University emerged from a dressing room accompanied by a tall, statuesque woman. She was well dressed. Cyrus recognized Wally's wife, Sally Lassiter.

Her bearing was tense but dignified; her face was ashen but dry-eyed.

Tom Whelan hurried to them.

"Tom," the president said, "would you take Mrs. Lassiter to the hospital now? The university will help with all arrangements."

Tom Whelan took Mrs. Lassiter's arm and they brushed by Cyrus and Guiterrez on their way out. They detected a faint whiff of expensive perfume. Guiterrez watched her go with a hooded look. "No tears there," he grunted.

He turned to Cyrus. "I'm going over to the west exits. We're setting up interrogation barriers there. You want to come along?"

"No," Cyrus said, still watching Sally Lassiter as she and Whelan departed the tunnel, "I'm going to stick here to talk to the players and the coaches."

16

"I'm relieved that the pretense of a happy marriage is over."

Sally Lassiter stood looking out of the tenth-floor apartment window. Below her the river sparkled golden in the sunlight. A chilly Saturday night had given way to a lovely Indian summer Sunday, and it had brought activity and movement to the river recreation area. Canoes and sailboats made sharp turns on the water; bicyclists meandered along the winding shore trails; in the picnic areas you could see the smoke rising from the barbeques. Families played games, dogs and people chased frisbees. It was a glorious Sunday along the river.

"We moved here two years ago. We sold our big house. I liked it because I thought Wally would be able to spend more time with me." Sally Lassiter turned back to Cyrus. "He spent less."

You could see the pretty-girl features beneath the older woman's handsome face. A jock's wife. But as the jocks' muscles go soft, so their girls' looks fade. Only strength of character can retain beauty. Sally Lassiter was still beautiful, Cyrus thought.

"How did you find out about Wally's other life, Mr. Wilson?" she asked.

"I talked with the assistant coaches after the game."

Silence.

"They knew," she said slowly. "Of course they would. His secretary Louise Gelman knew too, of course. It's a small town. I suppose even the players knew."

"Not all. The seniors knew something was wrong."

She nodded. "I knew that much too, but it took me a while to find out how he was solving his problems. It started three years ago with his first losing season. He hadn't recruited well that winter. He'd been top dog too long. He didn't think he had to go out himself. He thought the boys would come to him. They didn't. I tried to cheer him up. To tell him it wasn't that important. No one stays on top all his life. We had each other. But, of course, we didn't have each other at all."

She looked out the window at the river recreation areas. "I suppose you've met some of his girls, Mr. Wilson?"

"Not yet."

"You should. They'll tell you what happened to him." She hesitated. Then: "One night I saw him with a girl. We pretended we didn't see each other. I was driving to the Krogers market on Packard. He was coming out of Barney's Pub on Packard. He went for young girls, Mr. Wilson."

"Do you know any of their names?"

"No, thank God. For a while I tried to pretend they didn't exist. Then one night I had too much to drink and I confronted him with the girl I'd seen in front of the pub with him. He laughed. He said it was the girlfriend of one of his players. I pretended to believe that.

"Then another time I saw him with a different girl. You can take it from there, Mr. Wilson. Most people did."

"Do you know anyone who hated Wally enough to kill him?"

"Me." Her answer was blunt.

"Could you tell me where you were sitting during the game?"

She turned and stared at Cyrus. "Am I a suspect?"

"Anyone who hated Wally has got to be, ma'am," Cyrus said politely.

"Then, Mr. Wilson, you will have very many people to investigate. For a lot of people hated Wally. You don't get to the top of your profession without making enemies. You don't get there without stepping on a lot of people. Other coaches hated him, some of his players, fans, alumni, parents of players he cut, whose scholarships he took away, some reporters — in some ways Wally Lassiter was the most hated man I ever knew. And in others, the best loved too. He lived at the center of things and at a feverish pitch. When you live the way Wally lived, Mr. Wilson, you make admirers, you make enemies. He was a master salesman. He took people in. He took me in for years."

She smiled ruefully. "I sometimes think that if Wally had been born in this country a century or so ago, before there was the mania of football, he might have sold snake oil to pioneers. He talked boys into coming to Mid-East who had no business being here. He promised them the moon and when someone better came along he cut them without mercy, took them off their football scholarships.

"He maimed young people, Mr. Wilson. He was a coach who was supposed to build character. He destroyed it!"

She took a deep breath. "I'm running on. I'm not being much help to you, am I?"

"Could you tell me, for the record, ma'am, just where you were seated during the game?"

"In the president's box. I'm sorry. I thought you really knew."

"I didn't."

"You can call President Miller. He's home now. I know

115

that because he just called me before you came to see how I was."

"I shall, ma'am. By the way, did Mr. Lassiter have a study here?"

"Yes. He spent a lot of time in it too, going over scouting reports, videotapes of games, practices. He would spend hours in there with his football tapes."

"Would you mind if I looked through it?"

"Not at all."

She led him down the hall of their spacious condominium apartment to a small room at the far end. It looked like a coach's inner sanctum. Team pictures hanging on the walls. Pictures of Wally with other famous coaches. "Remembering a terrific clinic . . . " A picture of Wally receiving his National Coach-of-the-Year Award.

And then there were pictures of a lean, hard, snub-nosed Wally when he played for Mid-East. He had been an offensive guard. And his was a face that even then brooked no opposition. That would as soon run over you as spit at you.

On a big oak desk Cyrus found letters from high school coaches looking for jobs, recommending players — sometimes doing both in the same letters. There were invitations to Wally Lassiter to speak at high school banquets, coaching clinics in the summer, civic clubs, church groups, alumni groups.

There were letters from alumni castigating him for his play selection. Letters blessing him for trying to make Mid-East a football power again.

It was probably not unlike a study in the home of a GM president. This was a man who lived and worked in the public eye. A man of accomplishment, energy, ambition.

To the right of the desk was a Betamax videotape recorder, on a small table, and a monitor. Above the tape deck on wall shelves was a row of tape cassettes in small black-and-white boxes.

They were each labelled with a different game and the date. Cyrus took down last year's Mid-East–Indiana game. He turned on the TV monitor and pushed the On button on the recorder.

He slid the cassette in.

There was a shifting image, and then the Mid-East–Indiana game began. The kickoff was in a shower stall. A teenaged blonde was taking a shower. She was soon joined by an older man wearing only a beard. They were soaping each other when Cyrus stopped it and replaced it with the Mid-East–Notre Dame game of two years ago.

That game opened with a girl about thirteen years old being tied to a chair by a man. Then the man was joined by a woman and together they started ripping the girl's clothes off.

The best, though, was last fall's big game against Ohio State. Two girls were making love to each other in a variety of positions hard for anyone not a gymnast to conceive of.

"Are you finding what you want?" Sally Lassiter called through the door.

"Yes, ma'am," Cyrus said.

17

Lassiter's secretary Louise Gelman was a small, well-preserved woman in her early forties. Cyrus found her snipping the heads off dead flowers in the side garden of her house. She wore a beautifully tailored green pants suit and matching long green gardener's gloves.

"Yes," she murmured, "I've heard of you, Professor Wilson. And I guessed that you'd be here sooner or later."

The scissor blades flashed and a dead chrysanthemum head fell into a bushel on the ground by her foot.

"Why?"

"Because of what happened last Wednesday morning in the office."

Propelled by a tiny toe emerging from an Italian sandal, the basket moved along the ground. The scissors snapped and another dead flower fell into the basket. Cyrus was fascinated. He could visualize the years of practice that went into such apparently casual, but perfectly synchronized, movements.

"What did happen, Ms. Gelman?"

"Miss. I'm too old to be a Ms."

The scissors snapped and another head dropped into the basket.

"Of course, I didn't think about it till last night, when I heard on the news that someone had shot Wally. Then I remembered and I knew that sooner or later I'd have to tell someone about it."

Cyrus waited as two more guillotined flower heads dropped. Louise Gelman had perfected living alone; she controlled her environment; she would move at her pace.

"I don't remember exactly what time it was, but this kid burst into my office."

She contemplated a chrysanthemum head that looked alive to Cyrus.

"Perhaps he wasn't a kid exactly. But the past few years I've been thinking of them all as kids. Every year they get younger and younger. Perhaps he was in his twenties."

"A student?"

"I don't think so. He was too well dressed to be a student. But I wasn't really looking at his clothes. He was in a state of panic, and he had a big bandage on his face. He waved his hands at me and *demanded* to see Wally right away.

"I told him politely that no one saw Mr. Lassiter without an appointment. Not even his players. He went right on by me and barged into Wally's office. I can tell you, Professor Wilson, I was startled. It took me a minute to get my wits together. Then I went in after him. Wally was furious. He was shouting at the young man, but when he saw me, he calmed down and muttered: 'It's all right, Louise. I'll take care of this. Just shut the door.'

"I closed the door. After that I heard a lot of angry words. Wally is easy to overhear. Coaches have big voices . . ." She paused. "The young man was hitting him up for money."

"How do you know that?" Cyrus asked.

She smiled. And tiny but deep wrinkles appeared around her eyes and the corners of her mouth. They spoiled the well-preserved surface but humanized the inner woman.

"Because the young man came running out with a check in his hand. And he emerged faster than he went in. If that was possible."

"Was he scared?"

"I'd say so. You'd be scared too if you had made Wally Lassiter angry. And Wally was angry. He stormed around his office, kicking drawers shut and banging files with those big hands of his. He can get very physical when he's excited. Well, he stormed around for some time and then I heard him lock the door and make a phone call."

"To whom?"

"I couldn't tell."

"You tried to?"

She shrugged. "Yes. I'll admit it. I tried to. By this time I was curious, as you can imagine. I've worked for Wally Lassiter for ten years. I've seen a lot of people come through the office: athletes, coaches, salesmen, alumni, old ball players, pro scouts, reporters, TV producers, writers, trainers, fans . . . but that young man was a type I'd never seen before."

"What did he look like?"

"As I told you, he had a big bandage on the side of his face, so I couldn't really tell you what he looked like. But he was a type I'd never seen before in the office."

"What happened when Wally was done with his phone call?"

"He started getting mad all over again. Kicking drawers. That was when I decided to take a coffee break before *I* was on the receiving end of the famous Lassiter temper. You know, I can't believe yet that he's dead. I can't believe there was anyone in the world able to kill him."

"Do you have any idea of the name of his visitor?"

"No. As I said, he had no appointment."

"Have you seen him again since?"

"No."

"Would you know him again if you saw him? Or his picture?"

"It would be hard because of that bandage."

"Where did Wally bank?"

"Harbour Woods Bank and Trust."

"You were Wally's secretary for ten years, Miss Gelman."

"I started here a year after Wally became head coach."

"Did you like him?"

The question surprised her. She thought about it. "You know, no one's ever asked me that." The scissors were still poised in midair above the live-appearing chrysanthemum head. The sun sparkled merrily on the tips of the blades.

"At times Wally could be very likeable. The last few years have been hard."

"Have you noticed a personality change in Wally over the past few years?"

"Like what?"

"Well, what did becoming a losing coach do to him?"

She nodded. "It did everything to him. He couldn't face it. It made him into a completely different personality in lots of ways. His character changed, I feel — "

She hesitated.

"Into what?"

"Into something different," she said guardedly.

"Could you tell me about that?"

She shook her head. Cyrus waited. But she wasn't going to answer.

"Miss Gelman, what do you know about his marriage?"

She looked at Cyrus, trying to read something in his eyes. "She's an impressive lady, Mrs. Lassiter."

"What do you mean 'impressive'?"

"Coach's wives run to a type. She didn't."

"What type was she?"

"Her own type."

It was first down and thirty to go through Louise Gelman.

"How was their marriage?"

"You better ask her."

"Wally seems to have led another life after hours."

Louise Gelman's eyes were steady. He knew she had been expecting a thrust like that. "Is that so?" she replied.

"Do you know anything about that other life?"

"Nope."

"I don't believe you, ma'am," Cyrus said. "I've come here from Mrs. Lassiter's apartment. A man can keep his wife in ignorance where he can't fool his secretary. Though in this case Mrs. Lassiter is definitely not unaware of Wally's other life."

"What did she tell you?"

"He had mistresses."

"So what do you want me to say?"

"I want to know about his women. Mrs. Lassiter didn't know any more than that. I figure you must."

Louise Gelman's scissors wavered. She looked away from Cyrus toward the birdbath in a corner of the garden. A male cardinal was taking a bath. It was a pretty picture.

"I don't know any more than that either," she finally said.

"He's dead. I want to find his killer."

"How can that help you?"

"Anything might help. We're looking into all parts of Wally's life."

"Suppose it was just a nut that shot him. They shoot at presidents and popes without any reason. It could've been that with Wally."

"That's one of the things we hope to find out. But first, we're going to find out about Wally's life."

She was silent, contemplating the chrysanthemum head. "All right," she said, "but I don't know too much. And before I tell you, I want you to understand that he wasn't like this a few years back. It was the losing that got to him. You could see it happening. He just changed. He began fooling around with girls. Young girls. I mean girls his players' ages. He had a girl named Sue last year. This year he had one named Francine. I never saw either of them. But they used to call him up. I never said anything to him about it. I wouldn't dare. But they were professional whores. I could tell that. They both lived out at the Village Apartments toward Ypsi. Off the expressway."

"How do you know that?"

"I used to drive Wally there when the Lincoln was in the shop. They gave him a new Lincoln to drive every year. The dealer did."

"Did he tell you what he was doing when he went out there?"

She smiled, and the wrinkles aged her instantly.

"He said he played cards out there. That was good enough for me. Mr. Wilson, I lasted ten years with Wally because I minded my own business. Wally went through secretaries fast before he came here."

"How do you know?"

"I heard."

"How did you connect Sue and Francine with the Village Apartments?"

"When I picked him up he didn't smell of cards. He smelled of hooker. Hooker's Scent, I thought of it."

"Do you have last names for Sue and Francine?"

"They're only hookers."

"Hookers have last names."

"Not real ones."

"Give me their phony names."

She was annoyed with herself. She'd gone further than she had wanted.

The scissors flashed and the live chrysanthemum head toppled into the basket. A sandaled toe nudged the basket along.

"Sue Nelson. Francine Carter. Are you finished with your questions, Mr. Wilson? I do have a good many dead flowers waiting for me."

"Does the name Ricky Andrews mean anything to you?"

"No."

"How about just Ricky?"

"We've got two or three Rickys playing on this year's team."

"This Ricky wouldn't be a ball player."

"Then I don't know him. I would like to get on with my gardening, Mr. Wilson."

"One last question?"

She barely nodded.

"Could you tell me what's likeable about a college football coach, married to an attractive, intelligent woman, who likes to spend his time with hookers and looking at pornographic tapes with phony game labels on them?"

The scissors were poised in midair. She looked at him.

"So you found out about that too?"

"Yes."

She turned and looked at a dead chrysanthemum. She shrugged. "All I can say, then, is that Wally Lassiter had a tough job. And it didn't get easier for him as he got older. As for his marriage, I agree with you. She's an attractive woman." An enigmatic smile came over Louise Gelman's lips. "And that's all I'm going to say." She looked at Cyrus. "Do you know that old Indian expression, till you walk in another man's moccasins, don't judge?"

124

"But someone did," Cyrus said.

"Yes," she said angrily, "and sentenced too."

The scissors snipped. The flower fell. It missed the basket.

She stared disbelievingly.

Cyrus thanked her and left.

18

The vice-president in charge of personal accounts at the Harbour Woods Bank and Trust Company was an attractive, dark-haired woman. The name on her desk announced her to be Ruth Armendariz. She had sparkling black eyes that examined Cyrus's identification card closely. Then the eyes examined him. And finally she put in a call to the police department.

"I want to confirm a police identification card. The name on it is Cyrus Wilson."

She had a slight and charming Hispanic accent.

"Yes, I'll wait for Detective Guiterrez to call back."

She hung up. "Meanwhile I'll get the file," she said to Cyrus.

Cyrus watched her walk into another office. A sign of the times, he thought. Someone named Guiterrez is a detective first grade in charge of an important Michigan homicide investigation; someone named Armendariz is a vice-president in a Michigan bank. The country was making progress. You just had to quit reading the newspapers and look at life firsthand.

Ms. Armendariz came back with a folder in her hand,

walking as sexily as a woman could and still be a bank vice-president. She wasn't trying to be sexy. She just was. It was incredible, Cyrus thought, but perhaps no more incredible than his playing policeman.

"May I look at it, please?" Cyrus asked.

"As soon as Detective Guiterrez confirms your identification." She was polite but firm. "I don't doubt its authenticity, Mr. Wilson. It's just that" — she lowered her voice; her eyes sparkled mischievously — "you don't look like a detective."

"That's what makes me such a good one."

She laughed. The phone rang. "Ruth Armendariz," she said. "Yes, thank you for returning my call. He is sitting here with me." She explained her need for confirmation, listened, and then her luscious lips curved in wicked amusement. She eyed Cyrus. "I'd say pudgy," she said. She laughed and said something in Spanish. And ended with a "gracias."

"Detective Guiterrez describes you as being on the fat side, Mr. Wilson."

"He's much fatter than I am," Cyrus said.

"Somehow, from his voice, I doubt it. Do you know what date the check you are interested in might have been written?"

"Last Wednesday."

"Today is only Monday. It's probably not here yet."

"My hunch, ma'am, is that it was cashed very soon after it was written. Probably at one of your branch banks."

"Hmm. Here is one written Wednesday with a stop payment on it." She took a check with a paper stapled to it out of the file. "Could this be the one you're looking for?"

Cyrus regarded the name of the payee, turned the check over, and read the endorsed signature. Then he looked at the big STOP PAYMENT stamp on it.

"This," he said softly, "is more than I expected to find. What can you tell me about this stop payment?"

Ruth Armendariz punched the buttons on her phone. "Emily," she said, "could you give me some information on an S.P. #403181?"

"Ask her if the check was cashed or not, could you?"

"I'll have all the information in a moment. My guess, Mr. Wilson, is that — " she stopped. "Yes, go ahead." She listened, making notes on a pad. "That's fine. Thank you, Emily."

She turned to Cyrus. "Mr. Lassiter called at 10:45 Wednesday morning to stop payment on this check. The check was refused at our Baldwin Avenue branch after the computer indicated a stop payment on it."

"How did it end up in your file? Wouldn't the payee have kept it?"

"Ordinarily yes. Let me see about that."

A moment later Ruth Armendariz was talking to the manager of the Baldwin Avenue branch. She waited while the manager left the phone to talk to a teller. Finally the teller herself got on the phone and explained that when the stop payment was explained to the payee, he got very upset and ran out of the bank. The teller remembered the incident quite clearly because the man had a bandage on the side of his head.

All this Ruth Armendariz repeated to Cyrus.

"Do you have any questions for her?" she asked Cyrus.

"No. May I keep the check?"

"Not allowed," Ruth Armendariz said, hanging up. "However, I can make you a copy."

"Could I ask you not to mention this to anyone?"

"Bank records are confidential, Mr. Wilson, unless a court order dictates otherwise."

"You've been very helpful," Cyrus said. He paused. "I hope you don't mind my saying that you're the most unlikely banker I've ever seen."

She smiled. "That makes two of us who don't fit our image. Here's your copy."

"Thank you."

She dismissed him with a wave of her hand.

*

Cyrus used a pay phone outside the bank.

"Harbour Woods Chamber of Commerce," the receptionist said.

"I'd like to speak to Mr. Wilbur Evans, please. Cyrus Wilson calling."

A moment later Wilbur Evans was on the phone.

"Mr. Evans, this is Cy Wilson. We met the other — "

"Of course. How are you?"

"Fine. I remember your saying you'd be at band day taking pictures."

"Slides. I was there. Wasn't that horrible?"

"Yes, sir. I wonder if I could take a look at them. Eileen may have mentioned to you that I'm working with the Harbour Woods Police Department on these murders — "

"Oh yes. We all know that."

"The police have been looking at videotapes, film, pictures . . . I wondered if we could look at your slides."

"You're more than welcome to. I can pick them up this afternoon by five o'clock."

"Good. Were you shooting from the stands, Mr. Evans?"

"Some. And then I went down an aisle as close as I could to get some close-ups."

"Which sidelines?"

"Mid-East's."

"You didn't notice someone with a gun in his hand . . ."

"No, I didn't. A policeman questioned me. But the pictures might show something. It was just dreadful. I've

129

never seen anything like that in my life. I'm a little worried about all this, from the chamber's point of view. Time takes care of many things, but . . . well, it's disturbing."

"Yes, indeed. Well, thank you for your help, Mr. Evans," Cyrus said.

*

The corridors of the police department were jammed. A Lassiter investigative task force had been set up on Sunday that cut across departmental lines. On it were state policemen in the halls, city cops, county deputy sheriffs, and representatives of Mid-East University's Public Safety Department.

Mixing with the policemen were reporters from television, newspapers, radio, the wire services, and student newspapers. There were other people there, too: police buffs, stenographers, clerks, gofers with coffee and rolls —and standing out in the middle of the throng was a burly older man wearing a big Stetson hat. He put a clamp on Cyrus's arm as Cyrus tried to make his way down the hall to Guiterrez's office.

"Hold it, son," said the burly man, "you're Wilson, ain't you? The professor investigating this tragedy?"

"Yes, sir."

Porcine eyes glared at him. There was a wildness in the old man's face.

"I'm Cal Johnson. President of the Mid-East University Varsity Booster Club! I've been waiting for you, son."

The grip on Cyrus's arm was beginning to cut off his circulation. Although in his sixties, Calvin Johnson was a very strong man. Cyrus knew all about him. He had been an All-American football player for Mid-East University forty-plus years ago. The Varsity Booster Club that he headed consisted of former Mid-East athletes, many of whom now held high positions in Detroit professions and industry. Doctors, lawyers, businessmen. It was common knowledge that Wally Lassiter used these prominent "jock alumni," as they were called, to recruit athletes, wine and dine them and their parents and grandparents, and dangle in front of them promises of jobs after graduation if, by chance, they didn't make the pros.

"I want you to know, Wilson, that the Varsity Booster Club has just put up a reward of $25,000 to anyone who can help us apprehend the murderer of Wally Lassiter. This was a most heinous crime. Lassiter was an outstanding American. He was the most beloved and revered football coach in America. The Varsity Booster Club of Mid-East University stands foursquare behind this investigation and has raised $25,000 as a reward. You better be aware of this . . ."

He went on in the same bull roar, his voice echoing down the corridor. From the sly grins Cyrus was receiving as people went by, he could tell that Johnson had buttonholed just about everyone with his canned speech and he, Cyrus, was merely the latest victim.

"I can assure, Mr. Johnson, I'll be doing my best. The reward will undoubtedly be of help — "

Cyrus detached himself from the man's demonic grip.

"Don't give me any assurances, Professor. You find that killer. We've got the toughest schedule in the nation this year with a possible Rose Bowl bid at the end of it. Do you realize what that means?"

Cyrus nodded and slipped away as Johnson grabbed a radio reporter by her arm.

"I want the news of the reward put on the air, young lady."

One of the TV people from Detroit tapped Cyrus on the shoulder. "You're Professor Wilson, aren't you? The author of the John Agate mysteries?"

"No," Cyrus said, "the man you want is that older man back there talking to the young lady."

Two Harbour Woods policemen laughed.

Cyrus moved on through the throng of people.

"Turned up anything, Prof?" a reporter asked.

"Nothing yet," Cyrus said.

He slipped into Guiterrez's office. Tinker and Layne were sitting there with grim looks on their faces. Detroit was supposed to be the place for murders, not Harbour Woods, a college town forty-five miles away.

Guiterrez slammed the phone down on the hook. "Thousands of people sitting around a killer and no one has seen a man with a gun in his hands." He looked at Cyrus. "We got the report on the bullet. It was from a 7.65 Beretta."

"The person must be a hell of a shot," Layne said.

"He had to be close in," Guiterrez said. "Stood up and pointed like a lot of people point at things on the field, only he was pointing with a gun."

"With a silencer?" Tinker asked.

"In that racket a howitzer wouldn't have been heard." Guiterrez looked at Cyrus. "What's on the bank deal?"

"Sit back, gentlemen," Cyrus said. "I've got a surprise for you." He described his visits to Lassiter's widow and secretary and what had taken place the past Wednesday in the secretary's office.

"I went to check on the check this morning," Cyrus said cheerfully.

"You look like you pulled a gold ring," Layne said.

"I may have. The person Lassiter gave the check to was" — Cyrus paused to let it sink in — "Ricky Andrews."

They stared at him in disbelief.

"Come off it, Prof," Tinker said, "you're still back with the Browne case. Better shift gears."

"Look for yourselves," said Cyrus. He handed Guiterrez the copy of Wally's check with the stop payment attached. The two other detectives crowded in behind Guiterrez to look over his shoulder.

Layne whistled. Tinker shook his head in wonder.

Guiterrez nodded. "This connects Ricky Andrews with Wally Lassiter," he said. "Were you looking for this, Prof?"

"No, but I found some porno tapes in Lassiter's study at home. The adult bookstore sells them."

Tinker was floored. "Wally Lassiter with a collection of porno tapes. Who'd believe it?"

"A lot of people," Guiterrez said.

"Anyone who wanted him fired."

Guiterrez mused aloud. "Ricky was running some blackmail by Wally. Wally's a competitor. He decides to fight it. He puts a stop payment on it. So Ricky offs him. Is that your scenario, Prof?"

"I don't have a scenario, John," Cyrus said.

"Why not?" Tinker said, warming to it. "It gives Ricky a motive for shooting Wally. He's got one for Browne. It fits."

"It fits like shit, Tink," Layne said, walking back to his chair. "You don't shoot a guy in a crowded stadium because he stopped payment on a five-hundred-dollar check."

"Where I'm from, man, people kill for less," Tinker said.

"Not with 98,000 witnesses," Layne said.

"What 98,000 witnesses?" Guiterrez snarled. "I ain't seen one person who saw the head coach get shot in the stadium." Guiterrez looked at Cyrus. "What about Ricky's panic in the office? What about the bandage on his head? What in hell was that about?"

"I don't know," Cyrus admitted.

"You find that out, Prof, and I'll like what you just brought in. I'll like it a lot. But you got to work it out for us. And you got to do it fast. We got two guys murdered within five days. The first guy was a local biggie and the

133

pressure was on. The second guy is a national biggie and if we thought the pressure was on before, we ain't seen nothing yet. Murder is catching. Today two on campus. Who knows what the fuck will be tomorrow? Let's get this Ricky Andrews. If he didn't do it, he's a key to who did."

"Well, we got the all points out, John," Layne said. "We can cover the airports, the trains, the busses, but if he was running, he's gone."

"Anyone look at the videotapes to see if Andrews was in the crowd?" Cyrus asked.

No one had. There were mug shots of Ricky but no one had thought to see if Andrews was in the crowd.

"Christ, that's a needle in a haystack anyway," Layne said.

"I'm going to look at some pictures," Cyrus said. "I'm also going to poke into Ricky's business. Maybe I can find something there."

Guiterrez nodded.

"I been to the bookstore, Prof," Layne said, "there's nothing there for us."

"I wasn't thinking of the bookstore," Cyrus replied.

19

Cyrus found the manager of the Village Apartments in the first unit off the entry road. He was a bald, fat man with a ring of keys on his belt.

"You don't look like a cop," the fat man said, after checking Cyrus's identification.

He's the second person to tell me that today, Cyrus thought.

"Did Detective Tinker?" Cyrus said.

"Who's he?"

"He came out looking for Ricky Andrews the other day."

The fat man thought about it. "Oh yeah . . . him." You could see the wheels turning inside his head. "The black guy. *He* looked like a cop. Well, Andrews still ain't around. Least I ain't seen him lately."

"How about Francine Carter?"

The fat man nodded. "C Unit. Apartment 5."

"She a friend of Ricky's?"

"You move right in, don't you, Mister?" The fat man studied him. Am I here to make trouble for him was what he had to be thinking, Cyrus thought, and is my trouble going to cost him more than the trouble other people could give him?

"She's got lots of friends," the fat man said, carefully.

"Did any of them ever look familiar to you?"

"Mister, I try not to notice people's friends. You notice too much in a job like mine you're out on the street. There's a lot of unemployed people in this county. I like my job."

"When's the last time you saw Ricky Andrews?"

"When he paid his rent. Last month. He always pays in cash."

"How about Sue Nelson?"

The fat man's eyes narrowed. "She's dead," he said.

"What apartment was she in?"

He closed his eyes. "C Unit. Apartment 5."

"What a coincidence. Same as Francine's."

The fat man shrugged. "That's right."

"Did they know each other?"

"How do I know?"

"Who paid the rent on that apartment?"

"They did. The girls did."

"By check?"

"Cash." Pause. "Lots of tenants pay in cash."

"Did you ever see Sue and Francine together?"

"Hey, I told you, Mr. Wilson. I don't see nothing."

"That's right. You said that. It seems to be a healthy attitude."

"It keeps *me* healthy."

*

The young woman who opened the door in C Unit's apartment #5 gave Cyrus a brave smile. It didn't quite come off because she had the remnant of a black eye and a large yellowish bruise dominated one side of her face.

She was thin, with smeary lips, short dark hair, and wore

a loosely tied dressing gown over a bra and panties. In spite of the eye with its radiant yellow bruise, he could see that with the right makeup and clothes she could look electrifying.

Right now she was just scared. She kept looking past him to see who else was there.

"There's no one else here. I'm alone."

She looked at him. "Who are you?"

"Cyrus Wilson, Mid-East University Public Safety, working with the Harbour Woods Police Department."

"What do you want?"

"You're Francine Carter, aren't you?"

"Yes."

"I'd like to come in and talk with you."

"What about?" She had lowered her voice. There were two other apartments on that floor.

"Wally Lassiter," he said softly.

"Who's he?"

Cyrus just looked at her.

"Oh, hell," she said. "Come on in."

She closed the door behind him.

"Look, Mister, I don't know any more about it than what I saw on the TV. Some nut shot him in the stadium."

Cyrus looked around the apartment. Holiday Inn decor. Low bland yellow furniture. Low yellow lamps. An expensive stereo system and, from what he could see from where he stood, a mirror on the bedroom ceiling were the only items that would differentiate the apartment from a motel suite.

"See anything you like?" she asked sarcastically, drawing her dressing gown tighter around her body.

Cyrus sat down on a sofa.

"Why don't you make yourself at home?" she said.

"Miss Carter, I didn't — "

"*Ms.* Carter," she corrected him.

"All right, Ms. Carter," Cyrus began again, "I didn't come over here to harass you. But I'm investigating Wally Lassiter's death. And your name has come up as a close friend of Wally's."

"He had other close friends."

"We'll be talking with them. Won't you sit down, Ms. Carter?"

"I don't want to sit down," Francine Carter said. "And I didn't ask you to sit down."

Beneath the defiant surface he saw the fear still there. According to Tinker's research, she was all of nineteen years old.

"Who gave you the shiner?" he asked casually.

"I stepped into a door."

"Which one?"

"Any one you want to pick out. Look, I don't have to talk with you, Mister. I've got a lawyer. A good one."

"You might need him," Cyrus said. He took out his note pad and read: "Ms. Carter, Francine Carter, also known as Frances Conn, Felicia Carr, and christened Francesca Cacciopa at Holy Redeemer Church in Detroit about nineteen years ago. In her nineteen years," Cyrus intoned without expression, "Francesca Cacciopa received sixteen arrests for prostitution. In Detroit, Toledo, the downriver communities of Ecorse, Wyandotte, Trenton. And now," Cyrus lifted his eyes from the note pad and looked at her, "Francesca Cacciopa, a.k.a. Francine Carter, has turned up in Harbour Woods as the mistress of Wally Lassiter, famous football coach, shot and killed two days ago."

Francine Carter looked at him with contempt.

"Who're you trying to scare?" she said with a sneer.

"No one."

"I don't scare easy, Mister."

"Is that how you got the black eye?"

"Never mind how I got the black eye. That stuff you read. That's public record. It's got nothing to do with Wally's death. So you know what you can do with your pad."

"I didn't say it had, Ms. Carter. But with this background and your admitted relationship with Wally, it wouldn't be hard for the prosecutor to build up enough paperwork to put you in the can for a while."

She was silent. Then she sat down and crossed her legs. She had nice legs. She let Cyrus see them.

"What do you want to know?"

"When did you last see Wally?"

She took a pack of cigarettes out of the pocket of the gown and fumbled for a small silver lighter. "Smoke?"

Cyrus shook his head.

She lighted a cigarette and blew smoke at him. "Friday night. The team stays at the Harbour Woods Inn before home games. Wally drove over here from there. He stayed a couple of hours."

"Was he worried about anything?"

"He's always worried the night before a game. That's why he comes to me. That's why he takes me on the road with him. I relax him. I'm good. You ought to try me some time."

She smiled at him.

"I'm just a poor university teacher doubling as a cop."

"I got different rates for different folks."

"You'd lose money with me. Did Wally talk about anything beside the game? Did he ask you who gave you the black eye? Did *he* give it to you?"

She smiled. "Wally didn't hit his girls. He liked to use his hands on us but never where it showed." She winked at Cyrus. "He had horny fingers."

"Did he ask you about your eye?"

She sighed. "Not till after we had sex. I told him I

walked into a door. Wally wasn't interested. He doesn't come here because of my eyes."

"How long did he stay after you had sex?"

"Long enough to do it once more. Wally was active for an old guy."

"Between sex, then, what did you and Wally talk about?"

"I don't remember. I don't talk much and I listen even less. If you know what I mean. Wally likes to talk a lot. He can get upset after a losing game and then he really gets ranting and raving. He even cries about what went wrong. At first the ranting and raving used to scare me, but then I figured, hell, as long as he wasn't sore at me, what difference did it make? And then you got to figure when he's ranting he's not fucking and I like a coffee break every now and then."

"You don't remember what you talked about Friday night."

"He talked about the game. I faked listening."

"Has he ever mentioned someone who might be out to get him?"

"No one was out to get Wally unless he lost a game. Then everyone was."

"How long was Wally a client of yours?"

She thought about it. "Since January."

"How did you meet?"

"In a bar."

"What bar?"

"I forget which one." She smiled at him.

"Who pays the rent here?"

"I do."

"What about Sue?"

"Sue? Who's Sue?"

"Sue Nelson. She used to live here."

"Oh her." Pause. "She died."

"And you got her place."

"Anything wrong with that?"

"No. Not yet."

"Look. This is a nicer apartment than my old one. It's got a view of the lake. Want to look?"

"You took over Sue's apartment and you also took over Wally from her."

She was silent. Then she shrugged. "Okay. I did. So what?"

"So tell me about Sue Nelson."

His strategy was simple enough. Get her to talk about Sue Nelson, and it would lead to Ricky.

"What do you want to know?"

"What was she like?"

Francine Carter twisted out her cigarette. "If you really want to know, she was stuck up."

"In what ways?"

"She was snooty. She thought she was different from the rest of us. Maybe she was. She liked to read. And write poetry. She was always telling us how she was going to get out of the life and go to college. If — " She caught herself in time.

"If what?"

"If she could've."

"You were going to say 'if Ricky would let her.' "

"I don't know anyone named Ricky."

"Sure you do. He's the one that hit you." Cyrus leaned toward her. "He's also the one that shot and killed Wally Lassiter in the stadium Saturday."

"You're crazy," she whispered. "Ricky wouldn't have done that."

"Why not?"

"He's no killer. He'd hit me. Sure. But Ricky didn't kill Wally. Ricky never killed anyone in his life."

"What about Sue Nelson?"

141

"Who's been talking to you, Mister? She O.D'd. She offed herself. She was a junkie."

Francine Carter took out another cigarette. With shaking hands she lit it. "I guess you got me talking, didn't you?"

Cyrus sat back. "I guess maybe you better go on talking," he said softly.

She blew smoke out. "Maybe I better."

Francine Carter had first met Ricky in Detroit, where she had been working what the newspapers called the Cass corridor. He took her to a nice restaurant and treated her like a lady before he took her to a swanky motel in the suburbs. They spent a couple of days together. He talked her into coming out to Harbour Woods to work for him.

"I didn't have anyone looking after me on the street. And it can get mean for you if you don't have a man protecting you. Ricky had two other girls in Harbour Woods but he said he'd love me and look after me. So I came."

She laughed dryly. "He also told me a lot of his customers were unmarried doctors and lawyers and I might be able to marry one of them. He didn't have to tell me that. I didn't believe him. I was ready for a change. That was when I met Sue. She was working for him. And there was another girl."

Francine Carter never met the other girl. But she and Sue got along all right, as long as Sue didn't hand her that shit about poetry and how men were no damn good.

"I knew men were no damn good but I didn't think I was any better. She thought she was better than everyone."

After Sue died, she and Ricky talked about her taking over some of Sue's clients. Number one on the list was Wally Lassiter.

"I knew about him from Sue. She hated him. Wally didn't know that. He thought she was nuts about him.

Ricky set up a meeting with me and Wally over at Barney's." She smiled at Cyrus. "See, I finally remembered the name of that bar." She laughed. "I thought Wally might be rough, from what Sue told me. But I guess he was nicer to me than her. Maybe it was her looks that brought out the kinky in him."

"What did she look like?"

"Pretty. But she had kind of a snooty face. I mean, like she came from a nice family and a guy fucking her might think he was fucking a nice family. Some guys turn on to that."

"Did Wally talk about her?"

"Not a word. It was weird. It was like she'd never existed."

"And Ricky?"

"Yeah. Ricky talked about her a lot. Ricky liked her, until she agreed to be a witness against him. She could turn five tricks a night for him. She could handle the educated bums you get around here. She was smart. I'll hand her that. But she was screwed up. Even for someone in the business, she was screwed up."

"Did you get the feeling Ricky liked her best of his women?"

"No. He loved me the best," she said defiantly.

"Then why did he hit you?"

"I told you, I walked into a door."

"We're looking for Ricky for murdering Wally Lassiter and someone else. If you don't come clean with me, you'll come clean with a prosecutor down at city hall."

She was silent.

"Okay. He was scared. That's why he hit me."

"Scared of what?"

"I don't know. He wanted money and I wouldn't give it to him."

"When was this?"

"Last Wednesday."

"What time?"

"Noon time. He woke me up. He was moving fast and he was looking bad. He had a bandage on his face. He told me someone had tried to kill him the night before and he needed money to get out of town."

"Did he say who had tried to kill him?"

"No. He told me he'd just been to someone who owed him money. The guy wrote a check and then stopped payment on it." She looked at Cyrus, as the thought occurred to her. "Was that Wally?"

"Yes."

"Jesus. No wonder you're looking for Ricky. But he wouldn't kill Wally. He wouldn't kill anyone. He's just a . . . pimp, Mister. I been around *hard* guys. Ricky's not a hard guy. He had to be upset to hit even me — "

And with "even me" she broke down and began to cry. Wracking sobs that started from her belly. The tears running down her thin cheeks made her look mousy, adolescent, almost undernourished. Cyrus thought about Wally Lassiter, that great shaper of young people's characters, morals, bodies.

"Ms. Carter, do you have a key to Ricky's apartment?"

She nodded through her tears. Then she went into the kitchen and from a hook in the cupboard removed a key.

Cyrus took it. "Look," he said, "I have to ask you not to leave town. You'll be all right if you stay here. If you leave, a lot of cops will be looking for you."

"Leave?" she wept, "how am I going to leave? Ricky found my money."

Cyrus had two tens in his wallet. He gave her one. She stopped crying.

*

Ricky Andrews's apartment in another unit by the lake was larger and more elegant than Francine Carter's. It was also a mess. Clothes were strewn all over. Glasses, dishes, food all over the kitchen. Ricky had left in a hurry all right.

Cyrus started in the kitchen and worked his way to the bedroom. The drawers of the bureau there were open, clothes sticking half out. Cyrus dumped each drawer on the floor. In one drawer he found a small photograph in a silver frame.

It showed Ricky and a girl in a night club. The girl was grinning at the camera. There was something familiar about her. Cyrus took the picture out of the frame and slipped it into his jacket pocket.

Then he examined the contents of each drawer. In one drawer, under a pile of shirts, he found a wad of receipts, motel receipts, held together by a black clamp.

There were two pencilled names on top of each receipt. The top one read: Frank-Patty. The next one: Wally-Francine.

The receipt labelled Wally-Francine was dated a week ago. A Friday night. The Holiday Inn in Skokie, Illinois. That would be the night before the Northwestern game, Cyrus thought.

The receipt beneath that was labelled Henderson-Patty. And so the receipts went. Each one a motel. Each with two names on it. There were three girls' names that were repeated: Patty, Francine, and a Sally.

The receipts went back to the spring, last winter. Then the girls' names were different. Patty and Sally and Francine were gone. Replaced by a Sue and a Pam.

Ricky apparently ran three girls and kept records of their appointments with his clients. Wally's name turned up in a pattern of times and places. In the fall, and in motels in Columbus, Bloomington, South Bend . . .

Cyrus put the receipts in his other pocket. Unless he was

saving them as records for the IRS, Cyrus thought, Ricky Andrews was running, or planning to run, a blackmail caper.

That could get him involved with a killer, Cyrus thought. It might even force him to kill.

One step at a time, he thought. Be mercilessly logical and methodical. Like John Agate.

Cyrus searched through two more drawers before he found another item as interesting, or almost as interesting, as the various motel receipts. Strewn among Ricky's silk undershorts Cyrus found a bunch of address books. He thumbed through them. There must have been over a hundred women's names and addresses and phone numbers in them. In cities such as Detroit, Toledo, Chicago, and finally, New York. The New York names were faded.

Cyrus put the address books in his pockets. They could prove useful in the search for Ricky.

There was nothing more of interest in the bureau. Cyrus then went through the rest of the apartment. He found syringes, needles, spoons, rags, straps, medicine bottles with God knew what kinds of pills in them.

It was not unlike going through an athletic trainer's storeroom. Wally Lassiter, Cyrus thought, might have felt at home here, if Ricky ever let him use the place.

Which he probably hadn't.

When Cyrus was sure he'd found everything that was important, he locked the apartment. He kept the key and drove back to Harbour Woods. By way of Packard Road.

20

"I'll have a martini on the rocks and a grilled cheese sandwich," Cyrus told the waiter.

Barney's Pub was crowded at lunchtime. Packard Road was a busy four-lane connection between the cities of Harbour Woods and Ypsilanti. The pub got a lot of businessmen, truckers, salesmen. It was a good place to eat and drink if you didn't want to run into university people. A simple kind of macho place. Cyrus could understand why Ricky liked to take his hookers there.

The waiter brought the martini. He was grinning. "It's on the house, Professor."

Cyrus looked at him. Student. But not one he knew. "Why?"

"Ron says so." The waiter jerked his thumb at the bartender, a plump young man with a handlebar mustache. Cyrus recognized a former student of his named Ron Lieberman.

"Ron says you gave him a B last year when he deserved a D."

"Smartest move I ever made," Cyrus said. He rose with his drink in hand. "How about bringing my sandwich to the bar?"

"Sure thing, sir."

"How's it going, Mr. Wilson?" Ron Lieberman asked. They shook hands.

"All right, Ron. Thanks for the drink."

"The least I could do for the B."

Cyrus laughed. "How long have you been working here?"

"On and off since my sophomore year. I started as a waiter. I don't think I've ever seen you in here, Mr. Wilson."

Cyrus sipped his martini. "I avoid red-neck places as a rule. Good martini."

Lieberman laughed. "Same old Professor Wilson. Louie Cremona and I were talking about you yesterday. You remember Louie from the Whitman-Dickinson?"

"Of course. How's he doing?"

"Great. He saw the story in — "

"Ronnie!" came a cry from the other end of the bar, where a waitress had been waiting to catch his eye.

Liberman looked annoyed. "Don't leave, Prof. I'll be right back."

He went to make some drinks. When he returned he brought a beer for himself. The waiter brought Cyrus his sandwich.

"Hey, not bad at all," Ron approved. "'Grilled cheese and a martini. You remember the time you told the class you once ordered chablis with the Peter Pan special on a Howard Johnson's children's menu?"

"I got the idea from a Peter de Vries novel," Cyrus said.

"Yeah. We discovered that later. What I always wanted to know is did you really do it? Or were you just telling us a story out of a book?"

"No. I really did it," Cyrus said. "I always imitate literature in life."

Ron Lieberman beamed. "I figured that. Just like John

148

Agate. I read one of your kids' books this summer. It was okay. And then Cremona told me he saw a story in the MEU News that you were investigating the murders on campus for the university. Man, that's cool. Doing it in life just like you do it in books. That's using it all up."

Cyrus wasn't exactly sure what that meant or whether he was being complimented or not, but he thanked Lieberman anyway.

"I want to ask you something, Ron. Wally Lassiter used to drink here, I've been told. Is that right?"

Ron Lieberman wiped the bar in front of Cyrus. "I was wondering when you were going to get around to that, Mr. Wilson. I figured you were here for a reason."

"I should have given you an A, for intuition."

"Four Heinekins, Ronnie. Dark," the waitress called.

When Ron came back, he said, "Wally came here a lot, but no one was supposed to notice him."

"Why not?"

"He was with girls. He's married. That kind of bullshit."

Cyrus took out a picture of Francine Carter from the Detroit P.D. files.

"Francine," Ron said.

Cyrus showed him the picture of Ricky he'd removed from Ricky's bureau drawer.

"That's Sue. She O.D.'d. And died. And with her is Ricky baby."

"What do you know about him, Ron?"

"He deals. He's a pimp, too."

"Does he do business in here?"

"Barney'd throw him out."

"Bloody Mary, gin and bitters, scotch on the rocks, Ronnie."

Ron looked sore. "Be right back, Mr. Wilson."

It was like trying to get your car repaired while the mechanic was called away to pump gas.

Cyrus finished the sandwich and the martini.

Ron returned. "Want another, Mr. Wilson?"

Cyrus shook his head.

"It's free."

"No, thanks. Can we get back to Ricky?"

"Sure."

"When did you last see Ricky?"

"Last week. I forget what day it was. He came in and he was a mess. He'd banged his head somewhere. He wanted to borrow money from Barney. He said — " Ron stopped and stared at Cyrus. "Hey, you know what he kept saying. He kept saying Wally had double-crossed him. That Wally owed him money and wouldn't pay it. Wally'd stopped payment on a check of his. Jesus, you don't think Ricky plugged him in the stadium? Wow, I never put it together till now."

Ron Lieberman looked pleased with himself.

"Did Ricky leave right away?"

"No. After trying to hit Barney up for some bucks, he tried everyone else in the place. Even me. I asked him what a rich cat like him, driving an Alfa and all, needed money for.

"He said he was leaving town. He didn't like this city anymore. As for the Alfa, he didn't like that either. He was leaving it behind. Then he asked me if the airport limo stopped here on the way to Metro. I told him it never went by Packard. Just State and Washtenaw. I couldn't believe he was leaving that Alfa behind. That's an eighteen-thousand-dollar machine." Ron smiled. "Who says it pays to go to college?"

"Two light Strohs, Ronnie."

He shook his head. "She calls me Ronnie 'cause she knows I don't like it."

He drew the beers.

"Did he say where he was going?"

"No, but from his crazy behavior I'd say a long way from here. You think he killed Wally, Mr. Wilson?"

"I don't know."

"Jesus, what a world."

"Make it another Strohs, Ronnie," the waitress yelled loudly.

"Bitch," Ron said, as he drew the third Strohs.

*

John Guiterrez's ashtray was filled to overflowing. Next to it he had spread out the motel receipts Cyrus had given him. Ricky's address books he had already gone over.

"You did okay, Prof. I'll get some of these addresses out to New York, Chicago, Detroit. I think our boy's gone all right. According to Layne, he cleaned out the till at the bookstore last Wednesday. The creep that owns it won't sign a complaint. If I ever become a criminal, Prof, I'm going to rob adult bookstores."

"And have the Mafia on your tail, John? You'd do better robbing the A&P."

"Maybe. Anyway, he's spooked and he's run. And before Saturday too. Which should put him far from the maddening crowd."

"Madding," Cyrus said.

"Yeah? I always wondered about that. I read that book once. Or most of it." The phone rang. "Ask him to wait," Guiterrez said into it.

"I sent Tink off to check airlines, Prof, but I don't think Ricky went out under his own name. I just had another thought. Suppose he's been setting us up all this time. Telling people he's going out of town, cleaning out the bookstore? Maybe he's right here in River City. Maybe he stayed to bump off Wally. Maybe in front of 98,000 people is a smart thing. That's too many people. I mean, who've we met that saw it? No one."

Guiterrez looked down at the motel receipts. "You didn't find any with Arthur Browne's name on them?"

"No."

"Aint that a scream? The lawyer gets it for free; the jock pays."

The phone rang again. "I told you to — all right, send him in." Guiterrez hung up. "Some cockamamie deputy thinks he knows something. He can't wait. He's busy. He's got to check out a guy stealing gravel from the shoulder of a road in Lodi Township."

The office door opened and a young sheriff's deputy entered, looking tentative.

"What's up, friend?" Guiterrez asked, trying to put some kindness into his voice and not quite succeeding.

"I hate to bother you, sir. I know how busy you are but I talked to the sheriff and he said to talk to you personally. He said you were questioning everyone who was behind the Mid-East bench Saturday."

"We sure as hell are trying to. Were you there?"

"No, sir. Not during the game."

"That's good. I'd hate to think we didn't talk to a cop in that area."

"I was there in the morning, sir. I saw a man standing around in that part of the stadium, sort of looking about. It was raining, so he wasn't there long. But —"

Guiterrez tossed a mug shot of Ricky Andrews across the desk. "Is that him?"

The deputy studied it. "No, sir."

"What did your man look like?"

"He wore an orange-and-yellow rain slicker. It looked like he worked security in the stadium. It's not hard to get in there if you look like you're an usher." The deputy paused. "He wore those half-glasses. You know, the kind people look over at you. I thought it was kind of odd seeing an usher wearing them."

152

"Why?" Cyrus asked.

The deputy blushed. "I . . . connect them with professors."

Guiterrez laughed. "Okay. What was Mr. Half-Glasses doing there?"

"Nothing. Just standing there looking around."

"Standing where?" Cyrus asked.

The deputy swallowed. "Behind the Mid-East bench."

"What the fuck took you so long to get here?" Guiterrez snarled.

The deputy couldn't meet his eyes. "I guess I just forgot about him till I heard the city police were questioning people who sat in that part of the stadium."

"Where were you during the game?" Cyrus asked.

"On traffic duty on Saline Road."

"What in hell were you doing in the stadium in the morning?" Guiterrez said.

The deputy blushed again. "I'm a football nut, sir. I was on my way out to my post on Saline Road. I was early. So I went inside. It was as close as I was going to get to the game."

"How old would you say the man in half-glasses was?" Cyrus asked.

"Forties, sir. Maybe fifty. It was hard to tell. It was raining. And all ushers are about the same age. They're mostly guys who work around town. Football freaks. Like me . . ." he added, embarrassed.

"What's your name, Deputy?" Guiterrez asked.

"Delbert Schultz, sir."

"How long you been a deputy, Delbert?"

"A little under a year, sir. I was a fireman before that, but my wife made me quit. She thought it was too dangerous."

Guiterrez smiled. "All right, Delbert, better late than never. Give the secretary outside your name and home phone number. I'll call Sheriff Thompson and have you posted inside the stadium for all the next home games. I want you there early in the morning to see if you can spot the guy."

Delbert Schultz's eyes lighted up.

"Hey, you're not going there to watch football, Delbert."

"Yes, sir. I understand."

Guiterrez turned to Cyrus after the deputy left. "What do you think?"

"I don't know."

"I *know* you don't know, for Christ's sake. I was just asking you what you thought."

"I don't think, either," said Cyrus.

"That figures." Guiterrez looked down at the motel receipts, the address books, and the mug shots of Ricky Andrews spread across his desk. "It's hard to see a pimp shooting anyone. No less in a stadium. But a nut might do it. A nut would also bake a lawyer. Maybe we should be looking for a nut. A nut in half-glasses."

"Maybe," said Cyrus, "but I'd still like to get hold of Ricky."

"You and me both, brother."

154

21

Everything about Mary Louise Hillman was overflowing. Her voluminous purple robe, her pale skin, her language, her ideas . . .

"Limitations?" Her voice rose in liquid tones. "There are no limitations to sensations. As poets, our job is to find the appropriate language to convey subterranean sensations in experimental thought."

Eileen was silently grateful Cyrus wasn't present. He hated this kind of talk. It would bring out the cynicism in him.

"Don't be afraid of feeling. Don't be afraid of conveying feeling, my dear ones."

Mary Louise Hillman smiled at the cherubs in front of her and then, with a graceful gesture, she raised her beautiful celadon glazed porcelain Japanese tea bowl and sipped from it.

It was a gift, Eileen had read in *Newsweek,* from the Japanese government following her sensational poetry tour of Japan. Hillman had a great following among the Japanese. She must look like a rhinocerous there, Eileen thought.

Hillman set down the bowl, studied it for a moment, and then looked at her audience once more with a tiny, conspiratorial smile. "They say the sixties and seventies are passé. That experimenting with our minds and bodies is over. That we are now in for a period of buttoned-up thought, buttoned-up emotion, buttoned-up behavior. To that I say — " she leaned forward as a tiny but perfectly audible hiccup emerged, "unadorned bullshit!"

Nervous laughter from the class, some twenty of them in the third-floor seminar room of the library. The same library that would have the Hillman poetry manuscript wing built onto it with the foundation's munificent grant.

They were all graduate students. Poets and writers, each of whom had submitted manuscripts for the Hillman competition.

The famous poet swayed in front of them.

"For the artist — and that's what each of you is, or why else are you here? — there can never be retrenchment, never buttoning up. There is always outreach, exploration, the search for new sensations that can be conveyed in words and shared with others."

She steadied herself with one hand on the desk and lifted the tea bowl with the other and drank. She smiled at them. It was a smile that said: Look at me, I'm managing. Isn't it wonderful how we all manage things?

"If I have one thing to say to young poets and writers, it's this: don't be afraid. Cast your soul adrift. Then and only then will you be able to experience beyond language, beyond even senses . . ."

Cyrus would have said the woman spouted nothing but pedantic cant, Eileen thought. That she was a burnt-out case from an earlier era, a female Timothy Leary. She had published perhaps three volumes of poetry and parlayed them into a reputation as an established poet, thanks in part to the Hillman Foundation, which sponsored her college campus tours and which gave generously to colleges and universities. That would be Cyrus's point of view, thought Eileen. And until today she would have quarreled with it. For she liked Hillman's poetry. And the critics had hailed it. But now, seeing her in person, in those garish purple robes, using those exaggerated gestures and drinking God knew what in her Japanese tea bowl, Eileen wasn't so sure. I better reread her work, Eileen thought.

"And now, my darlings, I'll have more to say tomorrow in my talk after the awards. I don't want to shoot my wad right now. Tomorrow is," she beamed, "everything. In fact, although I'm staying on till the end of the week to deliver your honors convocation address, I can assure you that my talk tomorrow will be about what is closest to my soul. My honors convocation address is just that: an address. A public speech. Tomorrow, a short but private talk. Right now . . ." She picked up a piece of paper with that extra preciseness of someone who is compensating for having drunk too much. She put on her glasses. "Right now, I want to talk with the following people: Milton Kaplan, Eileen O'Hanrahan, Ruth Gardner."

Eileen's heart began to pound. She looked over at Milt Kaplan, a grad student who wrote poetry. And at Ruthie Gardner, who wrote both poetry and prose. What could Hillman want from the three of us? Eileen wondered. And hoped to God it was what she thought.

Eileen joined Ruth and Milton at the front of the room. Another student was asking Hillman who was her favorite poet writing today.

"I have no favorite poet, my child. When you get as old as I am, you stop playing favorite poets, seminal influences, and all that kind of garbage."

Hillman turned to the three of them. "My darlings, I want all of you to sit up front at the awards ceremonies tomorrow. Enough said?"

Eileen felt her blood rushing to her temples. Hillman's lubricious eyes rested on her.

"Our Irish beauty blushes adorably. You must be O'-Hanrahan. You remind me of myself . . . a while back. Now all of you, not a word to the others. Agreed?"

They stammered "of courses" and hardly dared to look at each other.

"You're all beautiful and I want to see more of each of you this week."

"Mary Louise," a voice called from the doorway.

A young man stood in the doorway. Slim, good-looking.

"Philip, darling, just in time. Remember dears, sit up front."

She pursed her lips and pantomimed a kiss to them and then walked unsteadily to the door. She took the young man's arm.

"My God," Milton Kaplan said, staring after them, "she's drunk."

"So what?" Ruth Gardner said. "Drunk she makes more sense than most people sober. Most poets are drunks, Milt. They have to drink in order to cope with their psychic pain."

"That is a lot of shit," Milton snorted. "I'm a poet and I don't have any psychic pain."

"That's cause you're a lousy poet," Gardner said. She was a tall, stringy-haired myopic girl with lots of energy. She would write wild, compulsive Gothic novels when she left Mid-East, Eileen guessed.

"Eileen," Gardner said to her, "did you see him? He must be her secretary."

"A weirdo," Milton said. "She's a lesbian. I'd look out for her if I were you, Eileen."

Eileen laughed.

"And why shouldn't *I* look out?" Gardner wanted to know.

158

And then the three of them laughed. They were all very excited and happy.

*

They stood in front of the six-story Harbour Woods Inn, a block away from the main campus. Flags representing various universities whipped in the late afternoon wind. It was sunny and cold and Philip Potter III was making Mary Louise stand outside to sober up. She was furious.

"I am sober, damn it," she yelled. "I'm feeling fine."

"Mary Louise," Philip Potter III said quietly, "you were drunk in that seminar. I stood in the hall and listened to you. You're absolutely losing control of yourself. Are you out of your mind drinking in front of students, in a university classroom?"

"Philip, you're really a drag," Mary Louise giggled. "In fact, I ought to make you appear tomorrow in drag." She threw back her head and laughed.

"Don't you know, darling, that when you give a university enough money you can do anything you like. And as for the big fucking honors convocation speech, I may decide to deliver that standing on my head. And they'll love it. For three million dollars, this university will adore it. They have leather patches on their souls, darling."

Philip Potter III winced. "I think you've had enough air now. We can go in now."

He was in charge of her. At least that was his "charge" from the foundation. And she knew it and let him. He could cut off her money with a bad report to the trustees. And several times he had come close to doing it. But cutting off her money meant cutting off his own money. So they existed together, linked in an uneasy alliance.

Though every year it got worse. Drinking, drugs, picking up men and women. He was getting old fast. He particularly dreaded this Mid-East venture. Usually they never stayed more than two days on a campus. But because the late Mr. Hillman's grandmother had graduated from Mid-East back in the 1890s, some trustee thought that it would be nice to give Mid-East a sizable building gift in addition to the usual Hillman writing prizes. And so they were here for over a week. Over a week in the provinces of America with Mary Louise flouting every convention she could.

Just last night he had spent most of the evening removing, under her direction, cocaine alkaloid from the hydrochloride salt. A doctor friend in New York had given her a large supply, and he was free-basing it for her. Last year it had been quaaludes; this year coke. She had promised him she'd be discreet about taking her drugs on a college campus. So today, instead, she had filled her Japanese bowl with vodka and fooled no one.

He understood her problem. She was constantly burning out, constantly needing more fuel.

They entered the lobby. And immediately he heard sounds he dreaded. The sounds of clinking glasses from the lounge.

"Phil, let's have a drink together."

"Mary Louise, you've had quite enough."

"Philip, join me and look after me or I drink alone," she said coyly.

And then, without waiting for an answer, she marched into the lounge. He hesitated and then went in after her.

There was no one in the barroom except for the bartender. But in an adjoining room a noisy party was being held. He could guess now what was going to happen.

He peered in.

Mary Louise was standing there with a waitress who was explaining to her that it was a farewell party.

"But I adore farewell parties," Mary Louise trilled. "Especially when I don't know to whom I'm bidding farewell.

Darling, get me a glass of Smirnoff's with only two cubes. Aren't you sweet? Philip, I see you hiding there. Put it on our room bill for her. Aren't they a happy bunch, Phil?"

Someone from the party had risen to make a toast. Philip Potter III knew that it would only be seconds before Mary Louise took over that job. She was clever with toasts. In seconds she would permit her immense energies to flow over them, helping them to adore her.

"Thank you, my dear," Mary Louise said to the waitress.

She lifted her glass high in the air. "To all you charming people," she sang out loudly, getting their attention. All heads turned toward her. "To your sadness and to your joy, to doors closing and other doors opening, to hellos and farewells, the stuff of life from which we are all made."

She *was* the hello, Philip Potter III thought.

"Come join us, Philip," she said, as she swept majestically down on the party of strangers.

22

After the seminar Eileen was simply too excited to work in the library as she had planned. She walked across campus, through the university's arboretum, and down to the river.

It was too early to go home. There would be no one there to share her anticipations. Cyrus would be out playing John Agate after teaching, Marie Genthon would be at work, Paul Genthon . . . Eileen felt uneasy around him. She knew he'd had other women into his apartment while Marie was at work. Ernst Mayer, the retired chemistry professor, would be in, but what would Eileen's winning a Hillman writing prize mean to an old chemist?

Arthur Browne would have been delighted. Enthusiastic! He would have stopped whatever he was doing, seized her hands and said: "Marvellous, marvellous, Eileen. You're on your way to fame and fortune."

Which was exactly what she wished to hear someone say.

She sat down on a rock at the water's edge. A girl was throwing a stick into the water for a labrador to chase. The dog made happy, wet noises as he swam.

Eileen smiled.

Tomorrow at about this time she would be sitting in the amphitheater on pins and needles, waiting to hear her name called out. If she won the top prize it would mean a lot of money. But it would mean more than money. It was prestige. It would help her get a good agent, perhaps even a publisher.

She could visualize the jacket copy on her first book. *Ms. O'Hanrahan is a winner of the prestigious Hillman Foundation Writing Award.*

God, she thought, smiling ruefully, I am a creative writer. It's a good thing Cyrus isn't here. He'd throw cold water on the whole thing. He'd tell me it's a bush-league writing contest and to just take the money and run.

She shivered. It was starting to get cold. The sun was going down. She picked up her book bag and walked back through the arb, across campus, and toward her house. People walked by quickly, heads down, hands in pockets.

Not one of them had the slightest idea that tomorrow at this time she would be an award-winning writer.

Oh, ego, ego, ego, she thought. This is what happens when you have no one to talk with.

Cyrus's apartment was dark, but a light was on in the Genthon's ground-floor apartment.

She knocked on their door. A moment later she heard Marie's footsteps. The door opened and Marie stood there, looking flushed and pretty. Have I interrupted something? Eileen wondered.

"Eileen, come in."

"Am I bothering you, Marie?"

"Not at all. I am all alone. I just got in."

Relieved, Eileen said, "It's just that I've had some wonderful news, Marie, and no one to share it with."

"Well then, cheri," Marie said, taking her hands, almost as Arthur would have done, "you must share it with me.

Don't tell me yet. I will make you a drink. But you must forgive if I do not drink with you. I think your friend Marie Genthon has already had one drink too many." She laughed, and went to the cupboard where the Genthon's kept their small but discriminating liquor supply. "We had a farewell party at the Harbour Woods Inn for a secretary. Such excitement. You like Cinzano sweet vermouth, Eileen?"

"I'd love it."

"It is softer than your American vermouths. But then I am prejudiced because I am French. See, this is the kind of drink I make. I pour it from a bottle."

Eileen sat and watched the lovely young Frenchwoman come toward her, a wine glass extended in her hand. "You take this and I will get a cup of coffee. No coffee and Marie will not be able to prepare dinner for her husband."

Eileen looked around while Marie was warming her coffee. It was a charming apartment, filled with all kinds of plants: ferns, pepperonia, philodendron, winter cactus, and a lovely jade tree that was Marie's pride and joy. She wondered if she and Cyrus ever got married what kind of place they'd have and whether it would be filled with such lovely plants as these. Probably not. Neither of them had green thumbs.

"There, you have your Cinzano and I my coffee. Chin-chin," Marie said.

Eileen sipped the vermouth. It was delicious.

"Now your good news, cheri."

"Marie, I think I've won a big writing prize." She told her about the Hillman competition, and the poet, and the awards ceremony tomorrow.

Marie listened intently, with a half-smile on her lips. When Eileen was done, she said, "Always when I hear your click-clicks upstairs, I think Eileen will be rich and famous someday. I am very glad for you. I hope it is a lot

164

of money tomorrow. Big bucks, as Paul likes to say. First prize. But, cheri, I do not know about this Hillman person. I do not think I like her."

Eileen looked at her astonished. "How do you even know her, Marie?"

"Not very well, to be sure, but what I have seen, I did not like at all."

"Marie, when did you ever meet Mary Louise Hillman?"

Marie looked at her watch. "About an hour ago," she said. "Eileen, the reason I do not drink vermouth with you now is that I have already had a lot to drink at a party. A farewell party for Verna Stubbs, who works in the city assessor's office. We were having a very good time until your friend Hillman joined our party."

"I can't believe this. Mary Louise Hillman?"

"That's who she said she was. And I believed it. She recited poetry and made toasts and flirted outrageously with everyone — men *and* women. She was drunk when she came in."

Mary Louise Hillman, thought Eileen, could have gone there after the seminar.

"At first we found her amusing. But then she became embarrassing. After all, it was a party to honor Verna, not Miss Hillman. The young man with her tried to get her to leave. They quarreled. She slapped him."

It could be no one else, Eileen thought sadly.

"And I know it was vodka she was drinking because she offered me some," Marie went on. "When she found out I was French she insisted on talking French to me. About sex. It was such an embarrassment for me, even though the others did not understand what she was saying. I tell you, cheri, she may be a good poet. But she is not a nice woman. I hope she gives you a lot of money. But after you take her money you should stay far away from her. No?"

Eileen smiled. Take the money and run. It wasn't Cyrus who finally said it. It was Marie.

*

Cyrus was hungry. He was a big young man and he liked to eat and he hadn't had a full-sized meal since the first murder. He suggested the Old Bavarian, which was a little fancier than the usual campus restaurants.

"But this is in way of a celebration," he said to Eileen. "Anticipating tomorrow's big check."

They were walking down Huron toward the restaurant.

"I am," Cyrus added, "truly excited for you."

"I'm getting there myself," Eileen said. She laughed. "Milton said the Hillman people gave out three thousand dollars at Berkeley last year. With inflation maybe it will be even more."

Cyrus laughed. "You're talking like a pro now, Eileen. Hillman may be a phony but that money of hers is real enough."

"Phony's not the right word. She's just . . . dissipated. And so unlike her poetry. That's the important thing, Cyrus. What she writes, not who she is."

"You are what you write."

"No. You like Hemingway's writing. Would you have liked it after you met him?"

"Sure."

"Liar. Anyway, she wrote a very lovely inscription to me in *Edges of Darkness.* That's her best volume."

"Wait a second, Eileen. Here's City Hall. Do you mind if I stop in here for a few minutes?"

City Hall lay between their house and the Old Bavarian. The police department entrance was right in front of them.

"You're really transparent, aren't you? Now I know why you picked the Old Bavarian. Some celebration."

166

"No, it is. In fact, I'm doing you a favor right now. I've asked that guy from the Chamber of Commerce, Evans, to bring over his slides of band day. They just came in. You might see some pictures you'd like for your brochure."

"You're always scheming, aren't you?"

"No. I'm just organized."

"You're not organized." she said, following him into City Hall, "you're simply devious."

"I'll accept that," he said.

Detective Layne was waiting for Cyrus in the task force office. He winked at Eileen.

"The chamber guy is set up in the screen room with his slides, Prof. Hello, Miss, how're you doing?" Without waiting for an answer, he said to Cyrus, "We got some beautiful calls today, Prof."

They walked down the hall to the screening room.

"One old lady called in to say Wally was gunned down by one of the helicopters that pull advertisements around the stadium."

"How did she know?"

"She saw it in a vision. It was the copter that pulls the potato bread ad. Also a scoutmaster from Pinckney called in to say he'd shot Lassiter because he thought it was time Mid-East began deemphasizing football."

"A scoutmaster," Eileen said. "My God."

"My sentiments too, exactly." Layne laughed. "I called the district council on him. They better check out his merit badges quick. Let's see, some more beauties . . ."

He took a piece of paper from his pocket.

"Got a call from an Ohio State fan who said he shot Lassiter as a mercy killing. A Mid-East fan told John he shot Wally because he lost the Rose Bowl six years ago. Why do you suppose he waited six years? Oh yeah, here's a cute one. Tink got an anonymous tip from a guy who said Wally was shot by a kid he cut from the squad two years ago. Tink looked the kid up. He's playing for Oregon this year. In fact, he scored a touchdown Saturday."

"I wonder why Wally cut him. How about the Beretta?"

"I've been running checks on all Berettas sold in the state for the past five years. Tink and Steve are looking into orange-and-yellow rain slickers and half-glasses. And we're going through the help: vendors, security, ushers, and so on. It'll take time. Let's see, *you* got some calls. It seems some paper mentioned you were *heading* the investigation."

Cyrus winced.

Layne chuckled. "It got John a bit upset, but he'll get over it. He's got a list of nuts who would talk only to you. I did fake being you for one guy who said a TV cameraman did it. One of those cameras on the press deck was a high-powered rifle. Anyway, I've left names and numbers that we got on your desk. Also you got a call from Tom Whelan, the university V.P., who wants you to call him back at home right away. And here's our pals."

Tinker and Guiterrez were sitting with Mr. Wilbur Evans of the Chamber of Commerce. A screen was up. A carousel projector turned on.

Evans rose courteously. "Hello, Eileen. This is an odd place to show you some of the slides I took Saturday. Hello, Mr. Wilson."

"I appreciate your coming down," Cyrus said.

"No, it's no bother. In fact, I find it exciting to be part of your investigation. Police work has always interested me. I only hope my pictures will be helpful to you."

"Let's get started," Guiterrez growled. "You're late, Prof."

"Oh?" Eileen said, and flashed Cyrus a look.

Cyrus shrugged.

"Lights," Guiterrez said. Layne flipped off the lights. "Go ahead, Mr. Evans."

"I must warn you again, I'm not a professional photographer. I could only get so close to the sidelines. Most of the shots are with a telefoto lens and some are probably blurry."

Like most amateurs he began with excuses.

"The first ones are mostly football action shots and they're not very good," Evans went on in his apologetic vein.

Cyrus saw that Eileen, bless her heart, had taken out a pencil and paper from her pocketbook. She was going to take notes on slides appropriate for the brochure. She held no grudges. She was a worker.

Viewing the football shots, Cyrus thought Wilbur Evans was right to apologize. Almost every one was out of focus. And in the ones that were sharp, Evans inevitably missed the main action.

But all of them sat up for the sideline shots. For these were good. There was Wally with earphones on looking grim. Wally in a marvellous shot, his hand on a player's shoulder, about to send him in.

Wally down on one knee.

Wally conferring with an assistant coach.

Wally shouting at an official.

Wally looking exasperated.

Pounding his fist onto the tartan turf.

Looking worriedly at his clipboard.

And even once looking fiercely at the camera.

"Mr. Evans," Eileen said, "these are all tremendous shots but we can no longer use them in a brochure advertising Harbour Woods."

"I understand," Evans said, and he laughed. "I've never seen the town that could be promoted by murder. But, of course, I had no idea at the time."

"Who did?" Layne said.

"Someone did," Guiterrez said.

"I do have some nice band shots," Evans said. "Would you like to see them?"

"Let's see them all," Guiterrez said.

Evans's band shots were good. Slides of kids blowing on their instruments, conductors waving batons, drum majorettes strutting, baton twirlers flaunting their skills, and a striking shot of the Mid-East University Director of Bands conducting the immense body of bandsmen and women from the top of his high scaffold.

"What about fans?" Cyrus asked. "Any shots there?"

He wanted that camera turned around on the first few rows. But that would be hard, since Evans was undoubtedly shooting from the first two rows.

"I have some," Evans said.

They were then treated to a series of slides showing students cheering, older alumni with clenched fists, ushers in orange-and-yellow rain coats.

'I want copies of all of those," Guiterrez said.

No half-glasses in sight, Cyrus thought.

"That's it," Evans said.

The lights were turned on.

"We can get football shots from the athletic department," Eileen said. "I've marked down some of the fan shots and band shots we might be able to use."

A true worker, she had forgotten about dinner and now she and Evans were talking about what would look best in the brochure.

Cyrus went down the hall to his office where he dialed Whelan's home number. Two teenagers answered the phone simultaneously on extension phones. Whelan came on a few seconds later.

"Get off," he snapped to his kids.

"Cy, thanks for calling. We've got more media pressure. I got a call today from Channel 8, Detroit. They want to do a longer piece for their weekend news about how a university goes on functioning despite two sensational

170

murders on campus. We're living in a fishbowl right now. The producer and his crew will be out tomorrow at one o'clock. He wants to look over the murder sites. The law club kitchen and the stadium. They want advice on what else to shoot. Can you handle this for us?"

"Don't our A.V. people have stock footage of the campus, Tom?"

"Of course they do. But this guy Fine, the producer, wants fresh stuff. He wants to cover daily events, a university going about its daily business."

Cyrus grinned but his voice was solemn. "Well, there's the Hillman lecture and awards for creative writing. That's going on tomorrow afternoon in the amphitheater."

"Perfect," said Whelan. "Feed them that. That's as remote from murder as you can get. You've got the idea, Cy. Run with it."

Run with it. P.R. talk. Enough to make you gag.

Cyrus found Eileen waiting for him outside the task force office.

"Where's Evans?"

"He had to go. Where were you?"

"Arranging a treat for you."

They left the building and walked down the block to the Old Bavarian.

"What sort of treat?" she asked suspiciously.

"You're going to be on TV."

"What are you talking about, Cyrus?"

"I just talked a Detroit TV station into coming here to tape the Hillman awards ceremony tomorrow."

"Are you serious?"

"Yes."

"Why?"

"To show the world a writer can be pretty as well as talented."

"You know you're extremely unfunny."

171

He laughed. "All right. They want to show a university functioning normally in times of crisis. I told them about the Hillman awards. Her whole visit here got national press. Naturally they latched onto it. They'll be here with their cameras."

"Oh, my God, now I'll have to worry about my dress and my hair. I've never been on TV before."

They went into the restaurant and waited for the hostess. It was a German inn sort of affair, dark wood, beer steins in niches, Black Forest pictures wherever you looked, and apple dumpling machen waiting on tables.

"You look fine. Just the way you are."

"What do you think about my red dress?"

Cyrus nodded. Seated at a table in the middle of the room was a man wearing half-glasses. He was in an animated conversation with another man.

"Cyrus, what are you staring at?"

"If I tell you will you lay off the John Agate routine?"

"Yes."

The hostess sat them at a nearby table. Cyrus told her about the deputy spotting a man who looked like he worked at the stadium but who was just looking things over. "All he could remember about the guy really was that he wore those half-glasses."

"Half-glasses are not uncommon," Eileen said. "My father wears them. You know someone else who does."

"Who's that?"

"Geoff Goldstein, chairman of your department."

"You're right. I never noticed."

She snorted. "And you're a detective? John Agate would have — no, I promised. I'll shut up about that. By the way, what did you think of Wilbur Evans's pictures? I thought they were quite good for an amateur."

Cyrus didn't answer. He was staring at the man with half-glasses. He was a businessman. An accountant. Visiting Harbour Woods for meetings of a chemical society, a refresher course in property law, perhaps a school administrator, maybe a —

"Cyrus!"

"Huh. Oh, I think your red dress will be fine," he said.

"Oh God," she said, "let's get something to eat."

They were saved from each other by the arrival of the waitress with menus.

23

There were students and faculty and townspeople drinking punch in the large reception room next to the amphitheater. Mary Louise Hillman had not yet arrived. The lecture–awards ceremony was scheduled to take place soon.

Eileen looked lovely in a bright red dress, a little lipstick, and her short-cropped dark hair. She wore the little gold pin he had given her last year on her birthday.

She was holding on tight to an empty plastic punch glass. She had finished the drink in one gulp.

"Nervous?" Cyrus asked.

Her answer was a crackling sound. She had split the punch glass.

"Damn. I've been trying so hard to keep calm too."

"By breaking punch cups?"

"No." She hesitated and looked at him defiantly. "By counting people in half-glasses."

Cyrus laughed. He leaned forward and brushed her cheeks with his lips.

"You look terrific."

"Don't you think it's an important clue?"

"Hey, who's John Agating now?"

"Well, I've got to do something beside worry about how much money I'm going to get, whether it will be first prize or last, whether publishers will pay attention to the award. So I decided to count half-glasses. I've counted three since you told me about it. There was the one in the restaurant last night. I saw another on my way to class this morning. And one in Kearsage Hall after class."

"Let's skip the half-glasses and get some fresh air on the balcony. Your pal Hillman probably won't get here till the second she's about to speak."

"She's not my pal, but I'll go along with you on the fresh air."

There were knots of people out on the balcony, which overlooked the campus. Autumn was holding beautifully, Cyrus thought. Gold, crisp, tangy — with the hint of cold weather coming in from the west. Somewhere in the Rockies it was beginning to snow. By next week snow would start to fall on Harbour Woods.

"Red alert," said Eileen. "Your chairman has spotted you."

Geoff Goldstein came up to them. He wasn't wearing glasses at all.

"Hello, Cyrus. Eileen."

"Geoff," Cyrus said in a measured tone.

"Did you meet your afternoon classes, Cy?"

"I did," Cyrus said, his face flushing. His measured tone hadn't warned Goldstein off. Cyrus didn't need this kind of bird-dogging at any time, and certainly not in front of Eileen.

But Geoff Goldstein, a prolific article writer on eighteenth-century literature, was a very stupid man.

"We're competing with John Agate these days for your boyfriend's attention."

Eileen's eyes danced mischievously. "So am I. By the way, Geoff, are you wearing contacts?"

"Yes," Goldstein said, pleased. "How do you like them?"

"Very nice, aren't they, Cyrus?"

"Yes," Cyrus said stiffly.

Goldstein turned to him. "The T.A. assigned to your comp class has left those essays from *Walden* in your box. He's also left a list of those who haven't handed them in. Hello, Archie, I didn't know you turned out for poets."

They were being joined on the balcony by Dean Archie Fields, looking like an old white rabbit hunched over his glass (not plastic — deans always managed this sort of thing so well) punch cup.

"Don't usually, Geoff. Hello, Cyrus. Miss O'Hanrahan. I'm turning out for three million bucks from the Hillman Foundation. And also to check the lady out. I've heard some strange tales."

"Such as?" Goldstein asked.

"Tippling in class. And elsewhere. I understand that poets on tour do that sort of thing, considering themselves sensitive creatures being paraded before the great unwashed. I don't mind her doing that even at this awards ceremony. But on Friday she's delivering the honors convocation address in full academic regalia, and that we can't have."

Goldstein smiled. "Do you have a speaker in the wings, Archie?"

"Me," the dean said reluctantly.

They all laughed. "Well, I hope she doesn't make a fool of herself today," Goldstein said. "I'm introducing her." What he really meant, thought Cyrus, was "I hope she doesn't make a fool of me."

"These are," Goldstein concluded, "difficult times for the university. Now, what in God's name is going on in there?"

A very bright light shone in the reception room. They all turned to see what was going on. And then, moving in a chain, they saw a television cameraman, connected by a wire to a second man with a machine strapped to his body. A third man appeared carrying the light on a pole.

The object of the camera's and light's attention now hove into view. Mary Louise Hillman in a flowing gown of sheer black chiffon with gold threads. An Iraqi court-style dress of ancient times.

"Is that her?" Archie Fields asked, stunned.

"I'm afraid so," Goldstein said.

At Hillman's elbow was her male secretary in a white turtleneck.

"And that, I take it, is her paramour."

"A veritable circus," said Goldstein.

"What in God's name are TV people doing here?" Fields asked.

Cyrus winced. He and Eileen, as very junior people in the university hierarchy, had stood by quietly. Now he felt Eileen's amused eyes on him.

Cyrus cleared his throat. "Channel 8 is doing a story on how a university goes on with its daily routine during a murder investigation."

"Who told them this Hillman person was routine around here?" Fields asked.

"I don't know," Cyrus lied. "But I think I'm supposed to look after them on Tom Whelan's behalf. If you'll excuse me."

"I'm coming with you," Eileen said. Once in the reception room and away from Goldstein and Fields, she broke into peals of laughter.

"Cut it out," Cyrus warned.

"You're a coward and a liar, John Agate."

"I'm aware of that. But where in hell did she ever get that dress? If she wears it to the honors convocation all hell really will break loose."

"Four," Eileen said.

"Four what?" Cyrus said, when a stocky, middle-aged man came up to them. He looked up at Cyrus. "You Wilson?" he demanded.

"Yes," Cyrus said, startled.

"You're doing a helluva job, I must say."

"I'm afraid you've got the advantage of me," Cyrus said politely.

"Sid Fine. Channel 8. You're the one supposed to be looking after me and my crew."

"Oh, yes. You seem to be doing pretty well."

"We'll know it when we play it back. That broad is drunk as a skunk, you know that?"

Hillman was now waving a glass in the air while she talked to four enraptured women and a microphone attached to the camera caught her words. The light shone brightly in her face.

"That's vodka she's got in that glass. She offered me some. You think she'll make a speech?"

"Just a few short words," Cyrus said. "The point of the ceremony in the amphitheater is the awarding of prizes. Miss O'Hanrahan here is receiving — "

"Damn it, that's enough of that light. Take your fucking camera and point it at someone else," Hillman yelled.

Her secretary appeared at her side. "Mary Louise," he said softly.

"Jesus," Sid Fine said, and he went over to the scene of the altercation. "Thanks, Miss Hillman. We got some nice shots. Now we'll take reaction shots of the crowd. Turn the light around, Timmie."

Cyrus shook his head. "Maybe this wasn't such a good idea after all." He looked at Eileen. "By the way, four what?"

"Four?"

"You said 'four' a while back."

178

"Oh, I saw a fourth person in half-glasses go by in the hall. I just caught a glimpse of him. He didn't come in."

"Smart chap. Here comes Archie and Goldstein to check on this mess."

Archie Fields and Geoff Goldstein were coming back into the reception room. Mary Louise Hillman's words had carried to the outside. As any good poet's would, Cyrus thought.

24

"You can begin now, Geoff," Barbara Goldstein whispered to her husband.

Goldstein always took his ceremonial cues from his wife, whose father had been chairman of the English department at Vanderbilt for thirty years.

A small, gray-haired lady with stern features, Barbara Goldstein watched her husband mount the three steps to the lectern. She watched him fiddle nervously with the lectern light, pour himself some water from the institutional brown carafe into one of the glasses and wait, a fixed smile on his face, as the buzz slowly died down in the amphitheater.

Mrs. Goldstein checked the TV camera crew. They were still getting in position. Their lights weren't turned on. She shook her head at Geoff. Not yet, she said with her eyes.

He nodded.

From the lectern, Geoff Goldstein could see the amphitheater rapidly filling. It seated about two hundred and fifty people. Goldstein spotted the members of his department and their wives. Graduate students, undergrads —

mostly women — and a variety of people from on and off campus. It was a good turnout, but not surprising, considering the amount of publicity generated by and about Hillman.

He wondered just how drunk she was. Would she make it up the three steps to the lectern? And would her words come out clearly? He could always cut her short. On Friday, at the honors convocation, it would be a different story. She would be alone before the world.

Goldstein glanced at Archie Fields. Archie sat with folded arms, like a judge. Archie, Goldstein knew, would not be afraid to go to the president and tell him Hillman was too much of a risk as an honors convocation speaker and to hell with the Hillman Foundation's three million dollars.

Goldstein saw Cyrus sitting next to Eileen O'Hanrahan. Cyrus Wilson was another problem he'd have to dispose of before long. Cyrus would definitely not be getting tenure, even if he did finish his dissertation. Cyrus Wilson was an amiable lout who had no business wanting to become a permanent member of an English department. Juvenile mystery books, indeed! He would be the laughing stock of the university if he gave tenure to someone who wrote children's books.

A bright TV light went on from the middle aisle. It was a good thing he was wearing his contacts, rather than his glasses. The lights would be reflected in his glasses. He looked much better in contacts.

Finally everyone was silent.

He cleared his throat. Don't begin with a sip of water, Barbara's eyes told him. Start strong.

"Unaccustomed as I am to appearing on TV," he said, and drew an obedient chuckle from the untenured members of the department, "I do think it's time to commence this happy occasion. As most of you know, the purpose of the Hillman Foundation Awards in Creative Writing is to acknowledge the talent of young people in the fields of poetry and prose fiction. In order not to have her audience in suspense about the winners, Miss Hillman has asked me to present them to you *before* her talk."

An appreciative hum from the audience.

"So, as each person's name is called, would he or she come forward to receive the award.

"Third prize of $750 goes to Milton Kaplan of New York City, a graduate student in English, for *My Father Sings And Other Poems.*"

Applause as Milton Kaplan, bravely masking disappointment, came up and shook Goldstein's hand. He received an envelope. On his way back to his seat, Mary Louise Hillman rose, blocking his way, and shook his hand also and said something to him.

"Second prize . . ."

In the seats Cyrus looked at Eileen. Her face was without expression.

". . . of $1500 goes to Ruth Gardner of St. Ignace . . ."

"Congratulations," Cyrus whispered, "you won it."

"Shsh," she whispered back fiercely. Her hands were poised, ready to clap for Ruth Gardner.

". . . for her collection of stories *U.P. Winters.*"

Applause. Eileen clapped hard. Cyrus grinned. "It's got to be over two grand for you."

"Shut up," Eileen said.

Hillman stopped Gardner also on her return to her seat and they stood talking, making Goldstein wait at the lectern. Everyone was looking at the poet in her black chiffon dress with the bright gold threads. Etched in sunlight where no sun is, Cyrus thought.

"And now, the first prize of $2500 . . ."

182

A collective gasp from the audience. Eileen's hand, icy cold, gripped Cyrus's.

" . . . goes to Eileen O'Hanrahan of Harbour Woods, Michigan, also a graduate student in English, for her collection of short stories entitled *Brooks Too Broad for Leaping.*"

A wave of applause swept over them. Eileen rose and walked quickly up the steps, pumped Goldstein's hand, shook hands with Hillman who leaned over and kissed her, and then, blushing, returned to her seat.

She did not look at Cyrus.

As the applause abated, Goldstein cleared his throat.

"Our congratulations to all three of these talented young people, as well as to all the others who entered the Hillman competition. And, of course, our gratitude to the person who has made all this possible — Mary Louise Hillman."

More applause, which Hillman acknowledged with a flashing smile and a wave as she half-turned in her seat.

"Although Miss Hillman will deliver a major address on the importance of the arts in America at our honors convocation on Friday, she has consented to conclude our ceremonies with a few words about poetry in America today."

Goldstein looked down at his notes.

"Mary Louise Hillman," he read, "was born in Middleville, Connecticut. She pursued her undergraduate studies at two New England colleges." Which meant, thought Cyrus, that she probably hadn't graduated from either. "After living in Europe for several years, she published her first volume of poetry, *Wildflowers,* which was highly acclaimed by critics. She has subsequently brought out two other volumes, one of which, *Edges of Darkness,* brought Miss Hillman a nomination for a National Book Award."

Goldstein looked up from his notes. He cleared his throat again. Barbara nodded to him. She knew he wanted to say a few words about the Hillman Foundation and the major building gift; he had worked out a metaphor of bricks and poetry, but it wasn't coming back to him. Best just to say "Without further ado — Mary Louise Hillman," but really the large foundation gift should receive maximum publicity, and there was a TV camera turned on him now! Bricks and words, no, mortar . . . There it was! Mortar and metaphor!

He smiled, reached for the glass of water and took a big swallow.

My God, thought Cyrus, he's going to talk more.

"Mortar and metaphor," began Goldstein, "are not often combined. However — "

A look of surprise appeared on his face.

Barbara Goldstein frowned.

" — today — "

And then Geoff Goldstein, who dominated departmental meetings with his endless speeches, who chaired session after session of Modern Language Association meetings with his tedious, droning voice, was suddenly fighting now to get out a single word.

Barbara Goldstein rose from her seat, her hand clutched to her throat.

Her husband's mouth began to twist as though it was being jerked apart by invisible strings. His face was turning a deep, blood red. His head and shoulders began twitching.

Someone in the amphitheater screamed.

Cyrus made his way down the aisle, moving as fast as he could. Barbara Goldstein was running up the steps.

And then, gasping for breath, Geoffrey Goldstein, professor of English and chairman of that department, fell against the lectern, knocking over the carafe and glass.

His wife reached his side first. "Geoffrey," she said, "speak to me. Geoffrey!"

Cyrus was there next, kneeling alongside Mrs. Goldstein. He could find no pulse in Goldstein's wrist. The chairman's face was rigid.

"Geoffrey, you've got to talk to me. Geoffrey, it's me — Barbara!"

Cyrus tried to fight down the panic rising inside him. It couldn't be. Not again. Arthur Browne, Wally Lassiter, and now Geoff Goldstein.

Someone he didn't know had undone Goldstein's jacket and shirt and was pounding on his heart.

Cyrus looked up. Archie Fields was standing there looking at him, calmly, as though he knew exactly what Cyrus was going to say. But I don't know for sure, Cyrus thought. He could have had a heart attack.

Cyrus stood up. "Better find a phone and get an ambulance, Dean," he said to Fields.

He looked to where Eileen was seated.

"God damn it, Wilson," Sid Fine, the TV producer, yelled at him, "get out of the way. You're blocking my shot of the body."

Eileen was sitting there with her eyes closed, her fists clenched.

"Is the poor chap all right?" Hillman was calling out, her bloated face looking worried. "Someone tell me. Is the poor chap all right?"

"The poor chap's dead," Cyrus said.

He picked up the glass and carafe. Both were empty.

He made his way back to Eileen, who sat there almost as rigid as Goldstein.

"Eileen," he said softly.

She wouldn't look at him. She knew. She knew and Fields knew and he knew too.

Gently he turned her face toward his. "Eileen, you have to tell me. What did number four look like?"

She stared at him.

"Come on, Eileen, what did he look like?"

But she couldn't talk. And afterwards, when she could talk, all she said was, "He didn't come in. He just walked by in the hall."

25

The windows of Professor Joe Swanson's office in the Pharmacy Building overlooked the heart of the Mid-East campus. Under the bright sidewalk globe lights — erected as a security measure after the Bandemer rape-murder of the year before — students hurried to the main library.

Joe Swanson was giving Cyrus a few minutes of consultation before his evening lab began. He was standing next to an old converted kerosene lamp, the light from which gave a beautiful hue to the cello bow he was holding. Joe Swanson, everyone knew, played the cello to relax between lectures and labs.

"Pernambuco," Swanson said. "The most beautiful wood in the world. The same guy who made Casals's bows makes mine. Now, you're a detective, Cy. Tell me, how does an onion farmer in New York State get hold of pernambuco to make cello bows for me and Pablo?"

"He used to be a bow maker in Italy before he bought the onion farm in New York."

Joe Swanson was impressed. "Right on the money. From now on I believe what I read in the papers." He laid the bow down and sat behind his desk, a genial cherub in a polka-dot tie. He poked his finger into the crease of one of his soft jowls. Behind him in a glass-fronted bookcase was his collection of old pharmacy instruments: a flagon, scales, mortar and pestle, calipers, measuring devices of all sorts, old gold-embossed books. Joe Swanson was the Pharmacy School's historian, a literate and cultured man.

"You know, Cy, I thought you might be over here when I heard the news. What is it, my friend? Are we having an epidemic of death? Is everyone on the faculty ticketed for destruction?"

"I doubt it, Joe."

"What could anyone have against Geoff Goldstein? Apart from the fact that he was an ass? I mean, if we killed off all the asses on the faculty who would be left to teach? I can't believe Geoff philandered." Joe Swanson squinted at Cyrus. "Did he?"

"The task force is talking with Barbara Goldstein now."

"When you say task force . . . you mean he could be linked with the Lassiter and Browne murders?"

"They're all members of the Mid-East faculty."

"Somebody is killing professors. And now you've come to see me."

"Joe, the chem lab downtown ran a test for us on the empty glass and the empty carafe. Hydrocyanic acid."

Joe Swanson sat there a moment. "So. Well, it's not hard to detect. It's not even hard to swallow. A little salty to the taste buds but not bad. The chemical dries up and leaves crystals behind. Add some acid and you come up with hydrocyanic acid. Apparently someone slipped a teaspoon of good old cyanide into Geoff Goldstein's drinking glass. And now the question is, who did it? An untenured member of the department. You, Cyrus?"

Cyrus smiled. "I've certainly got the motive. Tell me, Joe, where is cyanide available on campus?"

"Everywhere. Practically every research lab in this

building, the medical school, public health, the chemistry and biochemistry labs in the lit school."

Joe Swanson rose and went to his window and looked down on the campus.

"Cy, you can't go anywhere around here without running into cyanide. The college of engineering labs have it by the pound. So does the university's photographic services across the street. They use it for plating."

He turned and smiled wryly at Cyrus. "I used to keep a bag of it in my own lab until Harvey Haskell borrowed some. Do you remember Harvey?"

"No."

"Before your time most likely. A real character, Harvey. A professional sourpuss. Should have been a policeman, truly. Used to check the backs of students' watches for exam notes. Did everything but check their amalgam fillings when they came in to take exams. Then two things happened to Harvey. His wife left him and they caught Harvey, of all people, cheating on travel vouchers.

"Harvey had his revenge, however. He came into my lab one day when no one was about and stole a tablespoon of cyanide for his own use. Did Geoff turn cherry red before he died?"

"Yes."

"Lots of gasping, violent breathing?"

"Exactly."

"That's cyanide. Well, at least we won't have to listen to Geoffrey drone on endlessly anymore in faculty labs. It's a wonder he wasn't done in before. Who's next, Cyrus?"

Even the usually imperturbable Joe Swanson was coming unhinged, Cyrus thought.

"Joe, where can I get a list of labs using cyanide?"

"From chem stores. That's where they all get it from . . . supposedly."

"Why 'supposedly'?"

"All chemicals used on campus are supposed to be centrally purchased through chem stores. On the other hand, some people probably do business elsewhere. I'm just guessing. No matter what, you'll probably be investigating over a hundred teaching and research labs, most of which have practically complete public access."

Joe Swanson picked up his cello bow. "Did you know my bow maker was Italian or did you just guess?"

"No guess work," Cyrus said. "Pernambuco was the clue. It's Italian wood, isn't it?"

Joe Swanson looked at him disbelievingly. "It's Brazilian."

"Oh."

"Jesus," said the pharmacy professor, pointing the bow at Cyrus accusingly, "you certainly exhibit great skills of detection. Our lives are in good hands, aren't they?"

*

Cyrus walked across campus toward home. Now he wanted to get Eileen out of the apartment, get her back among people again. Back in the amphitheater she had practically gone into a catatonic state and Cyrus had had to ask a graduate student he knew to take her home.

The scene in the amphitheater remained vivid in Cyrus's mind. From a stunned shock of silence, there had come motion in all directions. Police, white-jacketed ambulance attendants with oxygen equipment. Hillman, with her secretary by her side, telling everyone in a drunken voice that tragedy had dogged her all her life. Barbara Goldstein, tearless and tense, talking rapidly as the attendants worked on her husband.

"I must get to a phone and call the children. We have a son in California and a daughter in Maine. We were going to move to Maine when Geoff retired. Boothbay

Harbor. We both love Maine. Geoff was in perfect health, wasn't he, Cyrus?"

Cyrus nodded.

"He walked four miles a day," she said grimly. "He prided himself on being fit. No one took better care of his health than Geoffrey. He never smoked. Was it his heart? A stroke? Why does that Hillman woman carry on like that? Really, I must call the children. I can call them from the hospital. They are going to take him to the hospital, aren't they? I know he's dead. Will someone please take me there? I want to be with him."

"Tink," Guiterrez said to the black detective. They conferred off to one side.

Cyrus looked back at Hillman. There would be no talk from her today. Yet, a cluster of students had gathered around her and were asking her questions about a female poetry cooperative in New Hampshire that she had founded and funded.

"No, darling, you don't have to be a lesbian to be a member but you might feel more at home if you were." She laughed.

Life went on.

The TV crew had left. In a hurry. They were rushing back to Detroit with videotape coverage that, Sid Fine assured Cyrus, "will win me a local Emmy. I owe you something for setting this up, Wilson."

Guiterrez had caught the last part of that and grinned evilly. "So you're setting this stuff up, Prof. You do good work."

"Where's the carafe and glass?"

"Layne took them over to the lab. Here we go again, don't we?"

Tink and Barbara Goldstein left with the ambulance.

"We may have an edge on this one, John," Cyrus said, nodding toward the poet.

"You think she was the target?"

"One of them was. If it was her there may be another attempt."

"When's she leaving town?" Guiterrez asked.

"Not till Friday. She's delivering the honors that morning at Stockton Auditorium."

"Jesus. She's gonna be hard to protect."

They stopped talking as Dean Archie Fields came up to them. "Cyrus, I just fielded a phone call for you. Tom Whelan is at the police station. They want you down there right away."

"Dean, would you do me a favor and tell them I'm busy? I'm taking Miss Hillman and her secretary to their hotel. I'll get to the police station as soon as I can."

Archie Fields looked at Guiterrez. "Why would anyone want to kill Professor Goldstein?" he asked. And when no one answered his question, he said, "Of course, I could also ask why anyone would want to murder Arthur Browne and Wally Lassiter."

"We're glad you're not asking that one, sir," Guiterrez said.

"Is someone trying to destroy the university?" Archie Fields went on. He was silent a moment. "I'll handle your phone call for you, Cyrus," he said and left.

They waited till the dean was out of earshot. Then Guiterrez said: "I'll have someone around that drunken broad twenty-four hours a day, Prof. But the Harbour Woods Inn is a sieve. There's a hundred ways in and a hundred ways out and a thousand guests coming and going. If she's gonna be around till Friday, how about getting her moved?"

"Good idea. I'll talk to Whelan about that. This may sound callous, John, but I hope Tink doesn't make too much progress with Mrs. Goldstein. As a target, Hillman could lead us to the killer."

*

Mary Louise Hillman and Philip Potter III had a suite of rooms on the sixth floor of the Harbour Woods Inn. They had a beautiful view at dusk. Cars moving on distant expressways surrounding the city, below them the lights of State Street with cars moving along slowly, playing fields lit up for touch football, lacrosse, rugby — a college town was alive at night.

Mary Louise Hillman glared at Cyrus as he stood by the window. She had a glass of vodka in her hand.

"I do not — N-O-T — want a policeman standing outside my door. I do not want to be moved to some dead university mansion. I want to stay right here and I intend to stay right here."

"Mary Louise," Potter murmured to her, "I do believe the detective is speaking to you in your own interests."

"He's not a detective, Philip. He teaches at this goddam redbrick university."

A most disagreeable woman, Cyrus thought.

"I'm investigating the campus murders, Miss Hillman," he said mildly. "And until we have proof that Professor Goldstein died of natural causes or that he and not you was the target of a murder by poisoning, then I'm afraid the Harbour Woods Police Department and university security are going to have to keep an eye on you. And to do that better I'm asking that you be moved to one of the university's own houses."

"You've run that record before, Mr. Wilson. And I'm telling you I like this place. It has a fine restaurant and a fine bar." She emphasized the last point by draining her glass and holding it out to Potter for a refill.

"Secondly," she said, "I *know* when people are having heart attacks. My own father had one and that's exactly what Professor Goldstein had. A heart attack. I understand it's in your interests to smell foul play. You get paid for foul play. But that was no murder!

"Thirdly, I've made a public spectacle of myself for

193

years and no one has taken a shot at me or tried to slip me poison.

"Fourthly, although you may not know it, Mr. professor-detective — and isn't that a riot, Phil, a university having its own sleuth, sort of like a Chesterton novel, isn't it? — although you may not know it, Mr. Wilson, I am a very well-loved person and a poet. And nobody kills a poet. Poets kill themselves. Thank you, darling." She took a fresh glass of vodka from her secretary. "Poets kill themselves via drink, drugs, loving to an excess, caring too much. They don't need other people to do them in."

She drank.

"And now, if you don't mind . . . " She put the glass down and stood up, "I am going to take a piss."

And out she went in her swirling black dress with the fine gold threads.

Philip Potter III sighed. "I don't excuse her behavior, Professor Wilson, but she has been under much tension."

"Tell me about that," Cyrus said.

"Oh, it's the usual thing. A tour of campuses. Readings. Awards. People adoring her. Wanting to touch her. Mary Louise loves living in the public eye, but it is a strain on us all." Potter smiled at Cyrus.

"You don't mind if I ask you what sorts of enemies she might have."

"Ask."

"I just did," Cyrus said, trying to contain his irritation. This was never-never land, he thought. A lesbian poet and her homosexual male secretary. It was clear the university had taken on an entirely new kind of benefactor. The price tag on a three million dollar gift might be very high.

"She has no enemies, Mr. Wilson. None. Indeed, Mary Louise has many people who love her and are grateful to her. You don't know this, of course, but her home in Middleville has long been a refuge to lost flower children.

I'm speaking more of the sixties and seventies than I am of today. But even today she welcomes all sorts of people. We've had more runaways than you would believe. The sick, the damned, the beautiful, the sensitive, the unloved. She takes everyone in. Mary Louise is generous. Volatile, yes, you've seen that for yourself. But kind and generous too. I sometimes look back to those wonderful and terrifying days of the seventies and think that perhaps Mary Louise was personally trying to make up for Viet Nam, brutal cops, racism, and repression. Mary Louise is a fine person, Mr. Wilson. She is sensitive and vulnerable. Hence her excessive drinking. I'm personally grieved that she is not letting you see the nicer parts of her character."

"Does the name Ricky Andrews sound familiar to you?"

"No. Who is he?"

"A local drug dealer," Cyrus said bluntly.

Philip Potter III blushed faintly. "We don't know people like that," he said.

He probably gets his drugs wholesale for her in New York, Cyrus thought.

"Do the names Arthur Browne or Wally Lassiter mean anything to you?" Cyrus asked.

Philip Potter III thought about it and shook his head. "I've never heard of either of them," he said.

He was probably the only one in Harbour Woods who hadn't, Cyrus thought. And the only one in the whole country who hadn't heard of Wally Lassiter.

"May I ask who they are?"

"Both of those men were murdered recently here on campus."

"Oh. Oh dear. Yes, now that you say that, I think I saw something on the TV news about that. But what does that have to do with Mary Louise or me?"

"It's just possible that Professor Goldstein did not have a heart attack or a stroke back there in the amphitheater.

It's possible he was poisoned. It's also possible that poison was meant for Miss Hillman."

"Impossible," Philip Potter III said flatly.

"Why?"

"Because, as I told you, Mr. Wilson, everyone loves Mary Louise. She — "

He stopped as the subject under discussion emerged from the bathroom pulling down on her dress.

"I say, do they have a bar in this safe house of yours?" Mary Louise Hillman asked Cyrus.

Philip Potter III looked surprised.

"One can be arranged," Cyrus said.

"Mary Louise," Potter said, "why have you changed your mind?"

A coy, mischievous smile played on her lips. "I've been thinking, Phil. Nobody has ever tried to bump me off before. I'm sure no one is now. But why not enjoy all aspects of it, including a new house and a police guard. Make him good-looking, Professor."

Philip Potter III shook his head. "You are really amazing, Mary Louise."

"But . . . " and Mary Louise waggled her finger at Cyrus, "suppose you find out that the professor died of natural causes and there was no poisoning, do I then have to move again?"

"No, ma'am. The university will be glad to put you and Mr. Potter up in good style."

"And do I get to keep my handsome policeman?"

"Incorrigible," breathed Philip Potter III.

Mary Louise Hillman laughed. A classic bitch, Cyrus thought. He wished Eileen were here to get this added dimension of her favorite poet. He wondered how Eileen was doing. It would be a while before he got back to her.

*

From the inn Cyrus walked to the police station. Whelan and Mazur were meeting with his uncle in the chief's office. Reporters were in the halls again with cassette recorders and microphones.

Cyrus walked quickly by them and down to Guiterrez's office. Tinker and Layne were in there with Guiterrez.

Guiterrez waved a yellow form at Cyrus. "Lab report on the water glass and the carafe. Cyanide."

Cyrus read it. He turned to Tinker. "How's Mrs. Goldstein?"

"Holding up real good," Tinker said. "I took her to the hospital and then home. There's a lot of people in her house now. Women friends with food. Her kids are on their way. She knows now. We got the autopsy report together in the hospital."

Layne tilted backwards in his chair and looked at the ceiling. "Arthur Browne, Wally Lassiter, and now a dude named Geoffrey Goldstein."

Guiterrez's eyes met Cyrus's. "How was the lady poet?"

"Drinking up a storm. We've got to move her. Probably to Brewster House."

Brewster House was an elegant home on the southeast side of Harbour Woods that had been given to the university by a wealthy alum. It was used now for small, elegant dinner parties and to put up special guests of the university. Hillman should probably have been put there in the first place, Cyrus thought.

"I'm going to talk to Whelan about it," he said.

Layne looked at him and Guiterrez with interest. "You guys think maybe Goldstein was a mistake."

Cyrus shrugged. "Tink," he asked, "did you ask Mrs. Goldstein if there had been any threats made on his life?"

"Yeah. None. She mentioned a few graduate students who were sore at him. A teacher in Arkansas who didn't get tenure a few years back and regularly wrote him nasty

197

letters. I asked her how her marriage was. She said there'd been times she'd like to have choked him but not poisoned him."

"Enemies on the faculty?" Guiterrez asked.

Tinker's expression was deadpan. "Only one in the department she thought had reason to hate him."

"Who's that?" Cyrus asked, curious.

"You."

Guiterrez snorted.

Tinker went on blandly. "Goldstein told his wife just the other day that he was going to see you did not get promoted. No tenure for you, Prof. Did you know that?"

"No," Cyrus said.

"Jesus," Guiterrez said, "you had a reason to bump off Browne. He was fiddling with your girl. Now you got a reason to bump off Goldstein. Give me a connection with Wally Lassiter, Prof, and I'll make the pinch right now. What do you say?"

"I think football at Mid-East should be deemphasized. Will that do?"

"Can't you do better than that?"

"Let me work on it a while."

"Don't take too long. We got the media on our backs."

"What about the lady poet, Prof?" Layne asked. "What's she like?"

"A drunk. A lesbian. Got a homosexual male secretary who says she is a Christ figure to everyone. Everyone loves her."

"Does *he* love her?" Guiterrez asked.

"He lives off her. If she's dead there goes his meal ticket."

"She got a will?"

"We can check on it," Cyrus said. "Tink, would you follow up on Goldstein? I think you better start going through the department. Talk some more to Mrs. G. And to his kids. A man's kids often know more about him than does his wife. And I can fill you in on some things."

"Like what?" Tinker asked.

"Like who really hated him around here."

"Did you, Prof?"

"No. I didn't hate Geoff. The only people I hate are lazy policemen who don't want to leave their desks to solve crimes."

Guiterrez laughed. "You better go down the hall and see that flack Whelan. He's upset."

"I don't blame him," Cyrus said.

*

More reporters had arrived and the corridor outside Chief Wilson's office was jammed. The chief's door was closed. A uniformed policeman stood outside it, guarding it.

The first TV news crew had arrived from Detroit. It was not Sid Fine's, Cyrus noted.

Two radio microphones were thrust in his face.

"No comment," Cyrus said, elbowing his way past them. "I'm not able to talk at this time."

"That makes three faculty members dead. We hear he was poisoned, Wilson."

"Do you have the autopsy report yet?"

The cop opened the door for Cyrus and shut it behind him.

Inside a council of war was going on. His uncle, Tom Whelan, and Rollie Mazur were sitting in the far corner of the room.

"Where've you been?" Mazur rasped at him.

"Seeing Mary Louise Hillman home."

"For God's sake, Cy," Whelan exploded, "you're taking Hillman home and another professor has been murdered. We saw the lab report. This is a nightmare, Cy. Someone is out to damage the university and they're doing it. You've got to stop these killings!"

"We're working on it, Tom," Chief Wilson said quietly.

"That's all I hear from you, Chief, is that you're working on it. It's not enough. It won't do. Rollie, you hear me. It won't do!"

Tom Whelan, red-faced, glared at them.

"Excuse me, Tom," Cyrus said mildly, "but I want to know if Brewster House is unoccupied now."

Whelan stared at Cyrus as though he had gone out of his mind.

"The thing is," Cyrus went on, "I want to move Mary Louise Hillman from the Harbour Woods Inn to Brewster House."

"This is the last straw," Tom Whelan exploded. "Our world is collapsing around us and you want to move a poet from a hotel to Brewster House. Cyrus, I got you released time from teaching to investigate these murders. Three faculty people have now been murdered — on university grounds! I'm not interested in moving Mary Louise Hillman anywhere."

Chief Wilson looked at his nephew. "You think she might have been the target, Cyrus?"

"I don't know. Perhaps."

Whelan stared at uncle and then at nephew, and then sat down. "My God," he whispered, "that would be awful."

Goldstein was certainly the preferred victim. Hillman was going to hand over to Mid-East a check for three million dollars.

"We're going to follow up both Hillman and Goldstein," Cyrus said to his uncle.

Mazur garbled something.

"What's that?" Whelan asked. "What did he say?"

"Rollie was merely reminding us," Chief Wilson said, "that Miss Hillman will be around till Friday."

"It's too tough guarding her at the inn, Tom. What about Brewster House?"

"If it's not free," Whelan said, "we'll make it free. But

why would anyone want to kill her? She doesn't have anything to do with the university."

He was moving on a fixed line, the way a university relations man should.

Cyrus glanced at his watch. "I want to go over to the pharmacy school and talk with Joe Swanson now. He has an evening lab. I think I can catch him before he goes to it." Cyrus turned to Tom Whelan. "Do you want me to talk to reporters outside?"

"Yes. Tell them — hell, you'll know what to tell them."

"Tell them nothing," his uncle said.

"But find the right words," Whelan cautioned.

"I wouldn't mention Hillman," his uncle said, and when Cyrus looked hurt, his uncle held up his hand in apology.

*

After telling the media people they were looking into connections between Goldstein, Browne, and Lassiter, but so far had found none, other than that they all worked for the university, Cyrus walked to the pharmacy school, where he talked with his old friend Joe Swanson about pernambuco cello bows and cyanic acid.

26

Joe Swanson had asked if it was an epidemic of death. As Cyrus walked back home he thought about that. It was every detective's nightmare. Randomness, the quantum theory of the universe, applied to murders. No pattern except perhaps copycat, no meaning except for shrinks.

He walked up the stairs of their beautiful old house and listened for a moment outside Eileen's door. She was playing Berlioz's *Symphonie Fantastique* on her stereo. She played that or Mozart when she was upset and wanted to get back in touch with herself.

He unlocked the door. She sat on the floor of her small living room, a book in her lap, looking like a small, erect rock in a swiftly moving stream. The music flowed around her. She was wearing the same attractive red dress she'd worn to the awards ceremony.

"Hello, Cy," she said, without turning.

He sat down next to her. "Hello, kiddo."

"Is Geoff dead?"

"Yes."

She was silent. "It seems we're developing a pattern."

"What do you mean?"

"You come home and I ask you is Arthur Browne dead? Or I ask you is Geoff Goldstein dead? And then I ask you if he was murdered and you say — "

"Yes."

She looked at him. She had cried for Arthur Browne, whom she liked. She wouldn't cry for Geoff Goldstein, who was only a pompous professor.

"Why, Cyrus? What would anyone have against Geoff Goldstein?"

That would warrant murder, Cyrus added silently. I don't know.

"Eileen, those half-glasses you saw going by in the hall . . . "

"It was a man. That's all I know. He went by so fast and I was listening to you and the dean and Geoff talking . . . "

"Tall man? Short man?"

"I think short, but I don't know. I know it sounds unreal but all I saw were the glasses." She shuddered.

For a moment Cyrus wondered whether he ought to tell her there was a possibility that Goldstein's death was an accident. That Hillman might have been the intended victim. But then he saw that the book in Eileen's hands was one of Hillman's poetry collections. *Edges of Darkness*.

"You're rereading her?" he asked.

"Yes. I'm still bothered by her as a person, but she wrote such lean, taut poetry. Listen:

> *My skull squeezes against reason*
> *I dread the madness*
> *I long to live in*

"She's good, Cyrus. She's true and honest. And I suspect that once she truly was in charge of her life. Look at this picture of her."

On the back flap of *Edges of Darkness* was a picture of a

much younger Mary Louise Hillman. A strong, handsome face. There was no fat in it, nor in her slender body. She wore a white blouse and a dark riding jacket and skirt. She was giving the photographer a happy smile.

Below the picture, a short biography:

Mary Louise Hillman's first volume, *Wildflowers,* won the prestigious Garrison Award from Yale University. Born and raised in Middleville, Connecticut where she continues to maintain a residence in her family's 120-year-old home, Hillman has published three collections of poems and numerous essays. Of her poetry, the critic Horatio Slote has written . . .

And on it went.

"For some reason," Eileen said, "she stopped writing. *Edges* is her last book and it came out six years ago. She stopped writing and her life fell apart."

"Maybe it was the other way around." He turned her face toward his and kissed her. "Had enough Berlioz?"

"I think so."

"How about some dinner then?"

She smiled. "All right. But let's not eat at the Old Bavarian. I don't want any more City Hall detours and I don't want to count half-glasses anymore."

"No more detours," Cyrus promised. But he wasn't sure about the half-glasses. You could, he thought dismally, see half-glasses just about everywhere.

27

Whiskey sours preceded a bottle of light Mosel from Anton Hammes's wine cellars in Aachen. Cyrus had cold poached salmon in lemon sauce, Eileen had the duckling in wine with mushrooms and orange slices. They ate at the Stationhouse, a small but elegant restaurant converted from the old Harbour Woods train station.

Afterward they walked across red-bricked Depot Street and up Division toward the house. Dinner had restored a degree of normalcy. The murders seemed far away. They talked about the real meaning of the Hillman competition: recognition and money. Cyrus wanted to know what Eileen would do with the money.

"Take you skiing at Christmas," she said.

"Do you mean that?"

"Yes."

"I'm your man. Your kept man."

They talked about skiing, about travelling, about visiting Eileen's family for New Year's. As they walked, students walked past them heading toward campus and the various libraries. Above them, in the maples and elms, a quarter moon played hide and seek in the dwindling leaves.

Between seasons, Cyrus thought, the best time of year.

"What are you thinking about, Cyrus?" Eileen asked.

"That this is a good town in which to live and work. We could do worse than stay on here the rest of our lives."

"Is that a proposal?"

"Almost."

"Almost, as the kids say, don't count."

Cyrus laughed. He pulled her toward him and they kissed. "Would you marry me?"

"Is that a real or hypothetical question?"

"Hypothetical right now. I couldn't afford to get married now. But as soon as I get tenure —"

She laughed. "Were you this careful as a child?"

"I was known as careful Cyrus when I was a kid."

"You may not get tenure for twenty years, Cyrus."

Cyrus smiled. "Sooner, now that Geoff is gone. Do you know what Barbara Goldstein told Tinker? That Geoff was not ever going to give me tenure."

Eileen looked at him. "Are they investigating you now?"

He shook his head. "I'm in charge of the investigations," he said, "and I'm only going to investigate myself when things get really desperate."

She pulled his head down to her. "I love John Agate very much," she whispered. "I don't care if you never get tenure, but some day I want to be Mrs. Cyrus Wilson."

"You will," he said, kissing her back. He rubbed against her and she pressed back. "Let's go," he said.

Lights were on in the second-story apartment of Ernst Mayer and in the Genthon's apartment downstairs. Outside on the porch a single bulb cast a pale yellow hue over the yew shrubs that bordered the house.

He kissed her once more before they went up the steps and suddenly her body, which was pressing against his, stiffened. He felt her back go rigid.

206

"What is it, Eileen?"

"Cyrus . . . " her voice was straining to keep calm, "there's someone in the bushes behind you."

"Okay," he whispered and, still holding her close, turned casually. There in the aura of light spilled onto the ground, he saw pant legs and dark shoes. The bushes hid the rest of the man's body.

"Okay," Cyrus whispered, "walk slowly and naturally up the steps and onto the porch."

"I'm scared. I can't move."

"Eileen," he repeated quietly, "turn around and walk slowly up the porch steps."

He released her. She turned and walked up the porch steps. Cyrus sighed loudly and made as if to follow her. Suddenly he plunged into the bushes and with a powerful jerk of his hands he yanked a figure out into the open.

Eileen screamed.

Cyrus slammed the man against the side of the porch. He ran his hands down the sides of his jacket, pants, searching for a weapon, then lock-gripped a pair of thin wrists and banged the man hard against the side of the porch.

The man called out: "For Christ's sake, quit it!"

He slumped over as Cyrus released him, covering his face with his hands. "Don't hit me. I come to talk to you. Jesus, don't hit me in the face. If you're Professor Wilson, I come here to talk to you."

Commotion above them on the porch. Both Genthons rushed out. Eileen was crying. Marie was holding her. Windows had opened in the house across the street. Eileen's scream had shaken up the neighborhood.

Cyrus pulled the man away from the porch and into the pool of light. They stood in front of the steps. It was a familiar face to Cyrus. He'd seen it in a half-dozen mug pictures. However, now there was a large bruise on one side. A bruise Cyrus had not caused.

"What is it, Cy?" Paul Genthon was leaning over the railing. "Are you all right?"

"It's okay, Paul," Cyrus said. "Would you and Marie take Eileen upstairs? I'll be along in a little while."

"Should I call the police?"

"No," Cyrus said. "This gentleman is an old friend. He just showed up unexpectedly."

Cyrus heard them leave. Eileen was still half-sobbing.

Cyrus looked at the slight, young man in front of him. "That was a dumb thing to do, Ricky. Hide in a bush like that."

Ricky Andrews looked surprised. "How do you know who I am?"

"I've seen your picture often enough."

"But you ain't a cop, are you? I come here cause I heard you weren't a real cop."

"That's right."

Ricky Andrews relaxed. He adjusted the lapels of his sports jacket. He wore a pink turtleneck. A thin, pinched, half-starved face. Eyes constantly in emotional motion: worry, fear, challenge . . .

"Sorry about scaring your chick, man. But it ain't safe for me to be showing my face around. You're the professor they put in charge of the Wally Lassiter murder investigation. Right?"

Cyrus decided not to give Andrews any wriggling time or space. "And the Arthur Browne killing too," he said. "The cops like you for that one too, Ricky."

Ricky Andrews backed off. "What do you mean, that one *too*? I didn't kill anyone, man. That's why I'm here. To help you guys. Why would I want to kill Browne? He was my lawyer."

"You made threats."

"Sure. I shoot my mouth off all the time. I'm a punk. But killing? I don't kill. Especially not Wally! Man, he was a golden egg for me. He was my retirement pension. You don't shoot pensions."

"Were you blackmailing him, Ricky?"

Ricky Andrews laughed. He took out a cigarette, lit it, and tossed the match into the bushes. "I guess you heard how I tried to hit him up for some money. No, I wasn't blackmailing him." He grinned recklessly. "Not yet anyway. He owed me money. And I needed it bad." His face grew serious. Somber. "I was scared."

Cyrus waited.

Ricky touched the bruise on his face with his cigarette hand. "That's another reason I come back. Someone tried to kill *me.*" He looked earnestly at Cyrus. The smoke curled past his ear.

"Tell me about it," Cyrus said.

"I don't know a hell of a lot. Look, can we go somewhere and talk? I got some ideas for you guys."

"Talk here. Talk now. Who tried to kill you?"

"I don't know who." Ricky hesitated. "It was last Tuesday night in the parking lot of my place. I think this guy was trying to kill me. Christ, he was trying to run me over. Then he tried to hit me. Shit, look at my face. He did hit me."

Cyrus recalled the conversation with Lassiter's secretary. Ricky's bandaged face; his near panic as he sought out Wally.

"What did he hit you with, Ricky?"

"I don't know what it was exactly. It wasn't a gun. It was like an iron pipe, only it was heavier than a pipe."

"What did this person look like?"

"I don't know that either. It was dark. No lights in the parking lot. I couldn't see his face. Most of the time I was covering up. Man, I thought I was gonna die. I couldn't believe it. In a goddam parking lot with this nut swinging that thing and calling me Satan pimp."

"Satan pimp?"

"Yeah. How do you like that? Satan pimp?"

"Was his voice familiar?"

"No. I thought it was just a screwball I'd run into in the parking lot by accident. That's what I thought. Later . . . " Ricky looked up shrewdly at Cyrus, "later I thought it might go deeper than that."

"What do you mean?"

Ricky took a deep drag on his cigarette. "Professor, let's you and me go get a drink and talk. This is no place to talk."

"We do it here, we do it now," Cyrus said.

"Why be so fuckin' hard, Professor?"

"People've been looking for you, Ricky."

"That right?"

"They want to know where you were last week on Monday night when Arthur Browne was killed."

Ricky shrugged. "No problem. I was in Pittsburgh. At the Holiday Inn at the airport. You can check that out."

"Why were you there?"

"We had a meeting of bookstore managers." Ricky laughed. "You and me, Professor, we're both in the book business, ain't we? You writing and me selling. Anyway, Harvey Miller, he's a guy from West Virginia, gets the inventory for the stores in this region. He wanted us to look at some new films. I got back Tuesday night and went right to the store with the two suitcases of film. I'm in the parking lot of my place after that, going into my pad, when this bastard nut tries to run me over."

"Who put the bandage on you?"

Ricky squinted up at Cyrus. "You heard about that? Okay I figured you might. A friend did."

"That's Tuesday night. Wednesday you went to Wally's office."

"Yeah." Ricky grinned. "Wally was a special customer of mine."

There was a reckless charm in the young pimp that would appeal to a lot of women, Cyrus thought.

"But the big shot wouldn't cooperate. So I had to get my money elsewhere. I got it and I went to New York. That's my hometown. The Big Apple."

"What were you running for?"

"I told you, man. Someone was trying to kill me."

"What made you think it wasn't just a screwball in a parking lot?"

Ricky was silent a moment. "Somethin' told me it wasn't just any screwball. Can I leave it at that? No, I guess not. Later, when I was in the hospital in New York I did a lot more thinking and remembering too."

"What hospital were you in?" Cyrus interrupted.

"The Cabrini Hospital down on 20th Street on the east side. It used to be the Columbus. I was there Friday through Monday. I got a receipt for those four days right here."

That put him there while Wally was being shot, Cyrus thought.

Ricky grinned at him, reading his thoughts. "That's right, Professor. I saw it on the TV in my hospital room about Wally. I also read the paper about that twenty-five-grand reward for info to catch Wally's killer. Well, in that hospital room I did some deep thinking and deep remembering. Here's what I come up with. I think the guy that tried to kill me could've been the same guy shot Wally and killed Browne. I think we're all connected."

"By what?"

Ricky smiled craftily. "Let's talk reward money first, Mr. Wilson."

"There's no reward money till someone's arrested and convicted. You know that. You either talk to me here and now, Ricky, or we go down to the cop shop and let them sweat you there."

Ricky twisted out his cigarette on the porch step. "You're a sweetheart, Professor. I come back and stand around in the cold bushes waiting to help you and you want to toss me to the hard boys. I could've gone right to the hard boys and got some coffee from *them.*"

"Give me what you know, Ricky, and if it sounds okay, I'll look after you. I'll protect you from the cops and from the guy you say is trying to kill you. Don't talk to me and we'll go down to the station and you'll spill to them for nothing."

"Okay. But if what I figure turns out right, I want the money."

"I'll see that you get it."

Ricky looked at him. "Can I trust you, Professor?"

"Yes," Cyrus said.

"Shit. What choice do I got? Okay, here goes nothing."

28

Ricky Andrews's story tallied with what they already knew about him. After the alleged attack in the parking lot, Ricky had gone to Wally the next morning to get money to help him get out of town. Wally's check had been held up by the bank. Wally had double-crossed him. Ricky got money elsewhere and went to New York City.

"Where did you get the money?"

"A girl I know."

"What girl?"

"I'd like to keep her out of this."

"Francine Carter?"

Ricky sighed. "She's in it. Okay. Francine. Yeah, her."

"Where did you stay in New York?"

"A friend of mine named Solly Rubin. Up on 85th Street, east side. Solly manages a disco joint. He told me the cops were nosing around our old neighborhood in Queens looking for me. My head was still hurting. I was throwing up. Solly got scared. He didn't want me dying in his place. And for all he knew I had bumped off someone in Michigan. He didn't want any part of that. So he took me down to the Cabrini.

"The Cabrini is a guinea hospital. The sisters don't ask questions. I was in the hospital watching the TV when the news come on about Wally getting shot in the stadium. I almost died when I heard that. They'd given me a head scan. They thought I could've had a brain clot. What they found was I had a bad concussion. So they made me stay in the hospital till Monday. I had nothing else to do, Professor, but put things together. First Browne, then me, then Wally. Shit, I ain't no cop, but I started thinking like one outa self-protection."

Ricky looked past Cyrus toward the street. There was a little traffic on the street. It never went to sleep, but it wasn't like New York. Nothing was quite like New York. Yes, it had taken courage for him to return here, Cyrus thought. Either that or greed. Or both. Greed that stimulated courage.

"I don't know the killer's name or even what he looks like," Ricky went on, "but I got an idea who he could be. Inside the hospital I kept coming back to the nut shouting 'Satan pimp' at me. It reminded me of my mother who used to tell me I was going to go to hell cause I didn't have Jesus in my heart. Remembering my old lady made something else click."

He paused. Here it comes, Cyrus thought. What it was that had brought Ricky Andrews back to Harbour Woods even though he knew he had to be a suspect in both the Browne and Lassiter murders.

"I remembered one night about a year ago I was sitting in Barney's Pub on Packard. I was drinking with this girl. Now don't go looking for her, Professor. She's dead. She O.D.'d back in January. Okay?"

Cyrus nodded.

"At that time I was setting this chick up with Wally for trips to away games. He needed chicks. She was supposed to go with him to California for the opening against

UCLA. Anyway, we're in Barney's, Sue and me, and in comes Browne. Not Wally. Browne. The dink lawyer."

"How did you know Arthur Browne?"

"Everyone on the street knew him. He ran Legal Aid. Of course I didn't know him like I was gonna know him come January when I got busted. But I knew *of* him. Right?"

"Okay."

"So my chick and me are sitting there and Browne comes in and he walks by us and then he comes back and he stares straight at my chick and he says, 'Cindy, is that you?'

"The guy's got a load on, I think, and I'm about to tell him to blow when I see my chick turning all kinds of colors. And Browne, he's still standing there and he says again, 'Cindy?' Just like that. Asking her a fucking question.

"My chick shakes her head. 'No,' she says, 'I don't know any Cindy. Go away, Mister.'

"But Browne he don't go. He's still standing there looking down at her and finally she gets up and yells at him, 'Will you get the fuck out of here?'

" 'Hey, take it easy,' I say, but what she says works. He takes off fast.

" 'You know that guy?' I ask her.

" 'I used to,' she says. And then she won't say no more.

" 'Hell, he's a hot lawyer in this town,' I say to her, but she won't talk.

" 'An' what's this Cindy shit?' I ask her. But she won't say nothing to that either. And I'm still trying to pry it open when in comes Wally and that ends it. You following this, Professor?"

"Yes," Cyrus said.

"Okay. We jump a week or so. I'm at her place. I got her a nice setup where I live." He looked at Cyrus. "Which you know all about since you met Francine. Right?"

Cyrus nodded.

Ricky shrugged. "Okay, so anyways she's shooting up one night and she starts playing that crappy Mike Douglas record about his daughter over and over and she starts crying and talking a blue streak. It turns out she's got that dink lawyer on her mind. And get this, Professor, she tells me the guy was her step-father once upon a time, and him and her used to screw afternoons after school when she was a kid. She was fifteen. Her mother was too dumb to catch on. Or maybe, Sue said, she didn't want to catch on."

Ricky looked at Cyrus to make sure he was believing all this.

"You heard that, didn't you, Professor? That dink lawyer was her step-father and used to fuck her regular. Him, the big lawyer!"

Cyrus watched him.

"Man, that's got to be news to you."

"Keep going, Ricky."

"You don't give back much change, do you, Professor?" Ricky laughed. "Well, okay, I like to store things like that away. You never know when information like that can make you money. Right? Anyway, she goes on and tells me that when she was sixteen her mother died. Cancer. There was no way the kid was going to live in the same apartment with that pervert. Right? So she takes off. She goes back East to live with her real father.

"But that don't work either 'cause the real father is too strict with her. He wants her to go to church with him. That kind of deal don't sit so hot with her. She's into dope and booze and fucking anything with pants on by now. Her old man is hassling her all the time so she leaves him. And after a while she works her way back here. And that was when she and me hooked up."

"What was she like, Ricky?"

Ricky was silent a moment. As Francine had been. And then gave almost the same answer she had.

"Different."

"What do you mean?"

"I mean 'different.' "

"Snooty?"

"Yeah. She could seem that way. But she wasn't. She had some class. She was smarter than most of my chicks."

"Why did she turn against you?"

Ricky looked at him. "You knew about that?"

"Yes."

He shrugged. "She was holding out on me. I look after my girls, Professor, but I don't let 'em hold out on me, if you know what I mean. We got a relationship. Sue was holding money out on me. She claimed she wanted to go to college, phony shit like that. And her a junkie and nympho. Talking about college. Shit, if it wasn't for me she'd be on the street. And they'd rip her apart on the street. A small chick like that. She was in the can in Detroit once overnight and the dykes were fighting over her. She was never so scared in her life she told me. She was stuck to me and she knew it. So when she left me, sure she was scared. She knew she wasn't ever going to make it back to where she come from. That's why she shot herself up. She knew what she was doing. She was getting out. A class bitch, but she never had her shit together."

Ricky looked at him. "What do you think, Professor?"

"Keep going."

Ricky gave him a crooked smile. "Okay. What I was thinking in that guinea hospital was maybe Sue told that straight-laced papa of hers about Browne. He'd come down pretty hard on her for her life, hey, maybe he come down harder on Browne."

"Could she have told him about Wally? Or about you?"

Ricky touched the side of his head gingerly. "Maybe

someone else told him about us. Or maybe he just found out. And he took care of Browne and Wally and he wanted to put me away too. And God damn it, man, he probably still wants to."

Cyrus pondered it. Greed could motivate courage; it could also stimulate visions, illusions, and connections in a mind already gone soft with junk.

From inside the house Cyrus heard the sounds of classical music. Eileen was playing Mozart.

"What was the real father's name?"

"I don't know."

"Where did she go when she went to live with him back East?"

"She never told me."

"Did she ever tell you her real name?"

"No. And I never asked. My chicks got lots of real names. I don't do cop work on them. They're loyal to me; I'm loyal to them. When I asked her about being Cindy she just said yeah she used to be Cindy but wasn't no more."

"Did she grow up in Harbour Woods?"

"She had to. Right? She was in high school when old Arthur was sticking it to her."

"Did you ever tell Arthur Browne you knew his step-daughter?"

Ricky grinned. "Nope. I was holding that in reserve. He didn't connect her with me when I come to him for help back in January. And then I was needing the man so bad there was no way I was gonna lay shit like that on him. He could've been sore. He knew I had chicks working for me but that wasn't what I'd been busted for. Why mix up things for both of us?"

Ricky looked at Cyrus with sincerity in his eyes. "Professor, I figure I *got* to help you find that nut. Not just for the dough but for my life."

218

"Does the name Geoff Goldstein mean anything to you?"

"No. Never heard of him."

"How about Mary Louise Hillman?"

"A chick . . . " Ricky took more time with that one. "Who is she?"

"A poet."

"A what?"

"A poet."

"Naw. Jesus, I don't know chicks who do that."

"Did Sue ever mention Goldstein's name to you?"

"No. I told you I never heard of him. Who's he?"

"A professor here."

Ricky thought some more. He grinned. "I got some professors I supply porno to. Pictures and stuff, but that name don't ring with me. What's he look like?"

Cyrus described Goldstein as best he could.

"He don't sound like any of my customers from the faculty."

It would be fun to find out who his customers on the faculty were, Cyrus thought.

"What's up with this Goldstein guy?"

"He was just murdered today."

Ricky's eyes widened. "Jesus. Another one. What the fuck is going on?"

"Did Sue ever mention Mary Louise Hillman to you?"

But Ricky was still digesting the Goldstein news.

Cyrus repeated the question.

"No," Ricky said. "I never heard of her. Or him. But Sue was a nympho. She could've fucked people I never knew about. Listen, Professor, there's a nut on the loose. I'm gonna have to look after myself."

His alibis would have to be checked, Cyrus thought, but if his story was true, and God knows it sounded right . . .

Cyrus reached a decision.

"How are you fixed for money?"

"I'm low. That's no shit. I got money due me from the store but I'm scared to go there. For all I know the nut has got it staked out."

"I'll get you money," Cyrus said.

"Serious?"

"Yes."

Ricky's eyes gleamed. "Now you're talking like my man. I knew I come to the right guy."

"But I want you close at hand."

"For twenty-five thou I'll *be* close at hand. You'll have a time losing me."

"Let's go then," Cyrus said.

"Where?"

"The Holiday Inn North. I'm going to register you there under the name of . . . John Agate."

"Who's he?"

"A friend of mine who won't mind. I don't want you leaving your room for anything. Not for meals, drinks, women . . . anything."

Ricky winked at him. "Anything you say, boss."

A pimp is a pimp is a pimp, Cyrus thought. But this one had a unique value. Especially if Goldstein's death had not been a mistake.

29

The air was cool and stale in Arthur Browne's apartment. A thin layer of dust covered everything.

Nothing had been touched in the bedroom. On the bureau was the small silver-framed picture of the woman and the teenage girl. Cyrus slipped it into his pocket, turned off the lights, and let himself out.

He left the key with Paul Genthon and mounted the stairs. Eileen was still playing Mozart. Now it was the music from *Elvira Madigan*. Last year they'd gone to see a rerun of that fine old movie. She had wept through it. The music alone, he thought, was enough to break your goddam heart.

He padded on to his own apartment. There he compared the picture he had just removed from Browne's apartment with the picture of the young woman in the night club with Ricky Andrews.

It wasn't obvious at first. The woman with Ricky was a poised, sophisticated-looking whore. True, there was a brittle quality that lay just below the surface.

The teenager in the silver frame was impish and mischievous, sticking her tongue out at the photographer.

But the structure of the face . . . and the eyes. The eyes of the teenager were old eyes. Knowing eyes.

He looked back at the whore. They were the same eyes.

Cyrus rang up the police station. Guiterrez had just come in from dinner. Cyrus told him about Ricky Andrews's reappearance and his alibis. They had to be checked: the Holiday Inn at the airport in Pittsburgh, the four days in the Cabrini Hospital in New York City.

"Christ," Guiterrez said bitterly, "if that's all true we lose our chief suspect. You got him with you right now?"

"No." Cyrus took a deep breath. This was the part of the call he hadn't looked forward to.

"I've just come back from registering him at the Holiday Inn North," Cyrus said.

"What?"

"Take it easy and listen. He won't be leaving there. He's motivated to stay there and scared to leave. He's registered under the name of John Agate."

"Have you flipped, Prof?"

"No. But to make sure he stays there, John, I want you to have a plainclothesman in the lobby around the clock."

"No way. He goes in the can for safekeeping."

"You won't be able to keep him there, John. He's scared of jails and cops. He'll get himself a lawyer and walk out. Once out, we stand to lose him again. Right now he's working for us. He wants that reward money. And he's scared for his life. He thinks one person killed Wally Lassiter and Arthur Browne. And he thinks that person wants to kill him." Cyrus related Ricky's parking lot story.

"Who is it?"

"He doesn't know his name. But he's given me some leads. I think he trusts me, John. He came all the way back here from New York City to see me. Now if you don't like all these reasons for keeping him in a motel, try this one. We can keep him there as bait. Just the way we're keeping a guard on Hillman. Only he's better bait than Hillman. We know someone tried to kill him. We don't know yet that anyone was trying for her."

"You don't *know* someone tried to kill him, Prof. You've only got his word for it."

"It rings true to me. His head is still banged up."

Guiterrez was silent. "I don't like it, Prof. It's too goddam clever. If we lose Andrews it'll be your head, not mine."

"Fair enough," Cyrus said. He laughed. "Now that Goldstein's gone I may get tenure after all."

Guiterrez laughed too. "Okay. I'll check his alibis and get someone out there pronto."

"What has Tinker turned up with Goldstein?"

"Nothing."

"Mrs. Goldstein ever hear of Ricky Andrews?"

"No. And Goldstein has no porno around in his study."

"Tell Tink to keep digging."

"He is. He's with the family now and he'll be talking with everyone in your department. So far you're still the number one suspect in the Goldstein murder, Prof."

"How's Hillman?"

"Trying to put the make on Officer Hansen. He's lucky he knows karate."

"What does Philip Potter the third do while that's going on?"

"I don't know. Hansen's too busy fighting off Hillman to report on Potter. You think we ought to keep an eye on him, do you?"

"Yes," Cyrus said.

"Done," Guiterrez said.

*

Eileen was lying on the bed. The bed lamp was on. Music was playing from her stereo.

"Hey," he said softly, "it's John Agate again."

"Hello, Cyrus."

He sat down alongside her. The red dress looked tired and worn. Her face was without expression. He owed her, he thought. Just as he had her bouncing back from Goldstein, Ricky pops out of the bushes. It was too much for her.

"I'm sorry . . . again," he said, and ran his finger along the side of her jaw. "You okay?"

"Yes. What happened down there?"

"It's okay. In fact, we've been looking for that guy. He's a local pimp named Ricky Andrews. He's a suspect."

"Cyrus — " She turned and looked at him. Her eyes were solemn. "Do I have to know about this?"

"Maybe not. But right now I need your help, Eileen."

"How can I help, Cyrus? I seem to be in the way all the time. Screaming, panicking — I just wish this would all go away."

"It will. Eileen, would you look at these pictures? Sit up and look at them. This night club picture, that's Ricky. The kid in the bushes. And that's one of his whores. Now look at the other picture."

"Cyrus," she said, taking that picture from him, "you stole this from Arthur's apartment."

"I took it, yes. Look at the young girl. It's the same person as the whore. The picture was taken when she was fifteen or sixteen. She's dead now, Eileen. She O.D.'d last January. The person I'm interested in here is the mother. Look hard at her. You spent time with Arthur Browne downstairs — "

"Cyrus, don't start that again."

"I'm not. Did Arthur ever talk about the woman and the girl?"

Eileen reluctantly faced the picture.

"She was his wife," she said slowly. "Her name was Josephine. But she's dead too, Cyrus."

224

"Did he ever talk about having a daughter?"

"A step-daughter . . ." She paused. "Must you dig all this up? Yes, I suppose you must. He had a step-daughter that he legally adopted. But after Josephine died, the step-daughter left him. He was very upset, he told me."

"Did he ever mention to you the name of the father? Or the daughter's previous name?"

"No."

"Or the wife's previous name?"

"No. He told me his wife had worked at the university." Eileen closed her eyes. "I can't remember where . . . wait . . . she had a job in something he was very interested in. Of course, she worked at the university theater box office. That was it!" Eileen looked at him. "Have I helped you, Cyrus?"

He took the pictures from her and tossed them on a nearby chair. "Yes," he said, and put his arms around her.

"Will it end soon, Cyrus?"

"Yes, baby, soon. I promise."

It was then that she began to cry. Hard, wracking sobs that worked their way up from her belly. She wasn't weeping, Cyrus thought, for a pompous professor or a debauched lawyer or a morally corrupt football coach. She wept for herself, who only wanted to write stories and live in a college town and having nothing at all to do with death.

"It will end very soon," Cyrus said, holding her close.

30

The leaves on the trees were red and gold. Michigan's license plates advertised the state as a water wonderland. But it was, Cyrus thought, truly an autumn state. A state of fall colors.

He pointed his car toward the Golden Knolls retirement village just off the freeway on the outskirts of town. Golden Knolls, which had started and gone bankrupt as a Methodist retirement center, had taken on new life when many retired university faculty and staff moved out there.

One of those retired university staff members was Pauline Frank, who for forty years had been known as "the ticket woman." Tall, hatchet-faced, unemotional, she had been office manager of the university theater ticket department.

Now she sat erect in a Victorian overstuffed chintz chair, holding her breakfast coffee in hand, and looking down her long, narrow beak at Cyrus, wedged tightly in a Boston rocker.

She appraised him with cold eyes. Then she looked away. At a series of color photographs on her walls —

the dunes at Sleeping Bear, the bridge at Mackinac, the cooling towers of the reactor at Charlevoix.

"Say what you will about nuclear energy and its dangers," she pronounced, "I think those cooling towers are magnificent structures. Especially when seen from the air. *Our* pyramids!"

Cyrus was silent. He knew she was considering his request and would get around to it in her own due time. Some of the stage had rubbed off onto the box office.

"What department did you say you were in, young man?"

"The English department. Though right now I'm representing the . . . uh . . . (it felt so awkward) . . . police department."

"How uncharacteristic of an English professor."

"Well," he said uncomfortably, "I don't have tenure."

"That explains exactly nothing," she said severely.

Cyrus would have squirmed if the Boston rocker had permitted. Fortunately it didn't. He was wedged in physically, as well as emotionally.

"You want to know about Josephine Browne? Well, I will tell you about Josephine Browne because wherever she is now, she cannot be hurt by any dirt anyone digs up. Though I think she was hurt enough in her time. By Arthur Browne and . . . ." She waggled a bony finger at the picture in Cyrus's hands. "By her. Her daughter Cynthia."

Pauline Frank looked away from Cyrus, toward the window.

"I never married. I never had children. But I can tell you, young man, it is a brave person who will bring up children in Harbour Woods. The high schools in this city were and probably are cesspools of drugs. I blame it all on the university too. That's the price one pays for living in a city that the university dominates. Marijuana all over the campus. That awful hash bash they have on campus every April first, attracting high school and junior high school children from all over. No wonder public school education has become a disaster area in this country. From the university on down!"

She glared at Cyrus before she continued.

"Josephine Browne was as ill equipped to raise a high school girl in this atmosphere as anyone. She tried. She drove Cynthia to school every day. She may have gone to her first class with her, to make sure she got there, for all I know. I gave Josie permission to be twenty-five minutes late to work each morning, for the express purpose of seeing that Cynthia went to class. Josie made it up at the other end. You ask what kind of person Josephine Browne was? She was a very hard worker. Conscientious. Dedicated and kindly. She was kind to people she may have hurt by being kind. Her husband, for example. She overlooked all his carryings on. Don't you agree, Professor Wilson, that it never helps an adulterer straighten himself out when his wife glosses over his affairs? Do you not agree?"

"Yes, ma'am."

"Arthur Browne was, if you'll pardon the expression, a bastard."

She looked belligerently at Cyrus. "Does that shock you?"

"No, ma'am."

"But then some of our finer people in Harbour Woods are bastards. Are you aware of that?"

Cyrus leaned forward. This could go on forever. He'd forgotten how much older people, isolated in retirement villages, like to talk.

"Ma'am, there is no record in Harbour Woods of Mrs. Browne's name by her first marriage. Would you know it, by chance?"

Pauline Frank turned away from him and looked at her

228

colored photographs. As if the past could be read there.

"No. Josie never talked about her first marriage and I never asked. She had more than enough to handle in her second. Trouble gravitates to certain people; perhaps they're masochists. I don't know."

"Was Cynthia's last name Browne when you knew them?"

"Yes. She had been adopted by Arthur Browne, for what that was worth. A beautiful little girl, Mr. Wilson. Intelligent too. But lost. Lost. Chasing will-o'-the-wisps. A lost soul . . ."

"Did you know where Mrs. Browne lived before she came to Harbour Woods?"

Pauline Frank closed her eyes. "She came from the East, I know that. And I know she had previous experience in a college theater ticket office." She opened her eyes and looked at Cyrus. "That's why I hired her over two other candidates. She had experience and experience is invaluable in our profession. Do you know how difficult it is to match tickets with a patron's problems, Mr. Wilson? Especially in a college town. It seems almost all our customers have arthritis in one hip or another, need an aisle seat, or have hearing problems or seeing problems. Why — "

"Do you remember what town that was?"

"Where she came from? No, I don't remember. But I do remember thinking that theirs was a theater romance. She met Arthur Browne in that town selling theater tickets. Something . . . " She frowned. "I hoped would never happen to me. Actors are a despicable lot. And Arthur Browne was an actor. A lawyer too, but mostly a bad actor. Ask him where — oh, dear, he's dead." She suddenly looked troubled. "I'm getting old. And just when you think age is only a numeral you forget things you shouldn't. I haven't been much of a help to you, young man."

"You've helped me a lot, ma'am."

"Have I? Then you're cleverer than you look. Well, I hope you catch the bastard that is trying to give the university a bad name. The university doesn't need that kind of publicity. It's quite able to ruin itself on its own, without any outside help."

*

Harbour Woods High School, at the intersection of Main Street and Stadium Boulevard, was a huge, sprawling brick complex that looked more like a factory than a place of learning.

It ran on for almost a quarter of a mile before it dribbled off inconclusively in a series of uni-strut structures that housed art studios, auto shops, drivers' ed classes.

Beyond them were athletic fields that stretched almost as far as the eye could see. Sports were big at Harbour Woods High.

"And don't forget drugs," Fred Schmidt said. "People think the drug days are gone. But they're worse now than they ever were. They're so 'in' now we've just about given up fighting them."

Schmidt was a powerfully built man with sloping shoulders. He had a large nose and sad, dog-like eyes. Years ago he was the head football coach at Harbour Woods.

"I gave it up after eight years. The pressure got to me. Even in a high school you have to win. I became a counsellor. I thought it would be easier than teaching math. It wasn't."

But he was proud of one thing. He always gave straight answers to bent kids.

"They may not have liked those answers, some of those little dope addicts, but with Fred Schmidt, they always knew where they stood."

"Where did Cindy Browne stand?" Cyrus asked.

The file on Cindy Browne was thin. It had taken Schmidt only a few minutes to find it. He was also proud of his filing system.

"When you get old, you can't count on your memory to serve you. No files and you're dead. Here she is. Cindy Browne. I can remember her all right. She was trouble with a capital T."

He moistened his index finger and turned a page, pausing to look at something. Not sharing. A kid with a fancy dessert, hogging it.

"Except for English, a borderline student. Terrible attendance record. Disciplinary action every other day almost. Home visits by her counsellor Mary Pattin. Mary's retired and lives in San Jose, California. You want her address?"

"It might be helpful."

"I'll have the secretary get it for you. Cindy's mother seems to have made quite a few trips to the counsellor's office. Let's see, there's a note here about her writing for the literary magazine, but she soon quit that. That was her only extracurricular activity. The big problem was keeping her in school. She was always ducking out after the first period."

"Did she graduate?"

"No. Lucky for us she transferred out her junior year."

"Does it say where?"

"Not here. I'll go on looking."

He turned a page over.

"Was her name always Cynthia Browne?" Cyrus asked. "Did she ever have another name?"

The question surprised Schmidt. "Cynthia Browne is all I have here." He looked at Cyrus. "Say, are you also working on the Wally Lassiter murder?"

"Yes."

Schmidt was silent for a moment. "What a shame that

was," he said. "Wally was a great man. Years ago he let me help out at his practices. I'd work with the boys on their warm-ups. Wally was a hard driver but he knew what he wanted. And he gave of himself. Completely. Now why would someone want to shoot him, I ask you. Talk about Lee Harvey Oswald . . . this country is going to hell, Professor. Straight to hell without any side trips."

"Do you see yet where she transferred to?"

Fred Schmidt bounced back to reality. "Let me keep looking." He licked his finger several more times. "Here's something. A record of her transcript, such as it was, was sent to Wilbur Cross High School in Middleville, Connecticut."

He looked up. "I'd guess that's where she went to. Wouldn't you?"

"Yes." Cyrus stood up. "I only wish the university's files were as complete as yours."

Fred Schmidt's honest face brightened. "Professor, I work hard at it. That's the reason they're in order. You never know when you'll need some bit of information from the past. These files can be gold mines. I wish I had more on the girl for you but, as you can see, she didn't hang around here very much."

The ten-o'clock bell sounded outside in the hall. Cyrus was late for the task force meeting at the police station.

"You've been very helpful, Mr. Schmidt."

Mr. Schmidt's handshake was a bonebreaker.

"I just hope you catch the lunatic who shot Wally. I'd like to see him strung up."

"What's the best way out of here?"

Schmidt smiled sourly. "There's no good way right now, Professor Wilson. We have three thousand plus students moving through these halls. I used to tell Wally he could train his halfbacks over here. My advice is wait four minutes and then run like hell."

232

Fred Schmidt laughed at his humor, and Cyrus joined in, as a way of thanking him.

From a phone in the main office of the school Cyrus called Eileen and asked her to read to him, again, over the phone, the back-flap copy on *Edges of Darkness*.

His mind was now racing along as crazily as Ricky Andrews's had.

31

The glossy Cretan maze caught Cyrus's eye. It gleamed at him through the clear plastic wrapper. It was unusual to find this kind of game in an airport gift shop, Cyrus thought, but perhaps not so surprising in Washington's National Airport, with its stream of erudite and cosmopolitan visitors.

The game with its literary overtones would be a good present for Eileen. It would also help him make amends for his precipitous departure twenty-four hours earlier from Harbour Woods.

A loudspeaker blared in the concourse. "Northwest Flight 175, nonstop to Detroit, now ready for boarding."

That was his flight.

"I don't need it wrapped," he told the clerk, "I'll take it as is."

Seconds later he was hurrying through the concourse.

The hunt was coming to an end.

Yesterday morning at the meeting it had sounded crazy to the task force when he told them he was leaving that afternoon for Connecticut to find the real father.

Tom Whelan grumbled. "This is no time to run off on

a wild goose chase, Cy. You've got Hillman under guard at Brewster House and she's causing all sorts of problems for the staff there. Goldstein's funeral is tomorrow afternoon and the whole faculty will be there and on edge. National TV news people are here — and you're running off."

"Cyrus wouldn't be leaving if he didn't think it necessary," the chief said, though Cyrus knew his uncle privately had his doubts. The killer was in Harbour Woods, not off in the East.

But now, Cyrus thought, three plane rides and twenty-four hours later, it was all worth it.

Cyrus passed through the electronic detector with an overnight bag, the Cretan maze game, and a two-week-old copy of *Newsweek.*

He boarded the flight. In his seat he looked at the brightly colored game. It was as appropriate for him as it was for Eileen, he thought. You could put me at one end in darkness with Theseus. Theseus who had made it out safely to sunlight by following a thread given him by the beautiful Ariadne.

My thread, thought Cyrus, *was* a woman. Sue Nelson nee Cindy Browne.

It was she who led him through the dark maze until he reached the sunlight of her real father.

Or, his terrifying darkness.

*

Just a little over twenty-four hours ago Cyrus had phoned the principal of Wilbur Cross High School in Middleville, Connecticut, asking for someone to meet him at the school around 7 P.M. Someone with access to school records.

At Bradley International Airport outside of Hartford he had rented a car and then driven south along the river, past dark fields containing faint but regular shapes of tobacco barns. Years ago he had flown here to attend his sister's graduation at Mount Holyoke College. It had been a smaller airport then.

He arrived in Middleville after seven and asked for directions twice. The high school was a new one, on the edge of town. There was a single, bright mercury-vapor light that cast an eerie pinkish glow over a dozen or so yellow school buses.

Near the buses a car was waiting with its lights on. From it emerged a man wearing a corduroy mackinaw and a fisherman's hat.

He looked to be in his mid-thirties. He had a cheerful face.

"Are you Mr. Wilson from Michigan?"

"Yes."

"I'm Ted Mayer. A twelfth-grade teacher. Mr. Schroeder, our principal, asked me to meet you. Come on in and I'll show you what we have."

*

The file here was even slimmer than the file in Harbour Woods.

"She went to Wilbur Cross less than a year," Mayer explained. "There's a notation here that says she moved away. And here's a typed letter from her counsellor. Cindy seemed to have been a troublesome student. Yet, the note says she showed promise as a creative writer. Wrote stories in the school magazine and she was invited to be a member of the Mary Louise Hillman creative writing workshop." Mayer looked up at Cyrus. "You know about that?"

"Not yet."

"Well, it was a local thing that used to go on here. And your Cindy seems to have been a member of it." Mayer

236

looked troubled. He turned a page. "Here's a note from the counsellor listing several meetings with the police about her."

"Who is the counsellor?"

"Martin Keppler. He doesn't teach here anymore. But Lieutenant Jarvis of the Middleville Police Department is mentioned here. And he's still around. Though we don't have the juvenile squad anymore." Ted Mayer laughed. "Thank God those days are gone."

"What about a parent or guardian?"

"Let's see . . . her father's name . . . odd, it's not the same as her's. Louis Wagner. He was — " Ted Mayer looked surprised and then impressed. "City manager of Middleville."

*

The Middleville City Hall was a two-story redbrick building on the square in the center of town. It was closed. Next door, in a large white frame house, was the police station. That was open.

In the front office, once a parlor, a patrolman sat behind a desk with a two-way radio in it. He asked for Cyrus's identification.

"Seems okay, sir, but I can't help you. There's only two of us on duty here and one car on patrol. Lieutenant Jarvis, he's number two, he'll be in at eight in the morning. A good place to sleep? The Middleville Inn's right across the square."

*

The Inn was a down-on-its-heels New England inn. Solid maple floors, beat-up wicker furniture, travel posters and black-and-white photographs of New England on the walls. While the clerk checked his credit card, Cyrus examined the pictures.

237

There was the inevitable covered bridge, a dam on the Connecticut River, the John Wesley campus right in the heart of Middleville, the Congregational Church on the square with its simple white steeple, an abandoned wool mill, some old houses with wide, flowing porches, including one that bore the following caption:

THE AUGUSTUS HILLMAN HOMESTEAD,
constructed 1793
Home of the Hillman Foundation
Lake Street, Middleville

"How far is Lake Street from here?" Cyrus asked.
"You're on it if you turn right at the corner," the desk clerk said, handing him back his card and a room key.

*

The Hillman homestead was as advertised both on book jacket and Inn photograph. Handsome, large, well cared for. A single light played on a small hand-lettered sign out front:

The Hillman Foundation
for Arts & Letters

Cyrus stood in the dark, looking at it. He'd come here because he couldn't believe it was a coincidence. Now he was more certain than ever that the pieces were falling into place. One didn't have to be a John Agate to sense it!

*

An Italian restaurant just off the square was open. Cyrus discovered that he was famished. He had an antipasto, lasagna, and washed it all down with a liter of bad Chianti.

Afterward he walked back to the Middleville Inn and had two brandies at the bar while he listened to two salesmen extol the virtues of Japanese cars.

A bus labelled Peter Pan Lines pulled up in front of the Inn. Cyrus watched a boy get off. All he carried was a squash racquet. He walked off into the darkness. Presumably to the college.

The Peter Pan Lines, he thought. Not a bad name for a trip into the past.

That night Cyrus slept the deep kind of sleep that John Agate also slept as he neared the solution of a mystery.

*

The city manager of Middleville was a short, barrel-chested Italian who punctuated his sentences with sharp finger stabs.

"You bet I remember Lou Wagner. Never forget him. He hired me. Wonderful guy. I got a picture of him right here on the wall."

It wasn't exactly a picture of Louis Wagner that the city manager took down. It was rather a shot of a group of men and one woman taken, he explained, at a ground-breaking ceremony for a shopping center.

"This was taken four years ago. That's Win Colfax, who was head of the chamber of commerce then. Next to him is Charley Hearn, the builder. He's from New Haven. That's Mrs. Bentsdorf from the county planner's office. There's Joe Mahaffey with the shovel. He was our mayor then — and there's Lou at the end."

Cyrus looked finally at Louis Wagner. The real father. A man of medium height with a quiet, nondescript face. He was the only one not looking at the camera. He was looking at the shovel in the mayor's hand. From the three-quarter's view of his face, you could tell little about it. A clerk's visage perhaps, a bureaucrat? A face without strength, without weakness, without anything. Perhaps shy, timid. Whatever, it did not look like the face of a religious nut, as Ricky had talked about him. But then, what did a religious nut look like?

As the city manager went on talking about the shopping center and what a good thing it had been for Middleville's tax base, Cyrus imagined half-glasses on Louis Wagner's nondescript face.

Then he tried to visualize this little man dragging Arthur Browne into an oven, shooting Wally Lassiter in a crowded stadium — it didn't fit. Not at all.

He turned to the city manager. "Did Wagner wear glasses?" he interrupted.

"Glasses? Not that I remember. Of course, Lou and I are at that age when our eyes start going bad overnight."

"Do you have any other pictures of him?"

"I'm afraid not. Whatever informal pictures were taken around here Lou took. He was an amateur photographer. You won't find many pictures of him. He was a quiet man. A behind-the-scenes man. A church-goer. He never called attention to himself and he should have because he was also an A-1 administrator. The kind they don't make anymore."

"Can I have a copy of this?"

"We wouldn't have one. But the newspaper might. It's their picture. The *Sentinel.* Right across the street."

It wasn't really a good picture; it wouldn't blow up well, or even reproduce well. But it was a picture of Louis Wagner.

"He was a crack administrator, Lou was, and in tough times too. College kids shooting up and high school kids imitating them. Always a town and gown problem here. Mill people and a fancy college. Oil and water. Lou handled it all. I got the promotion when he left but I can tell you: I was sorry to see him go, just the same."

"Where did he go?"

"Stoneville, Maryland. Near Washington. He became an assistant in the city administration there."

"What made him leave? He was running the show here, wasn't he?"

240

The city manager avoided his eyes. He gestured, palms out wide. "Bigger town. Better job. Better pay. What else?"

"Did you know his daughter?"

The eyes met his. "Okay. So you know about her. Well, she may have been part of the reason he left. She was a problem all right. But he was doing his best. There wasn't one of us here didn't think Lou was coping. He didn't have to leave on account of that. We thought."

*

"He did a lousy job with his daughter," Lieutenant Jarvis said. He was a wiry man of medium height, with a weather-beaten face and thoughtful blue eyes. He looked more like a farmer than a cop, thought Cyrus.

"Mostly because he never knew what was going on," the lieutenant went on. "In keeping it from the town, I kept it from him too."

He handed back the print of the picture Cyrus got from the Middleville *Sentinel.*

"When I told Lou his daughter was hanging around the wrong people, you know what his solution was? He'd quote the Bible at her. When I told him there were scandals in town that would hit the newspaper unless he got her out of town, that's just what he did. Only he went with her. I hear she didn't stay with him long after that."

Lieutenant Jarvis's thoughtful blue eyes searched the small office, as though looking for some concrete remembrance of Louis Wagner. Cyrus looked too. The office had once been a bedroom of the house. Dark oak doors, oak moldings at the ceilings, oak baseboards at the floor. It was quiet here. Just about the opposite of the Harbour Woods Police Station at this moment.

"Warning Lou like that I was doing a favor for myself. I was getting sick of trips to the high school. It was tough

241

trying to protect the reputation of a good city manager who didn't deserve a junkie daughter."

"Who were the wrong people she was hanging around?" Cyrus asked.

"There were plenty in those days."

"I was walking around last night and noticed the Hillman Foundation back on one of the streets. This is the poet Mary Louise Hillman's hometown, isn't it?"

The blue eyes narrowed, waiting. "That's right."

"Was she one of the wrong ones?"

Silence.

Finally Jarvis smiled thinly. "That's a big name in this town, Wilson."

"I see that."

"The Hillman family founded Middleville."

"She's out in Harbour Woods right now," Cyrus said. "A guest of the university."

"That right?"

"Yes."

Jarvis smiled bleakly. "I wish you'd keep her out there." He leaned back in the matching oak swivel chair. It was the kind of furniture, Cyrus thought, that one saw in prestigious old law offices. All the Harbour Woods P.D. had was steel and plastic.

"Lou's daughter came here from Harbour Woods, didn't she?"

"That's right," Cyrus said.

"And now you got people being bumped off right and left out there?"

Cyrus was silent. He knew that Jarvis was working it out in his mind. He looked at Cyrus and came to a conclusion. "Well," he said, "I had some problems here too. Mary Louise made my life miserable here with her freak show."

"Freak show?"

"That's what I called it and that's what it was. A freak

show. She took straight kids and bent them like nails. She used some kind of poetry workshop scam to recruit them. There wasn't much poetry but a helluva lot of pot. Wine and sex. Around here people closed their eyes to it because her name was Hillman. And Mary Louise could bring it off too. She could charm your balls off one minute and make you want to strangle her the next.

"The really bad part was the kids. They didn't know what she was doing to them. And she had to have them around. You're a college town cop too, so maybe you understand this kind of thing. I had it explained to me once by a psychology professor at the college. Hillman couldn't face growing old. She was a daddy's girl all her life. So her answer was to always have kids around her. Her peers. Make sense to you?"

Cyrus was silent.

Jarvis laughed. "Hell, I don't *know*. All I knew was that it was a relief when she moved her circus to New York City for a couple of years. That's where a sideshow like that belongs. They don't even know it's there. But then she came back. And it looks like she's back for good."

"Was Louis Wagner's daughter part of her group?"

"Yep."

"How close were she and Hillman?"

"How close would you like them to be?"

"Is Hillman a lesbian?"

Cyrus remembered her request for a handsome young cop to guard her.

"She's everything, Wilson. Man-eater, woman-eater, animal-eater. As corrupt as an old snake. She'd fuck a duck and talk to you about Ralph Waldo Emerson. Famous poet? She's a goddam disgrace to humanity."

The anger and bitterness in the small-town cop welled over.

"She's a drunk, a drug addict, and throws her weight

243

around every chance she can. Why the hell couldn't she have been the one that got bumped off in Harbour Woods?"

"Did Louis Wagner ever make any threats against her?"

"Lou? Threats?" Jarvis laughed bitterly. "They didn't go together. Lou was a quiet man, Wilson. He's just what he looks like in that picture. Won't look at a camera. Won't do anything to attract attention. The opposite of Mary Louise. No, he wouldn't make threats and he couldn't hurt a fly."

"His daughter died in Harbour Woods last January," Cyrus said. "Drug overdose."

Jarvis was silent. Then he emitted a faint sucking noise through his nostrils. The weather-beaten face looked harsh and unrelenting in the overhead light.

"I can't see it, Wilson," Jarvis said at last, with a shake of his head. "Maybe if he got drunk enough and Hillman was walking in front of his car, Lou might not hit the brake. But then you got that football coach's murder to explain, and the lawyer's. And I saw where you also lost a professor. That's an awful lot of killing to hang on little Lou Wagner."

"There may be connections," Cyrus said mildly.

"Sure. Three killings in a week's time and I'd be working on connections too. But not to Lou Wagner."

He seemed very sure about that. But then to make extra sure Jarvis rapped twice on his desk. He was lucky he had wood furniture, Cyrus thought.

32

On the way in from Washington's National Airport, Cyrus passed a sign. *Stoneville — Best City Spirit on the East Coast.*

In downtown Stoneville old Victorian homes stood cheek by jowl with new city buildings. The City Hall was an old 1910 type, heavy stone architecture, four floors high.

An elderly woman outside the city manager's office smiled at Cyrus.

"Can I help you?"

"I'm looking for a Mr. Louis Wagner."

"I'm sorry but Mr. Wagner's not here now. Can someone else help you?"

"When do you expect him back?"

"Mr. Wagner's on leave from this office."

"Oh . . ."

"Perhaps someone else can help you."

"No. I wanted to see Mr. Wagner," Cyrus said. "Is he in town?"

"I don't believe so. He took his vacation in August and then asked Mr. Shain for a leave. And he gave it to him."

"Mr. Shain is?"

"Our city manager. But he's in a meeting in Washington today. We have two other assistant city managers who are here today."

"Thanks," Cyrus said, dropping into a chair opposite this kindly and voluble older woman, "but I really came here to see Mr. Wagner."

She shook her head. "I'm certain Lou is out of town."

"Do you know where?"

The receptionist was about to answer him when suddenly she clammed up, her eyes became suspicious. "May I ask who you are, sir?"

Cyrus handed her his police identification card.

"Oh," she said, eyes widening. "A policeman from Harbour Woods." She glanced at him over the card. "Isn't that where those dreadful murders have been taking place?"

"Yes, ma'am."

"How awful." She handed him back the card. "No, I don't know where Lou went."

"Why did he take a leave, do you know?"

"No, I don't. He had vacation coming to him but he called Mr. Shain and asked for a leave. Without pay, of course. We expect him back any day now. And we need him back. Mr. Wagner is a wonderful administrator." She looked at Cyrus dubiously. "Your interest in Lou . . . it has nothing to do with the murders, does it?"

"Yes, ma'am, it does," Cyrus said gently.

She was shocked. "Oh. I hope not. Indeed, no. Of course not. Young man — " she fumbled in her pocketbook on the desk, "I can tell you one thing. Louis Wagner would never get involved in anything like that. He's a very decent man. A Christian. Why the very idea — " She took out a tissue and blew her nose. Her face had got red with emotion.

"Impossible. Absolutely impossible. I knew him as well

246

as anyone, sir. It's just not possible. My goodness. Lou Wagner is the essence of kindness. I can't think of anyone you should be *less* interested in than Lou Wagner."

"Do you have any idea where he is now, ma'am?"

"I told you before that I didn't," she said sharply.

"Ma'am," Cyrus said gently, "you told me you didn't know where he went. Perhaps you might know where he is."

"I don't," she snapped. "Nor does anyone else around here. Furthermore, Mr. . . . "

"Wilson."

"Wilson. I find these questions abhorrent."

Cyrus sat back. "By investigating Mr. Wagner I may find out he had no connection at all with the murders, ma'am."

She thought about that for a moment and then her face softened. She really wanted to be helpful, but Lou Wagner was a lovely man. To have him accused of murder, no, not accused, but even just connected . . . oh dear. "I am sorry. Please excuse me."

She blew her nose again.

"Could you look at this photo for me?" Cyrus asked, handing her the picture of the ground-breaking ceremony in Connecticut.

"Would you recognize Mr. Wagner from that?"

Her eyes went from face to face, finally settling on Wagner at the far end. She smiled. "That's him. Though it's not a very good picture of Lou. Typical of him not to look at the camera. He's a very private, self-effacing person."

Cyrus looked at her a moment. She was a helping kind of person and he wondered how far he could go with her.

"What did you do before you took this job, ma'am?" he asked.

She was surprised. "I taught high school English," she said.

"I thought something like that," Cyrus said. "You're very well spoken."

She blushed. "Thank you. I took this job four years ago, after a millage election failed. Since then the schools have done better, thanks to Lou Wagner. He helped us organize the last millage campaign. He really is a wonderful man."

"Would you have a better picture of him?"

"Let me think. Possibly . . . "

In another office Cyrus heard two clerks talking about a rain storm the other night in Virginia that had wiped out some telephone lines. Outside he could hear traffic moving along Stoneville's main street.

The elderly receptionist kneeled at a green filing cabinet, looking through some yellow folders in a drawer. She returned with a blue eight-by-ten-inch sheet of paper.

"It's as I thought. There is no photo. I thought there might be one attached to his job résumé but we're forbidden by law to ask for pictures of applicants."

"Could I have a look at his job résumé?"

She looked at Cyrus. "I don't see what this would tell you."

"Just for a moment, ma'am. It's really in Mr. Wagner's interests."

She hesitated and then handed it over. It was public record.

Cyrus read Louis Wagner's vita. He was born in Rochester, New York in 1937. Education in the Rochester public schools. Early employment: grocery store clerk, drug store clerk through high school. A B.S. in chemistry from Syracuse University. Master's degree in urban administration from the same university. Early career jobs: Hudson, N.Y.; Ithaca, N.Y.; Sharon, Conn.; Middleville, Conn.

There was no mention of family life. Marriage, divorce, or a child.

248

It was a bare-bones résumé. The résumé of a very private person, Cyrus thought.

"Thank you, ma'am." He handed it back to her. "Has Mr. Wagner changed much from the picture I showed you?"

She put the résumé back in the folder. "It's hard to tell from that picture."

"Does he have a mustache or beard, for example?"

"Of course not." She seemed shocked at the question.

"Does he wear glasses?"

"Yes. Though I've seen him without them. He has reading glasses, I think."

"Half-glasses?"

She looked surprised. "How did you know?"

"Just guessing. How about his personal life?"

"I knew nothing about it. None of us did."

She speaks too quickly, Cyrus thought.

"He had been married," Cyrus said. "I was up in Middleville, Connecticut, where, incidentally, they thought as highly of him as you."

"I'm glad of that."

"Apparently he was divorced."

She didn't look surprised.

"And had a daughter who, I gather, gave him worries."

The elderly receptionist sat very still. Then she reached into her pocketbook for the tissues. "Yes," she said softly, "he had a daughter that gave him many worries. I didn't know too much but I knew he had aggravation from her." She dabbed at her eyes. "She finally ran away."

"To where?"

"I don't know."

"Did he ever hear from her?"

"I don't know that either. Somehow, I think yes, though I don't know why. Lou never talked about her. It was through chance remarks that I even learned of his problems."

She wiped her eyes. Then looked at Cyrus.

"However, there is someone who might know more about his personal life than we did. Someone he was close to in Stoneville."

"Who's that, ma'am?"

"His minister. Soon after Lou arrived here he joined a church and worked very hard for it. His minister used to phone here quite often for Lou. Lou did a lot of the financial advising for his church."

"Do you know the minister's name?"

"It was Sand something. Sandstrom, Sandberg . . . something like that."

"The church?"

"That I do know. Lou was very proud of his role in the building of the church. It's The Good Shepherd on Stormville Road."

"Didn't I come in from the beltway on Stormville Road?"

"If you came up from the district, yes. And you can go past it on your way back. There's a shopping center across the street from it. It's red brick with a white colonial steeple."

"I'll find it. You've been very kind, ma'am."

"It's not hard to be kind where Lou Wagner is concerned. He is a very kind man himself."

"So everyone says."

"They speak the truth."

*

The Reverend Theodore Standifer had old, gray, pewtery eyes. They looked with curiosity at Cyrus.

"You're a policeman?"

"Yes, sir. Of sorts."

The old man smiled. "Curious the items one finds waiting on one's return from a retreat."

They were sitting in the pine-panelled pastor's office. Outside the windows in a stand of evergreens sparrows chirped away in the late afternoon sunlight.

"Why does a policeman from Harbour Woods, Michigan, want to talk about Louis Wagner?"

"There have been crimes committed in our city, Dr. Standifer."

The old man looked at Cyrus and if he thought the conversation had taken an unusual turn, he gave no hint. "What kinds of crimes?" he asked.

"Violent ones."

"As though committed by a madman?"

Cyrus's heart began to pound. "Yes, sir."

Dr. Standifer steepled his long, bony fingers and gazed at Cyrus over their tips. His eyes reflected nothing. Absolutely nothing.

"What do you want to know about Louis Wagner, Mr. Wilson?"

"Everything you can tell me, sir."

"He is a wonderful man. That is really everything, Mr. Wilson."

And nothing, Cyrus thought. He waited.

"But an answer like that is meaningless to a policeman. Let me elaborate, if I may. Five years ago I was called to this church. Louis came the year after I did. As though in answer to a prayer. We needed someone to manage our money. What little we had. Louis took over that chore. In a few years, thanks to Louis Wagner, we will be burning our mortgage on the front lawn."

He looked at one of the walls. There were photographs on it. Of different stages in the building of the church. There were no people in the pictures.

"Louis Wagner is a quiet man with an instinct for helping," the old man said. "It is a very important attribute in these unstable times."

He looked at Cyrus. "I admire Louis Wagner very much, Mr. Wilson. I would not want to see him come to harm."

"Will he?" Cyrus asked, curious to see what would come out of this strange role-reversal.

"I don't know. Perhaps that is up to God. As the sparks fly upwards, man is born into trouble . . . "

The gray pewtery eyes focused somewhere beyond Cyrus.

"In the Book of Prophets it is written of a burning fire shut up in one's bones . . . Do you know the Bible, Mr. Wilson?"

"As literature, sir, yes. As revealed word . . . " Cyrus let his words trail off.

Standifer smiled at him. "You read but do not believe, is that it?"

"Yes, sir."

"The rational man. The detective man. The man who seeks the tangible."

"Yes, sir."

"Many of us live on another plane, Mr. Wilson. Though we carry on with our mundane lives with hardly a soul knowing what dwells inside. This church, this room, was a sanctuary for Louis Wagner, Mr. Wilson. A harbor for his tortured soul."

Cyrus waited.

"A man may go mad with impunity if he be a president, a general, a senator — but let a humble Christian go mad and he will deliver unto himself his own worst punishment. Perhaps it is the tithe we pay for believing. For believing, Mr. Detective Wilson, is a great solace."

Cyrus nodded. He waited. The old man fell silent.

Cyrus asked, "Do you think Louis Wagner is capable of killing?"

252

The old man's eyes flashed. "Are you capable of killing?"

"Yes," Cyrus said, subdued before the fire.

"And so am I. And so is Louis Wagner and so is every man!"

The words rang angrily in the room and slowly fell to silence.

"What was torturing Louis Wagner, sir?" Cyrus asked quietly.

"His own guilt."

"Guilt about what?"

"His daughter. You know about his daughter, of course, or you wouldn't be here."

"Yes, sir."

"She died in your city last January and Louis blamed himself for that death. He was wrong. I counselled him. He had done all he could for the child. She was difficult, no, more than difficult, she was corrupt. He came here with her and I counselled her too. But there was an aberrant spirit inside her. One I could not reach. God ordained that she would leave this area, and when she finally did, he became a new man. He functioned again. At his job in City Hall. Here at our church. For four years Louis Wagner did good deeds for his community and his church. Without recognition, without seeking or wanting same.

"And then she came back into his life. Letters, phone calls . . . she tortured him. He didn't want her back. She would only drag him down into the pit with her.

"Such was my advice to him. Live, Louis, live, I counselled him. And you know, Mr. Wilson — "

The old man's eyes bore into his with a fevered intensity.

"I was wrong."

He took a deep breath. "In counselling Louis to look

after himself — if thine eye offend thee, pluck it out, to live for himself and his church and his community — I was counselling him toward his doom.

"She died in your city. She had recorded her sordid life in a journal he brought back. And he was not the same man after that. He worked. But he was a shell. Without a soul. Take a vacation, I urged. You haven't taken a vacation in years. Go somewhere. Take a cruise. Look at new trees, new birds, new mountains.

"He did. But as the poet said: we take our hell with us. He returned, and sat in this very same room . . . not long ago. We were to discuss the paving of our parking lot, and the bids that would go out on it. I was on the phone. And he was reading a magazine. A news magazine. When I got back to him, he had almost gone into a trance.

" 'Louis,' I said, 'are you all right?'

" 'The Lord has led me here today,' he whispered to me. 'I must go there and make amends.'

" 'Go where?' I asked, puzzled.

" 'Go where the serpents are gathering.'

" 'Louis, stop talking nonsense. What is this all about?'

"But he didn't answer me. He got up abruptly and left. I didn't see him the next day or the day after. The day after that, I think it was a Friday, I called Mr. Shain, the city manager. From him I learned that Louis had asked for, and been granted, a leave of absence. For two days I called Louis at home. There was no answer. Finally I went to his house. I learned that the neighbors were taking in his mail. He had stopped his newspaper delivery."

"Where do you think he went?" Cyrus asked.

"I don't know."

"Harbour Woods?"

"I don't know."

"Who were the serpents and where were they gathering?"

"I don't know."

"For God's sake, man," Cyrus cried out, "tell me what you do know. You were next to his heart."

The old man smiled with contempt. "You, a policeman, asking me that? What *I* know is not your kind of knowledge."

Cyrus walked over to a table in the rear of the room. There were several church magazines, *Readers Digest*s, and *Newsweek*s on it.

He turned to the old man.

"When did this last talk with Wagner take place?"

"After Labor Day. I know that because I wanted to talk business with him. Our church activities calendar was starting up again. Services were going back to eleven o'-clock from ten. Summer was over."

"What date was Labor Day this year?"

Standifer turned pages on his calendar.

"September seventh."

Cyrus began looking through the pile of *Newsweek*s. Their dates were about a week after arrival, he knew. Which meant the issue of September 14th would be arriving right after Labor Day.

But there was no September 14th issue. There was a September 21st.

He was aware that the old man was watching him.

"Do you know what you're looking for?" Standifer asked.

"Yes, sir."

"Perhaps I can help you."

Cyrus turned. "Is there a public library near — "

And then he saw what the old man was holding out to him.

"He left it behind."

Cyrus looked hard at the old man. And you held onto it, he thought.

Then Cyrus began going through the *Newsweek* of September 14th.

Outside the sparrows chittered in the dying twilight. Inside there was silence, except for the pages of *Newsweek* turning in his hands.

Finally, under the department of the magazine called "Newsmakers," he found it. He read it twice and then it was time to go. Time to run, fly, telephone, shout.

"Do you mind if I take this with me?" he asked Standifer calmly.

"No. I knew from the first that you would. All is preordained. Do you know the Book of Revelations, Mr. Wilson?"

Cyrus shook his head, thinking he should probably have said yes and fled.

"It is the last book in the New Testament. A book of great beauty and terror. In the spring of this year Louis became fascinated with it. With its promises of death, destruction, and the New Jerusalem. He was caught up with the revenge motif, with the death of Satan and his fiends. In this room last spring we argued by the hour on many evenings. He quoted Revelations and the God of destruction; I quoted the God of the Gospels, a God of mercy.

"It was hard going, Mr. Wilson. You are a policeman and perhaps you understand the thin line that exists between the hunter and the hunted, the policeman and the criminal, the Christ and the anti-Christ. He who would kill evil is also a killer, is he not?"

Clutching the *Newsweek*, Cyrus could only nod.

"All that spring and summer I felt my trusted Louis slipping through my hands. And then . . . ironically, sir, it wasn't the Book of Revelations that dispatched him. It

256

was the magazine you're holding in your hands. He is a good man, Mr. Wilson. I do not care what he has done. Louis Wagner is a good man."

The Reverend Dr. Standifer rose to his feet.

"Do you hear me, sir? Louis Wagner is a good man."

His voice thundered at empty air.

Cyrus was gone.

33

Cyrus found a phone booth in the shopping center on Stoneville Road across from the Church of the Good Shepherd. A steady stream of truck traffic obscured the church, except for the white steeple.

"Guiterrez," the voice crackled over the line.

"Cy Wilson. I'm calling from Stoneville, Maryland."

"What the fuck are you doing there, Prof?"

"I've got the name of our man. The killer."

There was a silence on the other end.

"Go ahead," Guiterrez said.

"Louis Wagner. L-O-U-I-S, W-A-G-N-E-R. He's a little man. Forty-five years old. He wears half-glasses. Probably holed up in a motel. Pick him up, John. Right away. I've got enough for us to hold him. He killed Browne and Lassiter. He killed Goldstein by mistake. Hillman was the target and still is. So's Ricky Andrews. Put some more people around them."

"Prof, are you sure about this?"

"Positive. I'll give you the details as soon as I get back. I'm on my way to the airport now. I've got a bad picture of him. It won't facsimile very well. I'll bring it with me. A little man in half-glasses. Louis Wagner."

"We'll find him," Guiterrez promised.

*

A little over two hours later, Cyrus left his car in the Harbour Woods City Hall parking lot and, heart pounding, ran into the police station. At last, he was coming face-to-face with Louis Wagner. He felt he knew the quiet little man well.

The police department corridors were deserted. It was a little after seven-thirty. A sergeant carrying a sandwich and a paper container of coffee nodded toward the chief's office.

"They're in there, Prof."

And so they were: his uncle, Guiterrez, Tinker, Layne, Rollie Mazur, and Tom Whelan in black tie. They did not have the air of hunters who had bagged their quarry.

"You didn't pick him up?" Cyrus said.

"No," Guiterrez snapped. "We've checked out every motel, hotel, and tourist home in the area. We've got people going through rooming houses right now."

Cyrus turned to Whelan. "Unless Wagner's picked up by tomorrow morning, I'd advise cancelling the honors convocation."

"Impossible. It's never been done in the one-hundred-and-sixty-five-year history of the university."

"Nor has an honors speaker been assassinated in the one-hundred-and-sixty-five-year history of the university."

"You don't seriously believe — "

"For God's sake, Tom, the man's a walking bomb. He came to Harbour Woods for one purpose: to kill. And that's exactly what he's been doing. At least now we've got his hit list."

Tom Whelan was shaken. "All right, Cy. You've made your point. Archie Fields has a canned speech. I'll talk to him." He picked up the phone on the chief's desk.

"John," Cyrus said to Guiterrez, "here's a picture of Wagner. He's the far guy on the left, looking away from the camera. It's not a good picture but you can crop it and blow it up."

They passed the picture around.

"Better explain it all, Cyrus," his uncle suggested quietly.

"Okay. That was Wagner's daughter who O.D.'d out at the Village Apartments last January. Her name was Cindy Wagner, though she went under the name of Sue Nelson. Ricky was her pimp. Her father Louis Wagner blames himself for her death. He also blames other people. Ricky. Arthur Browne, who was her step-father and apparently screwed her regularly when she was a high school kid here in Harbour Woods."

Layne whistled.

"Also on the hit list is Mary Louise Hillman, who ran a drug-sex group in Middleville, Connecticut. After her mother died, Cindy moved there to live with her father. Hillman did a number on her there, I gather. Anyway, Wagner, who was city manager of Middleville, had to leave town. He took Cindy with him. He got a job in Stoneville, Maryland. But the girl couldn't take his straight-laced ways and ran away. A couple of years later she turns up here in Harbour Woods, working as a whore for Ricky. And that was when she got involved with Wally Lassiter. Ricky lined her up with him. He was a steady customer."

Silence while they digested the short but pungent history of one Cindy Wagner.

"How did Wagner know about Lassiter and Ricky Andrews?" the chief asked.

260

"She left a diary."

Whelan put down the phone. "Archie's willing to speak. Now it's a matter of explaining this to Hillman. We're having a formal dinner at Brewster House right now, Cy. That's where I've just come from. Ms. Hillman is making a formal presentation of the foundation's check after the dinner."

"I'll go with you," Cyrus said. "I want to ask her some questions."

"Tink, make copies." Guiterrez handed the photo to Detective Tinker, who left the room with it.

"You do know, Cyrus, that if the dean makes the speech tomorrow," the chief said, "he'll be a target."

"Louis Wagner won't shoot him, Uncle," Cyrus replied. "If I read my man right, he's probably sick about Goldstein. But as long as we don't advertise the switch in speakers, we can probably catch him around the auditorium. Rollie, Stockton has got to be searched tonight, and the whole auditorium sealed off tomorrow. Everyone going in has got to be screened."

"Ye — es, I'll get — on — that," Rollie Mazur garbled. He picked up the phone Whelan had used.

"All right," said the chief, "we've got people out searching rooming houses. We've got Brewster House under guard. We've got people baby-sitting Ricky Andrews. Tomorrow, we check everyone going into the auditorium." His uncle looked at him. "Meanwhile we wait for him to move, is that it?"

"What the hell else can we do?" Guiterrez said.

"Maybe we can help him move," Cyrus said. "Wagner tried to kill Ricky once. Why don't we make it possible for him to try again?"

"Would he try again?" his uncle asked.

"Yes," Cyrus said flatly. "Nothing's going to deflect Louis Wagner now. He's a psycho pure and simple."

261

"What do we do? Advertise the Holiday Inn?"

Cyrus said nothing for a moment. Then the words poured out.

"No. We take Ricky out of the Holiday Inn tonight and salt him away in the county jail. We get word out — " He snapped his fingers. "I've got it. It's made to order. I'll tip Sid Fine a news story. He's the producer at Channel 8 who was in town yesterday. I tip him off that a suspect in the Harbour Woods murders will be showing up at the police station here at 9:30 A.M. to turn himself in as a witness. This guy claims he's not the killer but he knows who the killer is. He can identify the killer. Fine'll put it on the eleven o'clock news. The other stations will pick it up. Radio. The papers in the morning. If that doesn't bring Wagner out of the woodwork, nothing will."

"You're not really proposing to have Ricky Andrews marching in here," the chief asked.

"No. We'll get a volunteer from the department who looks like Ricky. Put him in a flak vest. We'll surround the area with sharpshooters. We can have someone play a lawyer with the decoy."

"Cyrus," his uncle said, "what you're doing is giving Wagner a choice between Andrews and Hillman. Suppose he chooses Hillman."

"Then," Guiterrez said with a wolfish smile, "he gets to shoot the dean."

"That's not funny," Tom Whelan said.

Rollie Mazur's voice box garbled out: "I . . . don't like . . . it. It's gambling with people's . . . lives. It's . . . bad . . . bad . . . " The words came clawing out.

"Right now that's all we've got to gamble with, Rollie," Cyrus said. "Tom, let me call Sid Fine at Channel 8, and then I'll go over to Brewster House with you. You can tell Hillman she won't be making the speech, but then I want to talk alone with her."

"Cy, are you really going to feed Sid Fine a false story?" Whelan was clearly disturbed by the idea.

"That's exactly what I'm going to do."

"I don't like it. It will make for bad relations for us with the media for years to come."

"You won't be here for years to come unless we catch Louis Wagner," Cyrus replied.

And Tom Whelan, thinking that over, agreed. Cyrus was probably right.

*

Over the phone from Detroit, Sid Fine was skeptical. "Let's run that one again. Tomorrow morning at 9:30 A.M. your number-one suspect is giving himself up."

"That's right. And I'm giving you an exclusive."

"Why?"

"Because we need some good publicity."

Fine was silent a moment. "Okay. We'll be there. If this is legit, Wilson, I owe you again."

"Don't worry," Cyrus said handsomely, "I'll collect from you."

He hung up.

"You've got a lot of nerve, Cy," Whelan said.

"Don't he?" Guiterrez laughed. He picked up a phone. "I'll let our people at Brewster House know you guys are coming. I wouldn't want either of you guys shot by mistake."

Whelan looked at Guiterrez to see if he was joking. He was not.

34

Brewster House sits at the end of a cul-de-sac off Geddes Road. It is a spacious stone house with a long looping drive. The grounds, maintained by the university's landscaping department, are lush and elegant. Even in autumn. Privet hedges line the approach to the house. Parked along the hedges were about a dozen cars.

Tom Whelan steered his Oldsmobile carefully along the drive. "All the trustees are here to accept the gift," he explained. He parked in a small area near the house, and they walked back toward the entrance. "I don't need to tell you how goddam nervous I am about this, Cy. If she makes a scene, I don't know what I'll do."

A figure stepped out of the shadows in front of them. It was a plainclothesman with a walky-talky. He checked them both out, nodded to Cyrus, and stepped back in the shadows.

"I've never been involved with anything like this in my life," Whelan went on.

Up the steps they went. Another figure detached itself from the shadows of the house.

"Hello, Prof," said a plainclothesman. "Is that Mr. Whelan with you?"

"Yes," Cyrus said.

"John said you were coming."

He opened the door for them. And still another police officer was on guard inside. This was the young one assigned to guard Hillman at the Harbour Woods Inn. Tall, sandy-haired, young — his name was Dennis Jones.

"How's it going, Dennis?" Cyrus asked.

"Okay, sir. They're in there eating."

Officer Jones indicated closed doors to his right through which could be heard the sounds of a dinner party: glasses, silver against plates, talk.

"Is she sober?" Cyrus asked.

Dennis Jones grinned. "Yes, sir. But I'm not sure she isn't a bit more aggressive sober than drunk."

"Defend yourself, Dennis," Cyrus said.

"I'm trying, Mr. Wilson. I'm married and have two kids."

Whelan winced. "What exactly do you want me to do, Cy?"

"Go in there and get her out. Don't answer anyone's questions. Just whisper to her that you'd like to talk with her outside the room for a moment."

"I hate this," Whelan murmured, but obediently he opened the doors and went into a brilliantly lit dining room. Cyrus saw a long, white tablecloth and some twenty distinguished men and women seated at dinner. Attending them were a half-dozen waiters and waitresses, mostly students.

The president of the university sat at the far end. To his right sat Mary Louise. Cyrus spotted Philip Potter III further down. Archie Fields was there, listening intently to a trustee.

Someone called out to Whelan as he advanced into the room but Tom didn't answer. He walked right to Hillman's side, bent down, and whispered in her ear.

"Really? Must I?" she said loudly.

Whelan's face flushed. But he continued to talk to her.

Cyrus turned to Dennis Jones. "How many people do we have here?"

"Four. I'm in here. Jerry's at the front door. Kelly Mintz is at the back door. And Dave Ragetti is patrolling the grounds. He watched you park. I think we've got it pretty well covered."

Mary Louise Hillman rose suddenly and announced to all that she would return presently. Philip Potter III rose too. Whither thou goest, I go too, Cyrus thought.

"Where can we talk with her?" Cyrus asked the young plainclothesman.

"There's a small library room across the hall, sir."

Cyrus walked across the center hall and looked into a small, book-lined room. One window. Heavy drapes. He parted the drapes. The window was locked. There were three chairs and a love seat.

"This will do," he said.

"What about the boyfriend?" Dennis Jones asked.

"He can come in too."

They walked back into the hall as Hillman emerged from the dining room. She stopped short when she saw Cyrus. "So. I might have guessed." She turned to the police officer. "Dennis the dull," she said scornfully.

The officer's face turned red.

"Mary Louise," Philip Potter III chided softly. He looked at Cyrus. "I take it this is your doing, Mr. Wilson."

"It is. I'd like to talk with you across the hall."

"Make it short and sweet, Professor," Mary Louise snapped. "I was brought up to believe that leaving a table in the middle of dinner is extremely rude."

She took her stance against a bookcase. She wore a simple yellow gown with classical lines. Her eyes were clear. Cyrus realized that he was probably seeing her sober for the first time. And, for the first time, he saw the lines of a younger Mary Louise Hillman, the strong, handsome face on the book flap.

Cyrus waited till Dennis Jones closed the door. Then he nodded to Whelan.

"Miss Hillman," Whelan began, and cleared his throat, "I don't know a diplomatic way to put this — "

"Just say it, Mr. Whelan!" Hillman said.

"I have to ask you not to deliver the honors convocation speech tomorrow."

She stared at him. "Are you out of your mind?"

Tom Whelan looked miserable, Cyrus thought, not without some satisfaction.

"For security reasons that Cy Wilson will explain to you, I've asked Dean Fields to deliver an address instead."

"That is absurd," Mary Louise said angrily. "I've stayed in this boring city a whole week in order to deliver this speech and that is exactly what I will do."

"We can have Dean Fields read *your* speech for you."

"And where am I while this is happening?"

This obviously was Whelan's second line of defense. "You can be called back to Connecticut on business."

"But I haven't been. My business is here." She turned to Cyrus with a look of exasperation. "I take it you're behind this. Am I to hear more about murders and poisons?"

"Yes, ma'am," Cyrus said politely, "you are. We believe that a killer is loose in Harbour Woods and intends to kill you. Professor Goldstein, we feel, did die by mistake."

"Poppycock! Detective stories. Killer-on-the-loose bullshit. You're trying to frighten me and I will not be frightened. I am Mary Louise Hillman and I do not cow easily. My ancestors fought Indians, Mr. Wilson. We pioneered this country. I intend to speak tomorrow on Literature and the Twenty-first Century. Let's return to the table, Philip. No empty threat of danger will stop me."

"Sorry, Miss Hillman," Cyrus said flatly, "but your speech is off."

Mary Louise looked hard at Cyrus for a moment and then turned to Tom Whelan. Her eyes were dancing malevolently. "Is it, Mr. Whelan?"

Tom Whelan said bravely: "Yes. We cannot put your life in jeopardy, Miss Hillman."

"Then," she said, "this is off too!"

She opened a small jet-beaded evening bag and took out a white envelope.

"Mary Louise, you can't be serious," Philip Potter III said.

"Oh, but I am, darling."

From the envelope she removed a check. "Hold my bag, Philip. One needs two hands to rip up a check for three million dollars."

She smiled at Whelan. "You know, Mr. Whelan, I once heard Laurence Rockefeller say there was a time he thought a million dollars was a lot of money. But even a Rockefeller never did what I am about to do. My only regret is that the media isn't here to film this. God knows the university got more favorable national publicity from my coming here than they deserve. This would go a long way to even that up. So, unless Mr. Whelan changes his mind . . . " She paused, looking at Tom Whelan, playing ring master with a check for a whip, and Tom Whelan was to trot, doglike, in circular submission.

Tell her to rip it up, Tom, Cyrus thought.

"Perhaps I had better discuss this with the members of the executive committee," Whelan said, and left the room.

"Yes, perhaps you'd better," Hillman said, laughing. She turned to her secretary. "Don't you just love to see academics dance for money?"

"That was exceedingly cruel of you, Mary Louise," Philip Potter III chided her. "I do believe both Dr. Whelan and Mr. Wilson are looking out for your welfare."

"Piffle. Whelan is looking out for money and Mr. Wilson is embarrassed by me. He doesn't like poets — oh, you can't fool me, Wilson — I see it in your eyes. You don't like naked emotion. And you really don't want a poet addressing your prestigious honors convocation. That's all your killer-on-the-loose business is about, isn't it? Tell the truth. Isn't it all poppycock?"

"No, ma'am," Cyrus said. "It's about a man named Louis Wagner."

He paused. Waiting.

"Is that supposed to mean something to me?" she asked.

"Yes."

"Well, it doesn't."

"I've just returned from Middleville," Cyrus said. Her eyes narrowed. "Louis Wagner," Cyrus went on, "used to be the city manager there."

"City managers," she said softly, "come and go. The name means nothing."

"He had a daughter named Cindy. Cindy Wagner. Does that name ring a bell with you? Go back three or four years."

"It means nothing."

"What about you, Mr. Potter?"

Potter shook his head sympathetically. "Sorry. But I've been Mary Louise's secretary for only two years now."

Cyrus looked at Hillman. Perhaps she had forgotten. How many young people had passed through her hands and through her drink-sodden brain? Perhaps she had a better memory drunk than sober. When sober her mind might block out unpleasantness.

"Cindy Wagner went to Middleville High School," Cyrus resumed. "She was part of your drug set." Her eyes registered no change; she watched him as a cat watches a

269

large dog — with hate and wariness. "Her father was city manager. Lieutenant Jarvis of the Middleville Police Department used to bail her out of trouble, really trying to protect her father's name. Does the name Jarvis mean anything to you?"

"The Jarvises," she said scornfully, "are Middleville's poor white trash. They traditionally become either public wards or policemen."

"What about Louis Wagner?" Potter asked.

"We're certain he's here in Harbour Woods and that he has been responsible for the three murders that have recently taken place. Wagner, I believe, is killing everyone who, he feels, has hurt his daughter. You're one, he believes. Indeed, your coming here was what tipped him over the edge and brought him here."

For a second he thought his words had pierced the imperious curtain and stirred the hard, poetic heart behind it. But her lips curled scornfully.

"As far as I'm concerned the names Louis Wagner and Cindy Wagner mean nothing to me." She hesitated. Something had stirred inside her. "Where is this girl I was supposed to have corrupted right now?"

"She died of a drug overdose in Harbour Woods last January."

Suddenly the fortress was breached. Pain appeared behind the ramparts. Hillman swayed for a moment. Philip Potter III went to her side.

"You do remember her, don't you?" Cyrus asked softly.

"No," she said harshly. "I grieve for the young and self-destructive. To be young is to be self-destructive. I am returning to the table, Philip."

She swept from the room.

"She knew her," Cyrus said to him.

"Yes, I believe she did." Potter turned to Cyrus. "Is her life truly in danger?"

270

"Very much so. We'll continue to protect her but it would be safer for everyone if she permitted the dean to read her speech and you and she left town. Do you think you can talk her into it?"

"No," Potter said. "I don't believe I can. When Mary Louise starts quoting her family fighting Indians, then I know her back is up. She can be very stubborn. And she *would* rip up that check. No, I suspect the only way you can get her not to deliver the speech is to reject the check. Would the university do that?"

"I don't know. Whelan went back there to confer."

"And isn't it true, Mr. Wilson, that if what you say is so, the killer will pursue her elsewhere — even in Connecticut?"

"I hope he'll be apprehended by then."

"But if he isn't. Then we do have to live with this thing, don't we?"

Cyrus was silent.

Potter smiled. "Better to take the three million and let her deliver her speech. You need the money and she needs the acclaim." Potter interrupted himself to put his finger to his lips.

From the dining room they heard the triumphant voice of Mary Louise Hillman.

"I am delighted that my speech will go on as scheduled. Hillmans never back down and I'm gratified that this great university will not be intimidated."

"So there," Potter said. "We'll all have to look after her carefully."

Cyrus nodded. Potter returned to the dining room. Cyrus went to find a telephone. The trap at City Hall tomorrow morning was now all important.

He phoned Guiterrez to tell him what happened and to make sure the arrangements for the Ricky Andrews look-alike were going through.

35

The alarm went off at seven.

Eileen groaned. Cyrus pushed in the knob and lay there staring at the ceiling.

"What time is it?" she said.

"Seven."

"So early?"

"John Agate's got to go to work." He looked at her. Her hair had fallen over her eyes. "Go back to sleep."

"You kept better hours when you taught English," she murmured into her pillow.

He leaned over and kissed her. "I love you."

She sighed and turned away from him. He pulled the covers up over her and got out of bed and padded into the bathroom. A ghastly face confronted him in the mirror. The result of a long night. They'd talked, made love, watched the eleven o'clock news on Channel 8, and heard the Ricky Andrews news item. At midnight they heard the item on all three Detroit channels. It was a hot news item, as he knew it would be. They made love again. After which she presented him with a batch of compositions left in his box by his teaching assistant, plus some papers and messages from students in his Whitman-Dickinson class, plus minutes of last week's department meeting about changing the requirements for the new doctor of arts degree. And then they made love again.

At about 1 A.M. Cyrus remembered the Cretan maze game and gave it to her. They sent out for pizza, played the game for another hour. It was complicated, the trip through darkness to sunlight. Eileen got through it before he did. In fact, he was still in darkness when he fell asleep around four.

*

The closer Cyrus got to City Hall, the more tension he felt in the air. Or was the tension just in him, he wondered.

To the unobservant eye nothing was changed. People were pulling up to the drive-in window on the north side of City Hall to pay their utility bills; the usual pick-up trucks and station wagons were parked as people went in and out of the building on their civic business.

But the police station entrance on the south side of the building was unnaturally quiet.

A man in workingman's clothes was leaning against the building reading a *Detroit Free Press.* He glanced at Cyrus and then looked back at his paper. He was a slow reader.

Across U.S. Bus. 23, on the flat roof of a dry cleaners, two men were examining an air-conditioning unit. They wore heavy parkas to protect them from the bite of the wind. Quite a cover, Cyrus thought.

It was a cold and sunny fall morning. The buildings cast sharp, dark shadows.

Kitty-corner from the police station was the Howell Brothers Building, a modern office building housing a stockbroker, law firms, an art deco–looking insurance agency, a travel agency. Plus the usual barber shop, gift shop, smoke shop, etc.

On its roof, too, were workingmen. They were examining an exhaust unit. Like the other workingmen he'd seen, they had no tools. Their proper tools, rifles, would be lying just out of sight below the roof parapet.

City Hall was ringed by the department's best marksmen.

Across the side street was the main fire station. In its red brick arches, several firemen loitered, all facing City Hall. All watching him.

In the parking lot, facing U.S. Bus. 23, was a white van. Inside it, a man was nibbling a sandwich.

On the sidewalk a man and woman strolled, her arm in his. They were walking around the City Hall. Around and around.

Cyrus felt a blast of warm air as he entered the building. There were cops all over the lobby. The whole police force, he guessed, was split between here and Stockton Auditorium.

Guiterrez, talking into his walky-talky, motioned with his free hand for Cyrus to come in and sit down.

"Let's get it straight," Guiterrez was saying into the instrument, "cleaners, Howell Brothers, fire, city — Tink's on the roof over my head. He's got the bullhorn. *He* talks. No one shoots unless Tink or I tell you to shoot. Tink's going to talk to the guy first. If he opens up, then we let him have it. But Tink talks first. Got it?"

"Roger," a series of voices answered through the static.

Guiterrez clicked off the speaker. "Well," he said with a shrug, "I've told 'em. Now let's hope the bastards follow orders and let's hope we can talk to the nut."

Let's hope the nut shows up, Cyrus thought.

"What about security in this building, John? Right here in the police station?"

"You got Jack Ruby on the brain, don't you?" Guiterrez smiled a ghostly smile. "I do too. Well, it's tighter'n a nun's ass. We checked out every room, every closet, we turned over trash cans. We been through the boiler, the subbasement, the basement, the elevator shafts, the equipment cages, broom closets, toilets. There's no way he's in here. It's out there he'll be. Take a look."

He showed Cyrus a rough map of the positions of all his sharpshooters. They included a position Cyrus hadn't spotted, above them on a second-floor terrace.

"We got field of fire in every direction. What's going to happen is this. Hal Layne and Johnny Powers — he's the look-alike from Narcotics — get out of the car here and walk this way through the parking lot. I got a man in the white van. They got to go by him. They walk slowly, and this gives Wagner time to see them. But he's got to show himself to do anything. If he's as nuts as you say, he will. He might jump out of a car and start shooting. If he does, Powers and Layne can duck behind this retaining wall right here. If he don't drop the gun when Tink hollers at him through the bullhorn, we — "

Guiterrez made the pull-trigger gesture with his right index finger.

"Layne is playing Andrews's lawyer. He's armed. So is Powers, of course."

"Did any TV people show up?"

"All of them. I put their vans in the garage downstairs. They're pooling their cameras. One camera's up on the terrace behind a bush. The other two are in the hall for when we book Wagner."

"Do the TV people suspect anything?"

"No. You did a great job. They think it's on the up-and-up. And it will be when we bag the bastard. They see it getting onto the network. Everyone's up for this, Prof."

A figure in motion caught Cyrus's eye. An athletic looking young woman in a yellow running suit came jogging by on the sidewalk. He saw a bulge around her waist. Not all the running in the world would remove that bulge, Cyrus thought.

"Sandy Mays. Vice Squad. She's a crack shot. She's gonna come running back the other side."

Guiterrez then informed Cyrus that he had put a patrolman with each TV crew. "All we need is for one of them guys to get hurt. By the way, Prof, you look like hell."

"I feel fine. What time do you have?"

"Nine-fifteen."

Cyrus checked his watch. "What time are Layne and the decoy due in?"

"Nine thirty on the button."

Cyrus looked out the window. Somewhere out there could be the quiet man. Blending in, invisible, a man who passed everywhere, like Walt Whitman's grass. *I bequeath myself to the dirt to grow from the grass I love, If you want me again look for me under your boot-soles.*

Cyrus's mind flashed across town to Stockton Auditorium and its five thousand seats. They would be filled for the honors convocation. Students, friends, parents, brothers, sisters, had travelled from small towns and large to listen to the poet Mary Louise Hillman and see their loved ones honored.

Hillman would be there now, Cyrus thought, having her academic robes checked out, smoothed over, in one of those basement rehearsal rooms. Tom Whelan would be hovering over her. Archie Fields would be there too, *his* speech tucked away in a pocket. And about all of them would be every security person the university could muster. Detectives and patrolmen in plainclothes would be throughout the auditorium and outside at every entrance and exit.

It was a war being waged on two fronts. And the hope was that the trap at City Hall would end it.

Guiterrez was called on his walky-talky. A VW had just double-parked outside the Howell Building.

"Keep an eye on it. If it's there another two minutes have Dunn and Cassidy check it out. If it's Wagner, grab him."

Nine-twenty-six by his watch and by the clock in the communications room across the hall.

The chief came into the office. He looked at Guiterrez and then at his nephew.

"You look awful, Cyrus."

"I'm okay."

"Layne and Powers are on their way, John," the chief said.

"Good," Guiterrez said.

He spoke into the walky-talky and heard something back.

"They're coming around the block now."

The three of them stood by the window. Swinging out of the traffic was a sharp, red Alfa-Romeo. It bounced brazenly into the parking lot.

Guiterrez grinned at Cyrus. "Nice touch, huh?"

"Yes."

"We had to hot-wire it." He barked into the walky-talky. "Our pigeons have come into the coop. What's on the VW?"

"It's moving now, John. It was a woman."

"Shit."

Out of the Alfa emerged two men. One was Hal Layne, carrying a lawyerly looking briefcase.

The other was the look-alike from Narcotics. Thin, wiry, he wore a tight-fitting tan raincoat and a wide-brimmed Borsalino hat.

"Don't he ever look like a pimp," Guiterrez said. "Cleaners, you got anything?"

"No."

"Howell roof?"

"Nothing, John. Just traffic."

"Fire station?"

277

"Nada."

"Tink?"

"Not a fucking thing, John. Wait. Hold it."

Cyrus and Guiterrez peered out the window. As Layne and Powers were making their way slowly toward the police department entrance, a short, older woman pushing a cart of groceries came toward them through the parking lot. She came alongside them.

"Watch the woman," Guiterrez barked into the walky-talky.

"Hal, be careful," Guiterrez added softly.

Layne saw the possible danger. His briefcase was in his left hand. His right hand was raised at belt level where his .32 revolver would be.

"She's too small," Cyrus said quietly. "Wagner can't be that small."

The woman was talking to herself. Her cart hit a crack in the parking lot. A bundle from the top wobbled and pitched out of the basket onto the ground.

"Watch her!" Guiterrez barked.

The woman bent to pick up her bundle.

Layne watched her. So did Powers. She put her bundle back in the basket and, still talking to herself, pushed the basket out of the lot and onto the sidewalk and proceeded east toward the campus section of town.

Layne and Powers continued walking. Seconds later they were inside city hall. Cyrus watched them enter on the closed-circuit TV hook-up.

Outside, guns in the doorways of the Fire Department and on the roofs of buildings were lowered.

And with the ease of tension came the inevitable disappointment. Guiterrez clicked off the walky-talky. "The bastard didn't show."

On the TV screen, Cyrus watched Layne and Powers walk by a cluster of policemen. The elaborate trap had failed.

"I'll explain to the TV people," the chief said gently. "I'll tell them it would have been a great story if it had worked. Don't worry about them, Cyrus."

"Nice acting," Guiterrez said to Layne and Powers as they came into the office.

"Nothing?" Layne asked.

"Nothing."

And then the last lines from Whitman's *Song of Myself* ran through Cyrus's head:

> *Failing to fetch me at first keep encouraged,*
> *Missing me one place search another*
> *I stop somewhere waiting for you.*

"We better get up to Stockton Auditorium, John," Cyrus said. "Our man has got a head start on us."

"Let's hope he'll be there," Guiterrez said.

Cyrus looked at him for a moment. "He'll be there," he said.

36

And he was. Huddled in semidarkness in a small space in the middle of a forest of uneven organ pipes, reading the journal by a small, naked light bulb hanging overhead. It was a perfect hiding place.

He had found his hiding place yesterday afternoon. He was taking no chances from now on. The unplanned death of the professor weighed on his mind. He was not used to making errors. Everyone always said that Lou Wagner did not make mistakes. But he had erred grievously with the death of the professor. And for that he owed God another debt.

There would be no slip-up this time. Wearing his green parka, he had left his rooming house about four o'clock. He stopped at a deli where he bought a sandwich and an apple. He would need food for the long night's vigil in Stockton Auditorium.

He put the sandwich and apple in one of the deep pockets with the book. In the other pocket was the gun with the silencer.

On his belt he wore a ring of keys. He would pass as a maintenance person.

That afternoon a chill wind was blowing. Not too many people were on the streets. But it was, as he guessed, busy around the auditorium. They were getting ready for the next day's program. A service truck was pulled up to the loading dock. Chairs were being unloaded. Next to the truck a florist's van was parked with its rear doors swung open.

He arrived at the loading dock just as four chairs were lowered over the side. He reached for them.

"They go on the cart," the man in the truck said.

He carried the chairs inside the building and stacked them on a cart.

"How's it going?" another workman asked him.

"Okay. And you?"

"Can't complain."

The fraternity of workingmen.

The chairs bumped up against the pistol in his pocket. A line from Revelations echoed in his mind.

For I will send unto thee a rod of iron . . .

A choir rehearsal was beginning and choir members in street clothes rubbed elbows with custodians and men bringing platforms up from the basement.

A workingman glanced at his ring of keys and asked him to help guide the cart onto the stage.

And so he crossed a beautiful golden stage. Thousands of blue seats ranging up to the second balcony stared mutely at him.

While the other man was unloading the chairs, he slipped off, walking through a door at the rear of the stage. It led into a narrow passageway. Off the passageway were rooms: rehearsal rooms, janitors' rooms, rest rooms, storage rooms. Might he find Mary Louise Hillman alone in one of these rooms tomorrow? The odds were against it.

And would it not be better to have her perish in the

limelight she craved and gloried in and had sacrificed so many innocent people to?

First, he needed a place to hide.

To his left was a stairway to the basement. He went down it and found himself in another busy area, a long, low-ceilinged gun-metal-gray room. There were people milling about everywhere he looked. Three men were wrestling a large lectern onto a platform lift that would take it directly up to the stage.

Beyond them was a caged area. In it a large grand piano, a small one, and many music stands. There was too much light there.

There were several rooms leading off from the open area. Rehearsal rooms, they appeared to be.

They also were too open.

He scoured the basement and subbasement floors, looking into the space below the stage. But it was filled with metal struts. Through the struts he could see the aisles and the seats.

Be watchful, and strengthen the things which remain that are ready to die.

It was prophetic how the two books flowed together. The Book of Revelations, which he knew by heart. The journal book which he read and reread and which guided his every thought and action.Past the choir members jabbering away nervously, past workmen, attendants, he moved, his keys jingling authoritatively. He went back up the stone steps.

Near the loading dock was a small stairway leading to a closed door. As he came up the steps, the door opened and a young man in shirt-sleeves emerged carrying a microphone and cable.

The young man eyed the ring of keys on his belt.

"You got a key to the loft? I'm ready to hang this mike now."

He smiled and shook his head.

The young radio engineer — for that was what he must surely be — frowned and walked impatiently past him to a supervisor in a hard hat leaning against a wall drinking coffee.

"Frank, I need the loft door opened."

"Sure thing, Stu," the supervisor said.

Coffee in one hand, the supervisor mounted the steps and unlocked the door. The young man immediately began to climb a steep ladder and soon disappeared from sight.

The supervisor closed the door and walked back to the loading dock. There he joined another man also drinking coffee.

When Wagner was certain the supervisors' attention was on a truck pulling up outside, he walked up the half-flight of steps to the room the young man had just left. It was a radio booth. Empty now. A porthole window looked down onto the golden stage. A beautiful view, but the booth would be occupied, and they would check on it. There was expensive equipment here.

As he started to leave he saw a fiberboard box under a table. It was filled with cables. A microphone lay on top of them.

To him that overcometh will I give to eat of the hidden manna.

He picked the microphone out of the box of cables. Holding the microphone in front of him he left the room. Below him the two supervisors were still drinking coffee, talking, their backs to him.

"Sorry," he called from the doorway of the booth, "Stu forgot to take this mike up there. Could you open that door again?"

"You radio guys," the supervisor grumbled, "can't you ever make up your minds ahead of time?"

Grumbling, the supervisor unlocked the loft door.

Grunting "Thanks, Frank," microphone in hand, Louis Wagner climbed a steep iron ladder into darkness.

*

He waited till his eyes grew accustomed to the dark. There was a skylight over the gray-green glass dome.

The roof of the sky was there. Looking up, he saw he was close to heaven.

Behold, he cometh with clouds; and every eye shall see him, And they also which pierced him: and all kindreds of the earth shall wail because of him.

Above him, the radio engineer was crawling up a horizontal metal ladder, a kind of catwalk, over the gray-green glass dome. He held a microphone and cable in one hand.

Louis Wagner climbed over a wood rail and walked over a plaster ceiling — the top of the rooms below — and melted into the shadows where the ceiling met the rough, unfinished outside wall of the auditorium.

He crouched there and waited.

The radio engineer had reached his destination. He lay on his belly, concentrating on lowering the microphone to the correct point above the stage.

He adjusted it, and then, finally satisfied, he crawled back down the catwalk across the dome glass and onto the plaster surface, and finally onto the wood-planked crosswalk. There he wiped his hands off on a rag. Then came walking back, walking within ten feet of where Louis Wagner crouched in the darkness.

The engineer backed down the ladder to the outside door.

The door opened and closed.

Louis Wagner waited.

And unto me was given a reed like a rod / And the angel stood saying, "Rise, and measure the temple . . ."

He was about to rise when a thunderous noise rent the air, almost knocking him down.

284

Panic rose inside him. His body began to shake. But then, slowly, he understood what was happening.

Someone had begun playing the organ. And the organ loft, below him, was filling the huge attic of the building with sound.

And as the voice of a great thunder: So I heard the voice of harpers harping with their harps.

He almost wept.

He felt uplifted. God was with him. God was watching over him.

He sat down and closed his eyes. He listened to the sounds of the heavenly instrument. He knew nothing of music. As a child his family had been too poor to give him such luxuries as music lessons. But little Cindy had been given piano lessons. And dancing lessons. There had been so much talent and sensitivity in his daughter. Such beauty and innocence.

His fists clenched and unclenched. He felt the weight of the journal in his pocket.

"We will be avenged, my darling. We will be avenged."

He lay back and let the music flow over him. Its rising notes built a sanctuary around him. No one and nothing could harm him until his mission was complete.

How long he lay there and listened he could not tell. He lost all sense of time. He dozed, he listened, and dozed. When he woke, the building was quiet.

He sat up refreshed, clear in mind about his next steps.

From some place in this area he would destroy the fiend Mary Louise Hillman. And he must also find a route of escape. For there were still two more who must die.

He climbed back over the wood rail. Looking down through a plaster grill he saw the blue seats of the auditorium. Through the grillwork to his left, he could see part of the stage. Flowers were in place. The choir stands were up. The seats for the dignitaries were set up. He could just see the edge of Mary Louise Hillman's lectern.

He glanced up at the glass dome. And the dome of heaven, in which the night sky now gleamed: stars, wisps of clouds drifting by, beckoned to him. The path of escape leads that way.

He climbed the ladder that led to the catwalk and then crawled, rung by rung as the radio engineer had, over the solid plaster section of the ceiling and then over what looked like a fragile film of glass that composed the dome.

With the stars twinkling down on him, he was a figure crawling between heaven and earth.

I am the Alpha and the Omega, the beginning and the ending.

He reached the small opening down through which the cable and microphone dangled. He peered down.

It was almost straight down to the lectern from here. A difficult shot.

He crawled on, over the crest of the dome, and now he was moving slowly down the other side. There were no openings there. Soon he reached solid ceiling again.

Down a catwalk, down a ladder, and up a wood-planked crosswalk, the twin of the one on the other side. But this one led to a solid door.

He opened it cautiously and found himself looking into a lobby. The lobby of the second balcony. Signs on the walls. Aisle sections. To his right a staircase and fire escape; to his left another staircase and fire escape.

He had literally crawled over the top of the auditorium.

This would be his path of flight when the deed was done. How all things worked toward an end. He was being looked after. Not only by God, but by Cindy. He was in Their hands.

Back on the other side of the dome he looked down at the myriad organ pipes reflecting in the light of the night sky. It was like staring into the bottom of a shallow ocean, a sea of trees. It was suddenly inviting.

He climbed down and entered the organ loft. And here he had truly entered another world, a dark and eerie world of tunnels created by the towering pipes. He felt his way through this maze, his feet moving slowly, tentatively, through an arid landscape. The dust of years had accumulated here.

He was sliding, probing, backing up, and moving forward in the dark. His hands ahead of him, feeling his way down one passage after another. Once a series of pipes blocked his way like soldiers, forcing him to back out and try another path. He moved up from one level to another and then down again, boxes and boards all of a jumble, forming makeshift steps.

But each minute he could see more easily. Each minute the darkness revealed its secrets.

And then, somewhere in a clearing in the middle of the forest, he saw a shelter for the night. A flat bench, a work bench, the length of his body, illuminated from above by a single little bulb.

He would remember this place. He would come back here.

He kept moving, a hunter in the forest, moving to keep an appointment with his quarry.

The pipes began to thin out. He saw the edge of the forest. And then through the grill he saw the blue seats of the auditorium. And he understood he had just circled the loft.

He took two steps forward and then froze.

He heard footsteps nearby.

He held his breath and looked down. A few feet below him a man was walking across the stage, shining a flashlight in front of him. It was a security guard. The flashlight shone on the lectern . . . and then moved on.

I know thy works and where thou dwellest / Even where Satan's seat is.

God had just told him where he should stand in order to smite Hillman.

At this spot he was no more than twenty-five feet above and behind where she would speak in the morning. From here it would be impossible for him to miss.

He waited patiently until the guard left the stage. Then, quietly, he worked his way back through the maze until he saw the workbench area again. He had to climb a box to get to it. But once there he saw he was beautifully hidden.

Now he could rest until the trumpets blew and Mary Louise Hillman stood before him on Judgment Morn.

He removed the pistol, the book, the sandwich and the apple from his pockets, and ate the sandwich and the apple. Then he folded the parka into a pillow and lay down.

He held the book up and read by the light of the single bulb:

Saturday, and I'm so depressed. What do I want from life? What do I want from people, what do I want from myself? Why must I always be wanting? What is wrong with me? Someone, please help me. Daddy, please help me. Don't turn me down again. I'm going to call you tomorrow. Please let me come home to you. I promise I won't bring shame on us anymore.

Written on the eve of her twenty-first birthday — the day before she died.

With trembling fingers he put his daughter's diary down. He had marked that passage. Read and reread it a hundred times. How could he have done that to her? Oh, what debts he owed God.

He closed his eyes. He could almost hear again the great organ playing and the heavenly hosts singing before God's fires that drove the serpents into the bottomless pits, before the seals were broken and the vials poured and the great shaking of hell began. They would all be there together then: Browne, Lassiter, Hillman, Andrews, and himself. All sinners. Destroyers of a precious child.

I am the Alpha and the Omega, the beginning and the end / The living and the dead / And the sea gave up the dead / And death and hell delivered up its dead / And they were judged every man according to their works.

Oh, my darling, my darling, darling, darling child . . .

Finally his tortured mind could stand it no more. It sank into blackness and Louis Wagner, huddled in the dense forest of organ pipes, found shelter for his soul as well as for his body.

He slept.

37

As the carillon bells played the Mid-East University alma mater, a long line of students, parents, friends, and townspeople moved slowly over the cold sunlit steps of Stockton Auditorium.

"How come only one door works?"

"Don't they know it's freezing out here?"

"Suppose it was snowing."

"They say it's supposed to snow tomorrow."

"We'll probably still be here."

"What are all the security people here for?"

"Maybe someone threatened to hijack the auditorium."

Cyrus and Guiterrez found Rollie Mazur at the Congress Street stage door. In his hard-to-understand gravelly voice, Mazur told them that his people had gone over the auditorium with a fine comb. "Balconies," rasped the voice box, "backstage . . . basement. If . . . the son of a bitch . . . is . . . in there . . . he's invisible."

"He hasn't ever had a problem going anywhere, except City Hall," Cyrus said. "Hello, Dean."

Dean Archie Fields, resplendent in his Harvard crimson

robes, paused by them on his way in. "I take it our speaker is all right, Cyrus."

Cyrus nodded.

"Good," the dean said. "Let's hope things stay that way. I still have a speech tucked away. Though I don't fancy delivering it. Excuse me, I have some deanly duties to perform."

He brushed by them.

"Those robes," Cyrus said. He turned to Mazur. "Have your people been checking who's inside those robes?"

"That's right," Guiterrez said. "The son of a bitch sneaked his way into the stadium dressed as security. That would be a natural cover for him here."

Mazur shook his head violently. "We're checking them . . . if . . . they . . . come dressed as . . . as . . . as pumpkins," he got out.

The faculty was gathering in the backstage area. The choir members were in simple black robes, checking scores with one another.

"Where is she?" Cyrus asked Mazur.

"Downstairs . . . room . . . two . . . fin-finishing breakfast . . . "

The plan had been to get Hillman out of Brewster House early and secure in one of the basement rehearsal rooms in case the trap at City Hall failed. Well, Cyrus thought ironically, the plan was working beautifully.

In front of room two, they found two policemen standing guard.

"Nothing, Lieutenant," one said to Guiterrez. "Only the waiters, her boyfriend, and Mr. Whelan are in there. We checked out the waiters. They're clean."

Cyrus knocked and they went inside a small, green, windowless room. Seated at an elaborately laid breakfast table with the university's finest silver service gleaming in an overhead light were Hillman and Philip Potter III. Two young waiters were clearing; Tom Whelan stood in the background looking tight-lipped and pale.

"Well," Hillman said to Cyrus, "have you caught your lunatic yet?"

"No, ma'am."

"Cy, I've told Miss Hillman that Dean Fields is still prepared to read her speech, or deliver one of his own."

"And I've told you no dice," Hillman snapped. "I will not be intimidated. I resent being handled like some packaged goods. I will deliver this goddam honors speech and get out of this town once and for all."

Philip Potter patted his mouth with a linen napkin. "Now, now, Mary Louise," he said soothingly. "These gentlemen are looking out for your welfare." Potter smiled brightly at Cyrus. "I've never seen so many policemen in my life. I'm sure your killer is not around."

Don't you wish it, Cyrus thought.

"Now I'd like some time to myself, gentlemen," Mary Louise Hillman said. "I hope *that* is not too much to ask. That includes you, Phil."

"Of course, Mary Louise." Potter folded his napkin and rose. Hillman stood too. She was wearing a robe with a fancy blue hood. Cyrus didn't recognize the ancestry.

"We'll be right outside your door, Miss Hillman," Tom Whelan said, mustering a nervous smile.

"I've no doubt you will. You can leave the water here, waiter. Is there a toilet around here by the way?"

"There's one on this floor," Tom Whelan said.

"I'll have a policewoman accompany you," Guiterrez said.

"No, you won't," Hillman snapped, "I go to the can alone."

Outside, Whelan wiped his forehead with a handkerchief. "My God," he murmured. "Just let us get this thing over with."

Guiterrez grinned wolfishly. "A real bitch, Prof."

"Now, now, gentlemen," Philip Potter murmured, "Mary Louise has been under considerable pressure. I'm sure everything will be all right. I shall wait right here for her."

"I'll stay with you," Whelan said. He was not in academic garb. He would not be part of the convocation.

"I'm going to have a look around," Cyrus told Guiterrez. "Why don't you double-check the auditorium. I'll take this area."

Guiterrez nodded. "Okay. I got to make sure my people are in place anyway."

Everyone who had been involved in the trap at City Hall was now at Stockton Auditorium.

"How does she get up to the stage, Tom?" Cyrus asked.

"The stairs," Whelan replied. "Rollie's going to clear the basement. By then the choir will be on stage and the faculty lined up in their order of procession. Terry Cleland from the Engineering College is the marshall. He'll have them in order."

Right now, Cyrus thought, it was chaos, with faculty, choir members, maintenance people, security people all jumbled together. There were too many people for the backstage and basement areas.

He could be among us, anonymous. In a choir, in an academic robe . . . a maintenance man.

There was nothing for it but to check out places he knew must have been checked: lavatories, storage rooms, cages, an area below the stage that was criss-crossed with struts and pipes and curiously littered with old cartons containing light bulbs, paper towels, packages of soap, clamps, braces.

The low ceilings of this basement area were skeined by steam pipes. Too narrow for a man to hide in. There was nothing in the pit that contained the pump and shaft that lowered the platform lift from stage to basement.

He was looking for a mousy little man. A nondescript little man. A man who passes for everyman. And a man who doesn't belong here.

Everyone looked mousy, everyone looked nondescript, everyone looked like he belonged here.

Cyrus went up the steps from the basement to backstage. Guiterrez was talking with a beefy man in a hard hat. He wore an identification badge on a plaid shirt that said Frank Panetta, Building Services.

"I'm telling you, Lieutenant," Panetta said, "I know everyone here. There ain't anyone I don't know."

There were two doors on the stairs going up from the backstage area. Cyrus pointed to the nearest one.

"What's behind that?"

"This is Cy Wilson, representing university security," Guiterrez explained.

"Behind that one is a radio booth."

"And the other one. The top one?"

"That leads behind the stage to the organ loft and the catwalk."

"Catwalk to where?"

"It goes over the glass dome and ceiling and ends up in the second balcony. We use the catwalk to change light bulbs and the engineers hang their mikes down to the stage from there. But them doors are locked, Mister. No one gets in there I don't let them in."

"Where are the engineers?"

"They're in the booth."

"It's . . . small," Rollie Mazur, who had come up behind them, garbled. "No . . . place to hide . . . in there."

"Let's take a look anyway," Guiterrez said.

As they went up the steps Cyrus could see into the auditorium. The ground floor was filled. The first and second balconies were beginning to fill up. Mary Louise Hillman was a draw.

On stage the choir had moved into place. Soon the organist would play the first notes of the alma mater, *Glory to Our University Fair.* Then the faculty, led by the marshall, the honored speaker, the president, and the deans of the various colleges would slowly march in to take their seats on the immense stage.

Panetta turned the key in the lock of the radio booth. "Coming in," he called through the door.

A small room, a porthole view of stage and audience. Seated at a console, his back to them, a young engineer was checking dials.

"Sorry, Stu." Panetta said, "These people are from security and they want to check out the booth."

"Well, they should've checked earlier," the engineer grumbled, turning on a tape.

"Why?" Cyrus asked.

The young engineer swivelled and fixed on them an irritated look. "Because some bastard ripped off my RE-15 mike. That's a four-hundred-dollar microphone."

He glared at them.

"Was that the mike you hung yesterday?" Panetta asked, puzzled.

"No, that was the choir mike. This was the speaker's mike. It ties into the P.A. system. It was down here in a box. And now it's gone. I had to put a cheap mike on the lectern."

"Which mike did your helper come and get?" Panetta asked.

"What helper?"

The organ began to play. Music flooded the little booth. "I got to go to work," the engineer said. He began adjusting dials, checking the tape recording.

Panetta said frantically, "He said you forgot to take a

mike up there. I opened the loft door for him. He had a mike with him."

The engineer spoke with his back to them. "I don't know what the hell you're talking about, Frank. I don't have a helper. You'll all have to get the hell out of here."

Outside, Cyrus grabbed Frank Panetta. "This helper, what did he look like?"

"Jesus, I don't know. There were lots of people here yesterday."

This from the guy who "knew everyone."

"Was he young? Old?"

"I've . . . got . . . a . . . pic . . . ture, Cyrus," Rollie Mazur garbled and handed Cyrus a copy of the print from Connecticut. It had been cropped. It wasn't a good picture. Louis Wagner, nondescript to start with, now looked fuzzy.

"Is that him?" Cyrus showed the picture under Panetta's nose.

"Jesus, I don't know. It could be him. It's hard to tell."

"Was this guy wearing glasses?"

"Glasses. Maybe. Yeah. He was. Those half-ones. That's what made me think he was an engineer. Our people don't wear — "

"He's in," Cyrus said to Guiterrez. "He's been here since yesterday. No wonder the trap at City Hall failed."

"Get that door open fast, Mac," Guiterrez snarled at Panetta.

"Yes, sir." Panetta ran up the steps.

"Rollie," said Cyrus urgently, "get Tom Whelan to call this convocation off immediately. And remove Hillman from the stage. Right away."

Below them two long lines of robed figures were moving slowly onto the stage as the choir sang in full voice. Mary Louise Hillman and the president came in behind the marshall. She was laughing, and saying something, as they moved out of Cyrus's view and onto the stage.

Rollie Mazur ran down the steps.

Panetta stepped aside as the loft door swung open. A narrow steel ladder confronted them. Guiterrez went up it first. Cyrus was right behind him. They were both stunned by the noise. The sound of the organ was deafening. Their eyes blinked in the darkness. Instinctively they both looked up toward the glass dome, and above it the skylight filled with the morning sunlight.

They could see where a microphone had been hung.

"I'm going up there," Guiterrez shouted at him over the music. "You check the loft."

Guiterrez jumped over a low rail. Climbed a second, shorter ladder, and ran along a planked walkway toward the catwalk.

Cyrus looked down into the organ loft. A large forest of dark, uneven pipes from which the university hymn swelled.

*

In the wings of the stage of Stockton Auditorium, Rollie Mazur cornered Tom Whelan.

"You've . . . got to . . . stop it."

"How can I?" Whelan said, shaken. "It's started."

"Talk to the marsh . . . all. Get him to . . . move her . . . off the stage."

"Rollie, I'm not prepared to do that."

And in truth Whelan looked ill prepared to do anything. He stood there stiffly. It had all been too much for the emotionally fragile Vice President for University Relations. Later someone would connect his paralysis with the fact that he was dressed in an ordinary business suit while everyone on stage was in academic regalia. He was a creature who all his life had sought to blend in.

Rollie Mazur had no such fears. He ran out onto the stage in full view of five thousand people. The choir was finishing the alma mater and the president of the university was preparing to introduce the honored speaker. Rollie Mazur buttonholed Professor Terry Cleland, the marshall of the convocation.

Their conversation was later recalled by several nearby faculty members.

"You've got . . . to . . . to get every . . . one off . . . stage," Mazur garbled through his mechanical voice box.

Professor Cleland, a distinguished metallurgist, regarded the little white-haired man with amazement.

"I cannot understand a word you're saying," he said. "Nor do I know who you are or how you got on this stage. However, sir, I can assure you that unless you leave immediately, I shall have you arrested."

The commotion alongside him did not escape the president's notice. He flashed a look of annoyance at them, but then as the organ sounds died, he rose to walk to the lectern.

Rollie Mazur gave up on Cleland and moved past the president's now empty seat and crouched down next to Mary Louise Hillman.

"Miss Hillman," he rasped, "he's . . . here. You . . . must . . . leave the stage."

Mary Louise Hillman looked down at Mazur with contempt. "I told you people that I will not be intimidated. And I will not!"

" . . . and so it is with great pleasure that I present to this honors convocation a distinguished person of letters, a poet, literary influence, and a friend to higher education all over this land — Mary Louise Hillman."

The applause rolled up from the audience.

Hillman grinned. Her eyes were shining.

"Miss Hillman," Mazur rasped, "you've got to—"

It was as far as he was able to get. Two strong hands fell on his shoulders. Two young faculty members, acting under Professor Cleland's direction, pulled Rollie Mazur to his feet and with swift dispatch ushered him off the stage.

Mary Louise Hillman, eyes shining, advanced to the lectern.

38

Cyrus looked into the dark maze of organ pipes. To the right was a grill of false pipes that looked out onto the auditorium. Looking at the bottom of the grill he could see onto the stage. Rollie Mazur was onstage, talking to Mary Louise Hillman.

Far above Cyrus, Guiterrez, pistol in hand, was moving up the crosswalk toward the catwalk over the green dome.

Cyrus entered the maze.

The music stopped. The ensuing silence was almost as deafening as the great sound of the organ. He halted. Had he heard something ahead of him? He strained to see into the darkness there. A line from Milton: darkness visible. But it was only visible in poetry. All he could make out so far were long, cylindrical organ pipes. He sensed they were still quivering from the music.

Somewhere inside this huge attic of the auditorium Louis Wagner, meek, mild, likeable, anonymous, was waiting. Waiting to kill.

And somehow, Cyrus thought, I've got to stop him.

He was beginning to see more in the darkness. A small light bulb was burning somewhere deep in the forest of pipes. There were little pipes and long ones, thin ones and fat ones, and a sort of path that wended its way through them all.

Cyrus walked forward slowly. As he did, the voice of the president of Mid-East University came clearly between the pipes, loud and clear.

He was introducing Mary Louise Hillman.

My God! Hadn't they got her off the stage yet? Were they going through with this?

He bumped into a metal pipe. The boards below his feet shook. He followed it to the left.

Below him he saw Mary Louise Hillman walk proudly toward the lectern, bearing before her, like a cupbearer, her speech bound in blue.

Cyrus wanted to shout "Stop her! Get her out!"

But the words wouldn't come. He plunged into the darkness, oblivious now to any noise he might be making.

"Mr. President," rang out Hillman's voice, "members of this great faculty, distinguished guests and, above all . . . "

Cyrus stopped. There was something ahead of him. Movement. A figure leaning forward against the false pipes, looking down between them. A gun with a silencer attached, resting between the pipes.

" . . . you students who have come here today to be honored for your achievements," Hillman went on.

"Don't!" Cyrus whispered.

A man's head turned. And finally Cyrus was face-to-face with Louis Wagner. A man he had been hunting for what felt like a long, long time. A man whose face and soul he knew by heart.

In the half-darkness Cyrus saw the mild face look puzzled, bewildered at this interruption. The gun still pointed at Hillman's back.

"Mr. Wagner," said Cyrus, trying to make his voice

calm and reasonable, his eyes reassuring as they locked on Wagner's puzzled look. "Put down your gun, sir."

"I cannot tell you," spoke Hillman, "what a great pleasure it is for me to be here to address you, not as a statesman but as a poet . . . "

"It's all over now, Mr. Wagner. Everything is going to be all right now."

Louis Wagner shook his head. "I'm afraid it's not over, sir," he said as quietly and politely as Cyrus had spoken, as though neither of them wished to disturb the speaker on the stage.

Wagner kept his finger on the trigger. Any sudden movement by Cyrus would be dangerous. The distance between them was too great.

"Poets," Hillman's voice echoed grandly in the loft, "are not often present at state occasions. In fact, they influence only after they are dead . . . "

"You see," Louis Wagner said quietly, "two more people must die for her."

Cyrus, cautiously, took a step forward, his eyes fixed on Wagner's. There were only ten feet separating them. If he kept conversing with the man, kept eye contact, and kept inching forward, in just a few seconds he could jump him.

"Two more?" Cyrus repeated.

"Oh, yes. The Satan pimp Ricky Andrews and then . . . myself. I am as guilty as the others."

"A very great writer," Hillman said, "wrote that in our lives politicians can do with our bodies what they will, but in death . . . "

"I've been to Middleville and Stoneville looking for you, Mr. Wagner."

And took another step forward.

" . . . we poets change places with the politicians. In death they die . . . "

"Everywhere they think very highly of you, sir. And they are all sorry about what happened to Cindy."

Louis Wagner's mouth moved. The words emerged apologetically.

"Yes, but it has been ordained that those who destroyed my daughter must also die. And now it is *her* turn."

"But in our death," Hillman rang out triumphantly, "we truly live!"

Cyrus jumped. But the deadly pfft of the gun beat him. Cyrus crashed into the man, sending him into the pipes. Cyrus reached for him but tripped over a loose board and then fell sideways between two series of metal pipes.

Below it was pandemonium. People running toward the lectern and the body that had fallen onto the stage floor. Gasps of shock and horror from the people in the seats.

Cyrus stood up and felt a hot blast next to his right ear. For a second he thought Wagner had shot at him, but then he realized it was Guiterrez running toward them, firing into the organ pipes ahead of him.

"Don't shoot!" Cyrus yelled, and then he started running down the passageway after Wagner.

Guiterrez's shot had reverberated throughout the huge hall. As he ran, Cyrus glimpsed hundreds of terrified faces looking up from the stage and the audience.

Another shot sped over his head.

"For Christ's sake, we can take him alive. He's not going to shoot at us."

He had his chance with me and didn't take it, Cyrus thought, pounding down the passageway. Thank God, he's mad. A sane man would have killed me.

If there was an exit at the other end of this passageway, then Wagner would have to climb a ladder to get out. They could haul him down there.

But the passageway wasn't going straight through. It began to wind its way back, going to the rear of the loft, up a level, down a level, with loose boards creaking beneath his feet. At one point Cyrus found he'd run into a dead end. Somewhere behind him Guiterrez also banged his way out of a false passage.

Ahead he could hear Louis Wagner's running feet. Wagner had spent the night here. He would know the maze by heart.

Cyrus found the main passageway again and he ran, his shoulders sideswiping organ pipes, his head low in case Guiterrez began shooting again.

And then, through a thinning series of pipes, he saw Wagner climbing the ladder. The same ladder that had taken them all down into the loft. Above it was the cross-walk that led to the catwalk.

Cyrus almost tripped on another loose board and then suddenly he was through the loft and out in the open. Wagner, on the cross walk, was nearing the catwalk.

Guiterrez caught up with Cyrus and shoved him aside. He was going to get up the ladder first.

Above them Louis Wagner was crawling on the catwalk now. He had almost reached the area of the glass dome and in seconds he would be crawling through the sunlight from the skylight above the dome.

Guiterrez stopped and aimed his revolver. "Wagner," Guiterrez shouted, "you're an easy shot now. Don't move!"

Louis Wagner, crawling up the metal struts, paused, and looked back down at them.

"There is no reason to shoot me," he called back. "I have no quarrel with you. We are not enemies."

And then, as though sure of their response to his reasonableness, Louis Wagner calmly turned his back to them and continued crawling up the catwalk.

He was going to make his escape via the second balcony exit, Cyrus realized. A careful man. A planner.

"Hold your fire, John," Cyrus said. "He won't shoot at us. And I can catch him."

Without waiting for an answer from the detective, Cyrus

ran up the crosswalk and began climbing the metal struts over the plaster section of the dome, climbing toward the glass cover.

"No, Prof," Guiterrez yelled, "we're not taking any more chances. He's got a gun. Wagner, stop right now or I'll shoot."

Louis Wagner went on climbing.

Guiterrez shot him in the shoulder.

Wagner turned, surprised. He looked with shock at the blood spurting from his shoulder. Then he looked down at Cyrus climbing toward him.

"Why did he shoot me?"

"You'll be all right, Mr. Wagner. Just stay there and I'll take you down."

"But I mustn't be stopped now. I must be allowed to go on. Don't you see? I have no choice. It was ordained. I don't understand—"

And then, pistol in one hand, Louis Wagner pushed himself off the metal rung and, balancing himself precariously, he stood erect. The pistol in his hand fell and skittered sideways down the thin glass of the dome.

He stood there, tottering, blood pouring from his shoulder wound.

"For God's sake, man, get down," Cyrus implored.

Louis Wagner raised his arms to the skylight and to the heavens that shone through it.

"Father, my work is unfinished. Why do you forsake me like this?"

And then Louis Wagner lost his balance and cartwheeled off the catwalk, fell onto the dome glass, crashed through it, and plunged sixty feet to the golden stage below.

There were screams, gasps, shouts from the people below.

Cyrus crawled the rest of the way up the catwalk to the gaping hole in the dome glass and looked down.

Louis Wagner lay just a few feet from Mary Louise Hillman's body. Sunlight streamed through the hole in the glass and bathed victim and killer in light so bright it was hard to tell which was which.

The maze had finally been run — by all.

39

"... And I saw a star fall from heaven unto the earth. And to him was given the key of the bottomless pit ... "

It had finally begun to snow. After threatening for two days. The old man stood bareheaded in front of the grave. In his bare hands he held two books. One, the Bible he was reading from, the chapter: the Book of Revelations. The other book, held below the Bible, Cyrus had let him read last night.

" ... and I saw a new heaven and a new earth: for the first heaven and the first earth were passed away. And I saw the holy city, new Jerusalem, coming down from God out of heaven, prepared as a bride adorned for her husband ... "

The coffin was pine. Paid for by friends in Stoneville, Maryland. The old man had flown out from Stoneville at his own expense.

"Behold the tabernacle of God is with men, and he will dwell with them, and they shall be his people, and God himself shall be with them, and be their God. And God shall wipe away all tears from their eyes; and there shall be no more death, neither sorrow, nor crying, neither shall there be any more pain ... "

A fifth mourner had arrived. He stood at a nearby grave, smoking a cigarette. Cyrus and Guiterrez looked at each other.

That this one should be the survivor, their eyes said.

"And he said unto me: it is done. I am the Alpha and the Omega, the beginning and the end. I will give unto him that is athirst of the fountain of the water of life freely . . . "

The old man's hands were shaking.

"Why doesn't he stop?" Eileen whispered.

Cyrus squeezed her hand. He hadn't wanted her to come. But she had read the diary, Cindy Wagner's diary, that they had found on the body of Wagner. The girl's writing had stunned her.

The old man continued. "Seal not the sayings of the prophecy of this book: for the time is at hand. He that is unjust, let him be unjust still: and he which is filthy, let him be filthy still . . . "

Cyrus looked at Ricky Andrews. The smoke from his cigarette curled upward to caress the wide brim of his Borsalino hat.

"I'm coming to the funeral, Mr. Wilson. I want to show you cops that I'm not all bad."

" . . . and he that is righteous, let him be righteous still. Behold, I am the Alpha and the Omega, the beginning and the end, the first and the last."

The old man lowered the bible.

"I would like now to read briefly from the final book of his life: the book of his daughter Cindy. For in the end, it wasn't God's word that guided Louis Wagner's last tragic acts, it was the tortured words of his daughter. I read a passage that Louis himself had marked."

What passage would it be, Cyrus wondered? One of the passages describing what Arthur Browne had done with her, what Mary Louise Hillman had done with her, Ricky

Andrews, Wally Lassiter? A blueprint of destruction for a distraught father. It had tipped him over the edge.

The old man read, "Saturday, and I'm so depressed. What do I want from life? What do I want from people, what do I want from myself? Why must I always be wanting? What is wrong with me? Someone, please help me. Daddy, please help me. Don't turn me down again. I'm going to call you tomorrow. Please let me come home to you. I promise I won't bring shame on us anymore."

The old man lowered the diary.

"Louis Wagner sinned against his daughter, against his fellow man, against God. But we are all sinners. Only a good man tries, even mistakenly, to redeem his soul. Louis Wagner was a good man."

Eileen was crying silently.

The old man looked at her from across the grave.

"Dust you are," he said, "and to dust you shall return."

He nodded to the grave diggers. The coffin was lowered hydraulically. Standifer bowed his head.

Eileen stepped forward and dropped a single red rose onto the coffin. She had bought it to put on the girl's grave. Guiterrez, hands jammed in his pockets, frowned at her act.

Cyrus walked over to the small stone of the grave adjoining Wagner's. It read *Sue Nelson 1961–1982.*

Ricky Andrews gestured at the stone. "That's why I come, Professor," he said. "I just wanted to show you that. You see, I take care of my chicks."

Eyes blazing, Guiterrez came toward Ricky. Cyrus held the detective off with his hand.

"You better leave," Cyrus said to the pimp.

"Sure. But I just wanted you to know."

"We know," said Guiterrez.

Ricky gave them both a mock salute, grinned, and walked off nonchalantly.

"I'm going to run him out of town if it's the last thing I do," Guiterrez snarled.

You'd like to finish Louis Wagner's work for him, wouldn't you, Cyrus thought.

Guiterrez looked at him and shrugged. "We got reports to make out, Prof. We recovered the other murder weapons from a trash bin behind Wagner's rooming house. An old-fashioned druggist's pestle and a jar of cyanide crystals. We also found a key to her apartment. He must have let himself in last January, found her body, and the diary."

"And started hunting," Cyrus said.

"I don't blame the poor bastard."

Cyrus said, "John, would you take care of my end of the paperwork for me? I'm finished playing detective."

Guiterrez tried not to look pleased. He was finally shed of the amateur detective whose work he reluctantly admired. Guiterrez nodded to Eileen, noting the frozen tears on her cheeks, and then he walked off — in the direction Ricky Andrews had gone.

"I don't like him," Eileen said.

"He's a good cop. He shot Wagner in the shoulder when he could have killed him."

"He did kill him, Cyrus."

"No. Wagner killed himself. He had two more on the list. He knew he'd never be able to kill Ricky Andrews now, but at least he could destroy himself."

"You have it all figured out, don't you, John Agate?"

"Please, Eileen. I'm all finished with that. Let's go."

"I want her diary."

"What for?"

"It's an amazing document."

"You'll have to ask Standifer for it. As Wagner's executor he gets to keep Wagner's things."

The Reverend Dr. Standifer looked up from his silent prayer. He said something to the grave diggers and then walked slowly around the grave and up to Cyrus and Eileen. The snow falling on his head made his hair even whiter.

"I am grateful to you, Mr. Wilson, for letting me know. Good-bye."

"Can I give you a lift to the airport, sir?"

"No. I prefer to go alone."

"Mr. Standifer," said Eileen, "could I have her diary, or make a copy of it?"

Standifer looked at Eileen for a moment, with those hard, pewtery eyes. He looked at her beauty, her youth, her openness, her sureness of self. The opposite of Cindy Wagner / Sue Nelson, 1961–1982.

"No," he said. "It is the work of the devil and it will be burned."

He walked on past them.

Eileen shivered. Cyrus put his arm around her. "Let's go," he said.

They walked together, arm in arm. They followed the figure of the old minister through the cemetery, out the gate, until they lost him in the swirling snow, a snow that would cover Harbour Woods in a mantle of pure whiteness.